ANTHEM

BOOK ONE OF NOTES FROM BOSTON

A. M. Leibowitz

Supposed Crimes LLC • Matthews, North Carolina

Published in the United States.

ISBN: 978-1-938108-97-6

www.supposedcrimes.com

This book is typeset in Goudy Old Style, licensed by Ascender Corporation.

"On the contrary, Aunt Augusta,
I've now realized for the first time in my life
the vital Importance of Being Earnest."

-Jack, The Importance of Being Earnest (Oscar Wilde)

CHAPTER ONE

"Trevor! Trev, get your ass down here and help me haul this thing up," Nate Kingsley hollered up the stairs.

"Yeah, haven't got all day!" another voice rose from the entryway—Jamie Cosgrove, one of their other soon-to-be roommates.

Trevor Davidson thundered down the stairs. "I'm coming, I'm coming!"

"That's what he said," the other two chorused.

Trevor scrunched his nose at them. "Nice, guys."

A neighbor stuck her graying head out of her door and snapped, "Keep it down."

Once she disappeared back inside, Jamie, who was still perched on the end of the couch they were supposed to move, snickered. Nate rolled his eyes.

"Does she expect us to be silent while moving furniture into the apartment?" he asked.

"Probably. Guess it's a good thing we're not right above her," Trevor said.

He took hold of one end of the beat-up couch, Nate took the other, and they ported it up the stairs. Jamie followed them with an armload of boxes, bringing snow and swirling wind into the entry with him. Trevor wondered how the four of them—including Jamie's friend Mack Whitman—were going to fit everything in. It was certainly cheaper to rent a nicer place together as none of them earned enough money for anything bigger than a studio. That was the price of being not-yet-famous musicians, working odd jobs and performing on the side. None of them were in a position to move out of Boston at the moment, so this arrangement would have to suffice. At least it was close to the T station, since Mack was the only one with a car.

It was just Trevor and Nate moving in; Mack and Jamie already shared the apartment, but they'd lost their previous roommates. Unable to afford the rent even on a cheap three-bedroom in Weymouth, Jamie and Mack had advertised for new tenants. After a mutual friend alerted Trevor to the opportunity, he had invited his oldest friend along for the ride, knowing Nate had to get out of his own bad situation.

They had been college roommates, and Nate had spent the entire previous year and a half going from couch to couch because his parents had no interest in letting him stay there, even if he paid rent. They were relatively liberal, but they thought making Nate leave home would force him to have a more stable job than performing opera. They were the kind of people who viewed the arts as consumables, not careers. Trevor counted himself fortunate his parents were more relaxed about having their grown son living at home. Then again, there were a lot of things Trevor's parents didn't know about him—by his choice—which might have made them feel otherwise. Nate was definitely one of those things.

To pay the bills, Trevor worked as the newly-minted Director of Music Ministry at a non-denominational church, having been promoted from his part-time gig as their pianist and Sunday worship leader. The title was a lot fancier than his paycheck, but it was enough to get by with a little help from his friends through rent-sharing. So far, it involved being the voice of the church's weekly worship podcast, and they'd already put out a couple of CDs of their music. They weren't popular yet, but the music had been a draw for people, and the church had doubled its size in the previous year after a mass mailing promoting the band.

Nate had a job as a barista at a local coffee shop a few blocks away. Trevor didn't discuss that particular occupation with the members of his church, nor did he suggest they frequent the shop. He had a very good idea what most of them would think of the owner—and of Nate, for that matter. Trevor sometimes wondered if Nate's sheer height scared the customers, but he never asked.

While Nate and Jamie worked on positioning the couch, Trevor set the boxes in the bedroom he and Nate would share. Trevor stepped out and nearly collided with Mack, who was in the process of taking two guitars into the tiny spare room they were using to house all their music equipment. Flattening himself against the wall, Trevor let Mack pass then returned to the living room.

Jamie dumped an armload just inside the door. "Who the hell had the brilliant idea to move in the middle of winter?" He brushed snow off his slim shoulders.

"It's not technically winter," Trevor informed him, pulling the boxes farther into the living room. "Three more days."

"Who cares? It's fucking cold out there." Jamie scowled at him and shook melting snow out of his spiky brown hair.

"Just a few more things and we're done," Nate said. "Home sweet home."

"Yeah, as soon as we unpack everything," Trevor replied.

"You mean we can't leave all your shit in boxes for the next however long we live here?" Jamie asked, toeing off his boots. "I wouldn't care."

"Not a chance. I refuse to live with slobs," Trevor told him.

Mack, appearing in the doorway, jerked his thumb at Trevor and said to Nate, "Was he this bad when you roomed together in college?"

"Yes," Nate said at the same time Trevor said, "No."

Jamie laughed. "If it bothers you that much, you're on permanent cleaning duty."

"I refuse to do dishes," Mack announced. "I get enough of that at work."

That was fair. Mack and Jamie worked at Legal Seafood, Jamie as a server and Mack busing tables and washing dishes. With his shaggy black hair, his multiple piercings, and his canvas of body art, he didn't exactly make the kind of impression the restaurant wanted to have on customers. Jamie, on the other hand, was the sort of adorable that made people swoon—all pint-sized, clean-cut, and blue-eyed innocence. If Trevor were honest, he'd have to admit Jamie was sort of pretty, in a boyish way.

Trevor rolled his eyes at all of them. "Do not put me in charge of cleaning. I *will* make you three suffer."

"You'd better listen to him," Nate said. "He means it." He shrugged. "At least our dorm room was always clean, though. Nothing like bringing a date home and having to shove dirty clothes under the bed on your way past."

At Nate's comment, Trevor's stomach tightened. None of them had talked at all about dating, and he wasn't sure if Mack or Jamie knew what Nate meant by "a date." He wasn't clear on what Mack or Jamie might mean, either.

"Well, there's my pet peeve," Jamie said, breaking Trevor out of his rumination. "You three had better let me know when you plan to have company. I absolutely do not want to walk in on any one of you going at it on the couch, and I don't need you all interrupting me if my boyfriend is here."

Trevor relaxed. So Jamie was cool and by extension, Mack as well. That made at least one place he didn't have to pretend to be a homophobic ass. Probably best to keep some of that from his employers, in much the same way he hadn't given his parents every detail on either his or Nate's relationships. He might not have known what his parents would think about Nate, but he was one hundred percent sure they would think Trevor had somehow tarnished his relationship with his girlfriend. They were a bit traditional.

He replied, "Fair enough. I'm sure my girlfriend will appreciate that." He ignored Nate's nudge. "Are we agreed, then? We keep the place clean, and we give a heads up on guests."

"Sounds like a plan." Jamie eyed Trevor, making his neck sweat. He couldn't possibly know anything, but it still made Trevor feel uncomfortable.

"Good. Then let's get the last of your shit and make this thing official with a pizza," Mack suggested.

"Right," Trevor said, and the four of them set off down the stairs.

Trevor lay on his mattress, a light from outside glowing yellow against the still-falling snow. He was glad to be wrapped in his thick, warm blanket. His thoughts drifted to Marlie, his on-and-off girlfriend of many years. They'd known each other since diapers, and they'd been together in one way or another since junior high school. Although they'd split up multiple times over the years and dated other people in between, they'd always come back to the familiarity of each other. They were currently in a holding pattern, mostly because Trevor needed to get his head straight about their relationship and where it was headed.

Over the years, they'd tried couple-hood multiple times, always resulting in calling it quits after a few months. This time, they'd stayed together for two years, both of them coming at it with more maturity than a pair of teenagers expected to go out because their parents were friends. For almost six months, Marlie had been hinting that it was time for them to make a more firm commitment. She'd said it would be a good career move, but Trevor knew there was more to it than that. She was dealing with a lot of pressure about their relationship, and he knew it.

He had to admit she was probably right about it being a good idea, though. They'd been together for enough time during their most recent phase they wouldn't be able to give the impression of having a sweet, chaste romance much longer. Two years was the upper limit on pretending they weren't sleeping together, and God knew the church loved a good sex scandal. Sadly, that included the very mundane truth that most relationships of any length involved more than cuddling and hand-holding. If the pastoral staff found out he and Marlie were intimate, he could face consequences ranging from making a formal apology to the church to losing his job. He'd seen it happen in other churches, and he had no doubt this one would be the same, whether they spelled it out or not. The one question he couldn't answer was why he didn't feel more enthusiastic about the prospect, despite the benefits he would reap personally and professionally.

With a sigh he turned over, listening to the slushy whoosh of the late-night traffic and trying to relax enough to sleep. The mattress dipped next to him, and he turned his head to look at his oldest friend other than Marlie. Nate planted an intentionally slobbery, wet kiss on Trevor's cheek.

"We did it! We're finally all moved in."

Breaking out of his melancholy, Trevor laughed and wiped his face then rolled so he was facing Nate. "Yeah. Ugh, I can't wait until we get all the crap cleaned up."

"Give us a few days before you start the lectures, okay?" Nate rolled his eyes, but he was grinning.

"Fine." Trevor reached out and put his hand on Nate's arm.

Nate hummed and leaned in to kiss Trevor lightly. They stayed with it for a few minutes then Nate slid his hand from Trevor's hip around to the front and dipped his fingers in the waistband of his flannel pajama pants.

"We should christen the new apartment," he murmured against Trevor's lips.

Trevor pulled back. "I don't think so." He jerked his head in the direction of the other bedroom.

"Oh, please. We did this in a dorm room with the thinnest walls ever. Are you saying you can't keep quiet for a hand job? Besides, Jamie's all right, and I assume Mack wouldn't care."

"I mean it." Trevor shook his head.

Nate huffed and withdrew his hand. He rolled onto his back and stared up at the ceiling; Trevor mimicked his actions. They were quiet for a few minutes.

Eventually, Nate said, "This isn't about keeping secrets from our very obviously cool roommates. Wanna tell me what's going on?"

"We need to stop." He looked over at Nate. "I mean, with Marlie and all."

"You've never been all that serious with her," Nate countered. "If you were, you'd have asked her to marry you already."

"I am serious!" Trevor insisted. "Besides, I think...well, with my job and everything..." He trailed off.

"I see." Nate scowled.

"I don't think you do." Trevor sat up and drew his knees to his chest. "Maybe this is part of my life I need to put behind me, you know? It's time to settle down with Marlie. Gotta get things on track."

Nate sat up too. "Put it behind you? It's not a faucet, Trevor. You don't just turn off your whole identity, and you definitely don't do it for a damn job."

"Who said anything about turning off my identity? I'm saying I'm not ready for that. Maybe I need to try having a real relationship for once."

"What do you mean by 'real'?" Nate asked. "Real because it's with a woman so you get the Jesus stamp of approval?"

"Don't you dare mock my faith." Trevor glared at him.

"I wasn't mocking. You should know me better than that." He sighed and ran a hand through his hair. "You didn't answer my question."

Trevor looked down at his hands. "No. Real because it's more than just messing with each other in bed now and again." He glanced at Nate, whose face was stony. "I've always been with Marlie, and I thought it was understood she and I would eventually stay together. What you and I did was great, but it's part of the past now. Fooling around between friends. Did it mean something else?"

Nate's head was tipped back, and his gaze was firmly fixed on the ceiling. "It's how I knew I would never be able to pretend to like girls." He cleared his throat. "Right from that first time when you slept over at my house." He looked directly at Trevor. "Don't kid yourself. I can't remember a single time you ever refused, until now. You liked it every bit as much as I did."

"Yes, but I'm telling you now I can't anymore."

"Because you keep refusing to admit you don't really want to be with her," Nate snapped.

"Did you even hear me? I'm not like you." Trevor huffed.

"Bullshit. If you loved Marlie that much, you'd have done something about it by now. Maybe it's time to stop lying to yourself and everyone around you."

"We've outgrown that, Nate. I get that you're gay and all, but I'm not. Before you judge me, please listen. I have to have a certain image, just like you do. My image doesn't happen to include secretly fooling around with you while building a relationship with Marlie." He lay back down. "That would be true even if you were a woman."

Nate settled down beside him. "Well, that last part I can agree with, anyway." He leaned over and kissed Trevor again. "I do feel sorry for you, though. You are severely restricting yourself. One of these days, that's going to come back to bite you in the ass."

Sighing, Trevor said, "I'll manage."

"I'll bet you will. Come on, one last time, then, before this ship sails?" Nate asked. There was a note of longing in his voice that made Trevor almost change his mind.

He wanted to say yes. It had been too long since he and Nate had touched each other, hands and lips moving until they found release. He wanted to reach for Nate and let himself fall into his hot kisses and sensual touches, to give back what he was getting. He wanted to feel smooth skin and rough stubble and coarse hair, their hands on each other until they'd relieved their pent-up tension. For a long moment, he lay there in the dark, staring at Nate's barely visible face.

"I'm sorry," he said. "I can't."

Nate nodded, but he didn't move to return to his own bed. Instead, he pushed until Trevor turned onto his side, his back to Nate, then settled down behind him. He curled around Trevor, and Trevor felt how aroused he still was. Instead of indicating he'd noticed, or that it had any effect on him at all, he pulled Nate's arm around his waist and rested his own on top of it. He relaxed into the mattress and let sleep overtake him.

CHAPTER TWO

Andre Cole gripped the phone tightly, barely restraining himself from shouting at the person on the other end of the line. *I hate this job,* he thought. Out loud, he said, "Have you tried uninstalling the program and reinstalling it?"

The customer gave him an earful, explaining why she couldn't possibly do that. Andre sighed. It was going to be a long day. By the time he hung up with the clueless woman, he was already drained and in need of a break. Out of the corner of his eye, he saw his coworker, Jagathi, smirking.

"Don't even start with me," Andre told her.

"I did not say a word."

"I hate this job," Andre muttered.

"That is the fifth time you said it since you arrived today. What has you all in knots?" Jagathi asked.

"Oh, maybe the fact that I sort of imagined I'd have moved on from fixing the first-world problems of luddites by now. Or possibly the fact that every single conversation I've had today could have been prevented by simply reading the damn instructions." Andre huffed.

Jagathi's features softened. "It's something more. I've known you too long."

For a moment, Andre considered telling her what was going on. They'd worked together in technical support at their company for almost five years, and Jagathi had been there during the aftermath of his wife's death. Yet now he didn't want to explain his sense it was time to get out, to cut his losses and move on. If he stayed on the Cape, he would never be able to let go. The problem was, he didn't have any idea how to make such a radical change—to take off without a sense of where he was going or what he would do.

"I—" he started, but he was cut off by his cell phone. A glance at the number had his eyebrows up. He raised his eyes to Jagathi and said, "Hang on a sec." With a nod, she turned back to her desk, and Andre answered the call. "Hey, Julian."

His friend Julian's warm voice came through the phone. "Yo, man. Are you busy?"

"Not particularly. Cross your fingers I don't get another damn call about our software not working right."

"That good?" Julian chuckled. "Well, I think you're gonna like the reason I'm calling you."

"Uh huh. I could use some good news right about now." He wondered if Julian was going to talk about his wife, Elisa, and their second pregnancy, but he decided Julian wouldn't be that insensitive as to phone him at work about it.

"My company's doing well," Julian said, and there was a note of pride in his words.

"I agree with you that's fantastic, but this has exactly what to do with interrupting me at work?"

"Thought you said you weren't busy."

Andre huffed into the phone. "I'm not. Look, I'm happy for you, but can you make a point before I get in trouble for taking personal calls?"

"Sure. This isn't a personal call, though. It's business." There was an obvious self-satisfied smile in his tone.

"Oh, really?"

"Mm-hm. I'm looking to hire someone with experience in technical support who also knows something about web design and building Internet platforms."

Andre sat up straighter. "You don't say." He'd been dabbling in a variety of web-based technologies for the last couple of years, taking the occasional freelance job, but he hadn't built up enough clients to branch out on his own.

"Do I happen to know anyone who's been my brother by choice for the last twenty years and might be looking for a new job?" Julian asked, oozing sugar.

"You might," Andre replied. "He might be very interested in the position. Would he need an interview?"

"He's having one as we speak."

Swallowing hard, Andre said, "And just when does he need to be back in Boston?"

"Right after New Year's, provided he gives his notice today."

"Won't be a problem."

Julian was most likely grinning like the fool he was. "Good."

When they ended the call, Andre turned to Jagathi, who was eying him curiously. "I quit," he muttered.

"Uh...what?" She blinked.

"I need to go tell Vaughan I quit," Andre told her. He leaned in and said quietly, "I got a better offer."

Jagathi broke out in a wide smile. "Always knew you were better than this. 'Bout time you moved on." She leaned in too. "Put in a good word for me?"

"Only if you want to move to the city."

She scrunched her nose then relaxed. "Maybe someday. Good luck, Andre. I hope my next desk mate is as good as you've been."

"Thanks." He stood up and grinned at her, feeling more alive than he had in the last three years. It was going to be a good day.

Andre blew on his coffee to cool it and looked across the tiny table at his sisters. He'd agreed to go shopping with them on the condition they help him hunt for an apartment, but he regretted the decision now that he was sitting in South Station trying not to look pained by the aches in his feet and his head. There was nothing he hated more than shopping, made worse by the festive holiday atmosphere. He felt he owed Trinity and Phyllice, though. This was the first time he'd asked to make a trip into the city with them since losing Dahlia, and they were more than willing to help him out.

On the plus side, he'd found a place almost first thing, a house for rent right in Weymouth. On the down side, he'd had to endure hours of crowds and noise and stores he didn't care about other than his sisters' one allowance into a secondhand music store. Now that he was comfortable and on the verge of being happily caffeinated, he crossed his fingers under the table in hopes the wicked duo didn't have plans to drag him anywhere else.

"What's the matter, baby brother?" Trinity asked, flicking her long braids over her shoulder.

"Nothing," Andre muttered.

Phyllice smirked. "Boy hates shopping." She patted his hand. "Don't worry—we're all done for now."

"For now?" he whined.

Trinity rolled her eyes. "Aren't you all supposed to like all this fashion stuff?"

"Aren't you supposed to drive a truck and wear flannel?" he snapped.

"That shit's for white ladies. You watch too much TV." She clicked her tongue. "For a half-queer, you sure are no fun."

"Don't call me that." He scowled at her. "If Grams ever heard you, she'd have your ass."

"So I won't let her hear me. You know I don't mean it." Trinity popped the top off her hot cocoa. She'd sworn off coffee the minute she found out she was pregnant, but she hadn't sworn off chocolate.

"Yeah, I do know," Andre replied. "Which is why I hate it. Can you just not?"

"Whatever."

"Yo." Phyllice waved her hand between them. "More pressing stuff to talk about right now. Andre, you gotta tell us more about this job. Thought we'd never get you back home."

He shrugged. "Julian finally got his business going." Chuckling, he added, "When I talked to him again, I got the feeling his main business is designing web space for bars. He had a huge account last year for a new gay club in Pawtucket."

Trinity laughed. "Julian is the straightest boy I ever met."

Andre snickered. "I don't think the owners cared." He pulled out his phone, did a quick search to pull it up, and handed it over to Trinity and Phyllice.

"Nice," Phyllice said.

"Here." Andre held out his hand for the phone. "Take a look at his own website." He pulled up Julian's app and passed the phone back.

While they were examining it, Andre took to people-watching. He might not have liked crowds, but he was fascinated by the passersby, especially in such a busy hub. There was a man in a long, elegant coat, running past with his phone pressed to his ear, oblivious to the angry glares as he knocked into people. Three women, their hands full of shopping bags, were talking loudly about their frustration with the men in their lives, their classic Boston accents carrying over the station's bustle. A skinny redhead with an incredible amount of excess energy had his fingers threaded with a significantly more reserved man, who resigned himself to being dragged through the station but smiled anyway. A tall, athletic woman with straight light brown hair in a low ponytail was seated on a suitcase, looking very much like someone out of a painting.

A youth with tawny skin and hair styled in short cornrows caught Andre's attention. The teen was a few seats over, knees drawn up and chin resting on them. A small drink and an order of fries sat untouched on the table. The young person had earbuds in, plugged into the phone laying in front of them, and their eyes were closed. The only other item in the vicinity was a worn backpack. The youth's coat barely looked warm enough to withstand a trip from South Station to the next building over. Andre was just close enough to see the tears sliding slowly down their cheeks.

The need to do something was in his blood, he thought. No one could have grown up in his household, headed by his formidable Grams, without developing a sixth sense. Andre nudged Trinity, who glanced over her shoulder then poked Phyllice, who was still going on about Julian's web site.

"I'll go," Phyllice said.

She rose from the table and stepped over to the teenager. Andre couldn't hear what Phyllice said, but next thing he knew, the youth was following Phyllice to their table. A bright pink t-shirt peeked out from beneath the worn jacket, and tears had streaked the little bit of makeup the teen had on. Andre moved Trinity's shopping bags from the chair to under the table. The child slumped down and looked around at them.

"Uh...hi." It was barely more than a whisper.

"You've met Phyllice," Trinity said, gesturing at their oldest sibling. "I'm Trinity, and this is Andre. What's your name, honey?"

"Lina," the youth mumbled. "Lina Hawling."

Andre knew he needed to say something to put Lina at ease and make an affirmation. "Lina, what pronouns do you use?" he asked.

The relief on Lina's face was almost immediate. "She and her, please."

"It's nice to meet you, Lina," Trinity said. She looked down at Lina's phone. "What are you listening to?"

Lina's cheeks turned a slightly darker shade. "They're a band I used to like. Uh, back when I lived in Seattle."

Andre exchanged a look with his sisters and said, "You came all the way from Seattle?"

"No." Lina shook her head vigorously. "Just from Worcester. We moved, um, a few years ago."

Her hands shook, and Trinity took one while Phyllice took the other. Lina relaxed slightly, and they let go. She picked up her drink and took a sip then made a face.

"Where are you headed?" Phyllice asked, even though all of them knew the answer.

"I-I don't know." Fresh tears pooled in her eyes.

"Okay, honey. It's all right." Trinity put her arm around the girl. "We can get you somewhere. Will you trust us?"

"I don't know," Lina repeated.

Trinity rubbed her shoulder gently, and Lina leaned into her, laying her cheek against Trinity's breast.

Phyllice adjusted her angle so she looked Lina in the eyes. "Our grandmother has a place in Quincy. It's for people who need some help for a bit. All she asks is that you help out there while you stay and look for something else. Do you think you could go there?"

"I...um..." Lina reached into her pocket and pulled out a little money. "I don't know if I have enough for the T."

"It's okay," Andre said. "I'll spot you, and if you really want to, you can pay my Grams back. She'll know where to find me."

Lina nodded. "Okay." She still looked a little lost, but she'd stopped crying and was attempting to eat the little bit of food she'd gotten.

"We were headed that way anyhow," Trinity said. "We'll ride with you and make sure you get there safely." She looked up at the board. "There's a train leaving soon. We can just make it."

"Thanks."

They all stood, and Trinity reached for her bags. They were mostly full of baby clothes, but she pulled out a stylish jacket and handed it to Lina.

"Put this on. You'll need something warmer than what you've got now, and I was planning on giving this to Grams for her place anyway."

Andre looked at her sharply, and she shook her head slightly. He backed off. If this was what Trinity wanted, he wouldn't stop her. Lina wrapped herself in the coat—which was a good two sizes too big for her undernourished frame—and shouldered her backpack. Andre and his sisters led Lina back out of the station to the waiting trains.

All they could do was get her there; the rest was up to their

Grams and Lina. Andre said a quick prayer as he fell in line with the others, undecided whether or not he hoped this was the last time he would see her.

Two weeks later, Andre sat at his desk, throwing things into a box. He'd stayed until after Christmas, spending time with his parents and sisters before taking the last few days to tie up loose ends at work. When he signed out at the end of the day, he would head to Boston to spend New Year's Eve at Julian's house before going over to sign the lease on his town house in Weymouth.

He pulled an old notice off the corkboard behind his computer monitor and almost gasped when he saw the pictures he still had pinned underneath. One was of his wife, Dahlia, looking positively radiant. Pregnancy had agreed with her, though she'd had double the cargo. She wore a flowing peach sundress that flattered her smooth, brown skin. A wide-brimmed hat shielded her eyes, but Andre recalled their dark, sparkling depths as clearly as if she were standing right there with him. He swallowed the lump in his throat and pulled off the picture, gently placing it on top of the other items in the box.

The other picture was of the babies on ultrasound. Andre had always thought they looked like grainy blobs, but the tech had assured them those really were human fetuses. They'd had good, strong heart beats, and one had been sucking her thumb. Even Andre could see that. When they'd found out from the ultrasound that both babies were girls, he'd gone a little wild with shopping, buying both matching pink dresses and matching very tiny pink Red Sox jerseys. Of course, he also hadn't been able to resist the Minecraft-themed footie pajamas, the SuperMario plush dolls, and the itty bitty baseball gloves, either. Dahlia had only laughed at him and suggested he slow down until after the babies arrived.

Andre couldn't help it, though. He'd known since he was four years old that he was going to be a daddy one day. His sisters had confiscated his "baby," and he'd cried until Grams made them give it back. It wasn't even a real baby doll—just a hand-me-down 1980s Black Barbie given to him by one of the women Grams worked with. He'd carted her around with him everywhere, wrapped up in a paper towel like a blanket, hollering at anyone who threatened to replace her with something they considered more appropriate for a little boy.

Dragging himself out of the memories, he sighed at the reminder of why he was packing everything into boxes and getting the hell out of Dodge. It didn't matter that it had been three years; it felt like yesterday he'd gotten the phone call that changed his life. His wife and unborn baby girls were gone. Everything after that was a blur. Months dragged on. There was nothing but work and work and more work. It no longer mattered how much Andre hated his job; it was a paycheck, and it meant at least eight hours in which he could dwell on something other than the constant reminders of what he'd lost.

He'd immediately donated every last baby-related item in the house, cleaning out the place where there had once been a nursery. Gone were the brightly colored decorations and the tidy shelf with all the bins of baby-care items. The second bedroom stood empty— no furniture, no clothes, no toys, no diapers. Dahlia's things had been more difficult. He'd kept a few sentimental items, but the rest he'd returned to her mother. There was no point in keeping them, and he knew she would want them. He had effectively created a void, with one unfurnished bedroom and another stripped to half its earlier possessions. He'd kept anything they purchased together, but all the things she'd brought into their home were gone.

Meanwhile, Julian had fussed; he didn't seem to know how to conduct himself around Andre. His own wife was newly pregnant, expecting their first, and they'd just begun to tell everyone. Andre was glad for them, but he had to admit he'd been grateful for Julian's hesitancy in talking about it at first. Once Elisa was in the later stages, when all the really exciting things happened, Julian had been bursting with news and the urge to share it.

When Julian had moved his wife and infant son to Boston to start his own web design company in Braintree, Andre hadn't been able to bring himself to be upset. The constant reminder that his oldest friend was living the life Andre had wanted was too much. They hadn't spoken much for the first year he was gone. As time went by, though, they'd patched their relationship. It was hard to stay angry with the man who had become like another member of Andre's own family. It was worth scrapping his entire life on the Cape and taking a chance on Boston if he could work with Julian.

"You okay?"

The voice broke his reverie. Andre looked up and shook his head to clear it. "Sorry. Just lost in thought for a minute." He offered a small smile to Jagathi.

"You know, we're going to miss you around here," she remarked.

"You'll survive." Andre chuckled.

"The company will. *I* will probably be stuck with a desk mate who has no sense of humor."

"Probably, knowing your luck." He stood up and put the box on his chair, nearly finished with his cleaning. "You'll have to make up for it."

Jagathi laughed. "I will try to keep whoever it is entertained with my adventures in online dating. Want to join me for lunch and I can fill you in on the latest one?"

"Do I even want to know?" Andre asked.

"Yes. Trust me, you do." As they stepped away from his desk, she looped her arm through his and continued speaking. "It all started with this message I got..."

CHAPTER THREE

Mack and Jamie's band, the Creepy Crullers—who even knew what that name meant—were playing a New Year's Eve gig. They'd left hours earlier. Nate had also taken off. One of his castmates from his latest opera was having a party, and although Nate had offered to bring him along, Trevor had declined. Instead, he was sitting alone in the apartment, trying not to dwell on the fight he'd had with Marlie after Christmas which had resulted in her not calling him since. He could have gone into the city for First Night festivities, but it wasn't a lot of fun alone, and he wasn't in the mood.

Even moping was too much effort. Trevor flipped on the television, ordered takeout, and popped the top off a beer, settling in to watch whatever mindless thing he could find. Nate surprised him by breezing in around ten. Trevor sat up from his half-doze on the couch. He'd had one too many beers, and he felt sloshy when he propped himself up. By Nate's unsteady gait, he wasn't in much better a position.

"Have fun?" Trevor asked, yawning.

"Was okay." Nate's words slurred a little. He held up a bottle of champagne. "Brought this home, though."

Trevor groaned. "I've had plenty." He waved his hand at the beer bottles littered on the floor around the coffee table, and he nearly knocked over the mostly full one still sitting there.

"Me too," Nate agreed. He stepped farther into the room and plopped down next to Trevor, slinging his arm over Trevor's shoulders. "Why are you home alone?"

"Didn't feel like going anywhere," Trevor replied, shifting so he was angled toward Nate.

"You still thinking about Marlie?" Nate's eyes crinkled, and he furrowed his brow. "Geez. What did you guys fight about this time?"

Trevor grunted. "I'm not even sure. Her parents are pissed I haven't asked her to marry me yet. Why'd you leave the party so early?"

Nate dropped his arm and stretched so his six-foot-three-inch frame was sprawled over most of the couch. "Asshole who came with someone caught his date hitting on me, and he tried to punch me. It got ugly."

He didn't elaborate, and Trevor didn't ask, even though he had a hard time picturing anyone trying to take Nate. His head buzzed, and he leaned to rest it on the back of the couch. Nate slouched sideways so his head was on Trevor's shoulder, and he flipped channels on the television for a few minutes. He huffed and turned it off.

"This is boring. Come on, let's go somewhere." He shoved Trevor.

Groaning, Trevor rubbed his eyes. "What did you have in mind?"

"Mack and Jamie are playing that place on Boylston. We can go there."

Trevor sat up and blinked at Nate. "That's a gay club."

"Your point?"

"Why would I want to go there?"

Nate rolled his eyes. "First of all, our roommates are playing. Second, what's the big deal? You go, have a drink–" He looked at the beer bottles on the floor. "Or not, whatever. You get groped, find someone to kiss at midnight, and come home."

"Yeah, alone, because you'll find someone to take you back to his place. No thanks." Trevor shook his head. "And you know I'm trying to–"

"Yeah, yeah." Nate waved his hand dismissively. "You're trying to be a good Christian boy. I never said you needed to fuck some random guy, just have a bit of fun. I promise, I won't leave you stranded. And if there's no Prince Charming, I'll lay one on you to ring in the new year. Come on. We can't just sit here like a pair of old farts, watching television all night." He stood up and held out a hand.

Trevor accepted it, and Nate hauled him to his feet. With a sigh, Trevor gathered his empties and lined them up on the kitchen counter. When he turned around, Nate's eyes were crinkled with amusement, and Trevor couldn't help chuckling.

"You win. Let's go."

They rode the packed T inbound, squashed between the other revelers on their way into the heart of the city for First Night, then the even more packed Red Line to Boylston. The club was several blocks from the station, tucked between a couple of other buildings and with a line out the door. Trevor had only been to a club once before, the last time Nate dragged him out. He'd been as uncomfortable then as he was now. Reminding himself that at least Mack and Jamie were there somewhere, he wrapped his arms around his waist and stomped his feet to keep warm.

Eventually they were inside, and Trevor was hit by how crowded it was, even so early. It was more like an old-style bar than one of the newer clubs, dim but not dark and full of polished wood furniture. The whole inside was decked out for the occasion with multi-colored twinkle lights, balloons, and silver confetti on all the tables. First Night celebrations were in full swing, the music thumping under the buzz of talking and laughter. He was surprised to see such a mix of people and range of ages. The Creepy Crullers were already playing; the better-known bands weren't scheduled until after midnight. Nate and Trevor wriggled through the throng to the bar.

It only took three minutes for someone to make a move on Nate. Trevor wasn't surprised; Nate's height was intimidating, but he was good-looking and outgoing. He turned to Trevor to ask permission with his eyes, and Trevor nodded. He turned back to the bar and picked up his soda, hoping he could just blend into the scenery until Nate got back or it was time to leave. After being jostled from behind one too many times, he faced out into the crowd and took to watching people come in.

Trevor remembered what Nate had said, and he considered whether there was anyone who interested him, at least for a dance or two. It couldn't hurt to relax, and Nate was right that he wasn't expected to do anything he didn't want to—or at least, anyone who treated him with such little respect probably wasn't worth his time.

After a while, Trevor gave up. He simply wasn't cut out for making connections with strangers, and he felt out of place. Just as he was about to find some corner to hide in, two men walked in, and his attention was immediately on them. It might have been because their interaction resembled his and Nate's so strongly they caught his eye.

The taller one, who had hair and skin almost the same shade of light brown, was shoving on the other one, who looked as though he wanted to be just about anywhere else. Trevor choked back a laugh. The shorter man allowed himself to be propelled toward the bar. He was slender, dressed in loose-fitting well-worn jeans and a v-neck shirt complemented by a pair of wire-framed glasses. His smooth skin was a rich, dark umber, and he had closely cropped hair and stylishly trimmed facial hair. Trevor averted his gaze just as they maneuvered up beside him, not wanting to be caught staring.

He heard the taller man order a drink, and he kept an eye on them in his peripheral vision. They were both Trevor's idea of attractive, especially the smaller one. Trevor always had appreciated what Jamie called the "sexy geek" look. The alcohol must have affected him more than he'd anticipated because one half of his mind hoped the man would approach him while the other half argued back he'd better keep his distance. He drew his lower lip between his teeth and tried to focus on something—anything—else, but it was impossible when he was sitting a few feet from someone so appealing.

Trevor decided to do nothing. The guys weren't even looking his way, too busy wrapped up in their own conversation. Up until then, no one else had approached Trevor either, so he assumed he was safe from any advances, wanted or not. Shoulders slumped, he turned back to his drink. He always had Nate, if the evening didn't go anywhere interesting.

Andre scowled at Julian. By leaning in close, he could speak without yelling. "You didn't tell me you were bringing me here," he hissed. "What the hell are we doing at a gay club?"

Julian grinned and dragged him right up to the bar. "It's obviously not for me, my man." He clapped Andre on the back. "This is for you. I knew you weren't ready for women, but you needed something."

"This wasn't exactly what I had in mind when I said we should go and let your wife get some rest." He didn't correct Julian about whether or not he wanted to be with women; Julian didn't need to know about the times over the last few years he'd needed to feel another heartbeat next to his. Whether it was round breasts and hips or muscular lines and planes hardly mattered when he was in the mood to connect.

"You don't have to get laid. Just have a couple shots, get groped, kiss a hot man at midnight, and call it a day." He snorted. "Besides, it wasn't my idea."

"Oh? Whose was it?"

"Elisa's."

Andre's eyebrows rose. "She was worried you'd pick someone up? Damn. Didn't think she was the jealous type."

"She's not. This was about you. Before she went to bed, she told me I should bring you here. I guess her friend's man plays in one of the bands that's on tonight or something."

"I think she just told you that so you wouldn't flip your shit 'cause she thought you'd cheat on her," Andre suggested.

Julian shrugged. "Yeah, probably." He scanned the room then nodded at a tall, well-dressed brother. "Him."

Andre was about to say he wasn't bad when the man glanced their way and clearly gave Julian a once-over, eyes raking his entire body. Sighing, Andre replied, "Obviously out of my league."

"All right. Someone else then." Julian peered around Andre. His eyebrows rose, and a slow smile spread across his face. "Sexy over there's watching you."

Andre followed Julian's gaze. "You think he's hot?" He snickered. "Thought you were straight."

"Mm. I can recognize man candy when I see it." He laughed. "Elisa points it out. I got that first one, but he wasn't into you. Maybe this guy."

The man at the bar wasn't half bad, for a white guy. He had wavy, dark blond hair that hung almost to his shoulders, and Andre could see he was muscled but in a softer, almost curvy way—a bit on the chunky side. Despite the scruff on his chin, he had boyish features, but his mouth was turned down and he sat hunched on his stool. Andre almost smiled at how the man looked nearly as out of place as he felt. There was no way he was eying Andre or any other man there.

Andre scoffed. "He's probably just hoping I'll leave him be."

Julian shoved him. "Don't be like that." A dirty smile formed slowly on his face. "Five bucks says he's looking 'cause you wear that 'hot nerd' thing so fine."

"No."

"Yes. Go talk to him."

Julian yanked on his arm, and Andre nearly lost his balance. The other man glanced over, and Andre got a full view of his face. When their eyes met, the guy shrank back a little and developed a charming blush. He hastily looked away, causing Julian to laugh.

"Baby, get your ass over there and ask him to dance or something."

"Or something," Andre muttered, but he got up. "What are you gonna do?"

Julian waved a hand dismissively. "Sit here till I get hit on, then let the poor soul down gently." He offered a wicked grin. "Or maybe I'll go dance. You know I don't care."

Andre narrowed his eyes at Julian before turning around and sidestepping over to the blond guy. He hated to admit it, but the guy was his type, and Julian was right—he needed to just let go for a bit. Loud music, cold beer, and a hot body pressed against his could be just what he needed. He sidled up to the other guy, whose eyes widened comically when he saw Andre. He opened his mouth like he was about to say something, thought better of it, and clamped his lips shut. Andre shook his head. They were both out of their element, and knowing that put him at ease.

"Hey," he said. He nodded at the guy's glass. "What are you drinking?"

"Moxie," the man said then snorted. "Boring. Sorry."

"You in the mood for something stronger? How about just a beer?"

"Uh...sure." The man blushed again.

Andre ordered a couple of Sam Adams. When they showed up, he held his out to the blond man. "Cheers." They clinked. "What's your name?"

"Tr—Trey," he stammered.

So, they were playing that game. Andre could spot a fake a mile away. "Fine, then, Trey. I'm...Antoine."

Trey—or whoever he really was—ran a hand through his hair. "I'm sorry. I suck at this. I was just going to stay home and mope tonight, but my friend dragged me here." He waved at the band. "We know those guys."

Andre didn't ask how they were associated. Instead, he nodded. "We seem to be in the same boat." He took a swig of his beer and leaned closer. "Would you be offended if I said your friends aren't that good?"

Trey jerked, and his eyebrows shot up. His lips curled upward on one side, and his eyes glinted with mischief. "Not at all. I thought it was just me. This isn't my kind of music."

"Oh yeah?" Intrigued, Andre tilted his head. "What do you like, then?"

"If I'm out to be entertained, I like jazz. I wanted to be a jazz pianist when I was a kid." He laughed. "Don't know why I'm telling you this."

Andre tilted his chin. "So, you play?"

"Yeah. Not jazz, though. At least, not anymore." Trey silenced himself by taking a drink.

"I like a little jazz myself. There's a great place not that far from here. Weekends, they have open mike. You should check it out sometime." Andre's throat tightened. He hadn't meant to let it slip; the jazz cafe was where he'd met Dahlia. He brushed the memory away.

"Maybe I will."

The music changed, and Andre set his empty glass down on the bar. The new song was tolerable, though it wasn't one he recognized—probably one of the band's own tunes. It was slower, mellow with a longing refrain about missed chances. The lead singer wasn't bad when he wasn't screaming the lyrics. Andre turned to Trey and said, "So what do you say? You in the mood to dance?"

Trey shrugged. "Yeah, okay."

He downed the rest of his beer surprisingly fast, and Andre raised his eyebrows, but Trey didn't seem to notice. He followed Andre away from the bar and out among the crowd. It was too tightly packed for Andre's taste, but he focused on Trey, and in no time they were moving to the music. Trey was surprisingly agile, leaving Andre content to let him lead. It didn't take long to be caught up in the rhythm and the motion; they moved closer together, and Andre draped an arm around Trey's shoulder. Trey stiffened, but he gradually relaxed into it and slipped his arm around Andre's waist.

Whether it was the alcohol or the heat or the press of Trey's body against his own, Andre wasn't sure, but the tension felt good and his whole body was alive. The vague thought that he now owed Julian five dollars popped into his head, but he brushed it off so it wouldn't spoil the moment. The music and the booze coursed through him, and he leaned in closer. He and Trey were pushed together partly by the crowd and partly of their own volition.

Inhaling deeply, he took in the scent of Trey's skin, a heady combination of sweat, soap, and alcohol.

Andre took a chance. He leaned up to speak into Trey's ear. "It's customary to kiss someone at midnight."

Trey's breath tickled his face. "And how close are we to midnight?"

"Close enough."

Trey slid his cheek against Andre's, the rough stubble creating delicious friction just before their mouths joined. It should just have been a brief kiss, something to welcome January first and no more. Except once they'd started, it was like wildfire. Andre sensed a change in Trey, almost an animal hunger. He kissed Andre feverishly, and Andre returned it with equal intensity. They were tangled in each other, panting, their mouths and hips moving together and Trey's tongue exploring Andre's. Trey's palm made slow circles on Andre's back, and Andre ran his fingers under Trey's thick blond hair to touch his neck. For the next several minutes, Andre focused only on how good Trey's body felt against his, the sounds of the band and the crowd fading into the background.

When Trey tried to slip a hand under Andre's shirt, Andre gasped, and something clunked back into place. "Not here," he said between breaths.

Trey grunted in agreement and backed off a little, but they kept sneaking in smaller, breathless kisses while Andre debated further. He wasn't planning on going home with Trey nor asking him to come back to Julian's place—both Julian and Elisa would kill him. They could do the next best thing and simply find somewhere marginally less public to make out for a while. Andre slid his hand down Trey's wrist to touch his hand. He tilted his head in question, and to his surprise, Trey nodded.

They escaped through the crowd to the narrow hallway where the bathrooms were located. It wasn't ideal, but it was good enough. The hallway was nearly empty. They paused along the wall to kiss and grope a bit more, allowing the fire to build between them. When they finally stumbled into the bathroom, Andre almost didn't care anymore who else was in there with them.

To his relief, there was an unoccupied stall. The moment the door was latched, though, Andre just stood there, undecided. This hadn't been in the plan, and now that it was a reality, he wasn't sure anymore. He stared at Trey, his heart hammering in his chest. He thought he should move, but he was rooted to the spot. The spell was broken when Trey yanked on his shirt, causing Andre to stumble into him. The heat of Trey's chest against his was Andre's undoing. He looked into Trey's eyes for a split second before crashing their mouths together.

Greedily, they kissed and licked and nipped. Trey shifted so Andre was flush against the wall with Trey leaning on him. Trey's leg brushed against Andre's crotch, and he groaned, already stiff. He adjusted so they could slide together, grinding against each other. Trey's hand wandered down to squeeze Andre's backside, and Andre grunted. He thrust faster, wanting something to relieve the building ache.

He was too close. Even in his booze-addled state, he didn't want to come in his pants. He slowed down his rocking just as Trey reached between them to unfasten both his jeans and Andre's.

"Oh, God," Trey said. "God, yeah. Come on. Want this so damn much."

The eager words lit a fire in Andre, and he pressed his mouth against Trey's throat, sucking lightly. Trey was eagerly yanking at their clothes, moving just enough to begin pushing Andre's pants down. Just as Andre was about to participate, Trey dropped to his knees, dragging down Andre's jeans and underwear as he went.

"Wh-what are you doing?" Andre asked. All he'd counted on was a hurried hand-job, which would have been plenty, as far gone as he already was.

"What's it look like?" Trevor replied, but both his hand and his voice shook.

Andre looked down at him and frowned. "You ever do this before?"

"N-no."

Oh, Lord, help me. No wonder he'd seemed both uncomfortable and eager. "I don't want to be your first. You're gonna regret it. We've been drinking."

By that time, Trey had fully exposed Andre. He ran one finger lightly over Andre's erection, drawing a shudder. "I'm not too drunk to know what I want." He hovered for a moment. "Your cock is real nice."

Andre almost laughed. It came out as a strangled hiccup as he tried to stop it. "What?"

Trey shrugged. "I like your dick. It's different from...it's different." He toyed with the foreskin, sliding it back and forth.

"Haven't you ever touched anyone uncut before?" Andre drew a shuddering breath, trying to stem the rising need in case Trey freaked and called it quits.

"Uh-uh." Trey blushed again. "I haven't been with a lot of people." He held still, every exhalation making a warm puff of air against Andre's skin. "You want me to stop?" He looked up at Andre.

After a few tense heartbeats, Andre replied, "Not unless you want to."

Slowly, probably because he was inexperienced, Trey brought his mouth into contact with the tip of Andre's penis. At first, all he did was tease, licking a little and exploring. As he gained confidence, he lavished attention on Andre, using his tongue to elicit filthy sounds and make Andre buck his hips. Surprised and somewhat confused by Trey's skill, Andre moaned and twisted his fingers in Trey's hair, tugging a little. Trey brought his free hand down to untuck himself from his jeans, stroking himself while he sucked. Andre leaned back, parting his legs and thrusting his hips outward. Trey bobbed his head faster, and Andre began to pant.

"Damn...oh, damn..." he muttered. "Better pull off. I'm about to nut."

Trey moaned around his mouthful, magnifying Andre's need for release. In front of him, Trey rapidly pulled on himself until he shot hard between Andre's spread knees, hitting the stall behind him. He moaned again, and that did it; Andre came explosively, straight into Trey's mouth. Trey spluttered and drooled most of it back out as he withdrew.

For some time, neither of them moved, gasping and shaking. Slowly the other sounds in the bathroom brought them back to their senses. Andre's head felt more clear than it had when they'd come in, and from the expression on Trey's face, he was feeling the same way. Trey sat back on his heels, trying to wipe his mouth clean. Andre looked at the mess and suppressed a huff of annoyance, knowing it wasn't entirely Trey's fault. He clicked his tongue and started cleaning up.

"I'm sorry." Shrinking back, Trey rose to his feet and leaned heavily against the wall, his pants still open and his softening cock poking out.

Andre took a deep breath and tried to relax. "Nah, it's okay." He gave a short laugh. "I did warn you, and I'd say it was worth it. Felt damn good."

"Yeah," Trey said. "God. It did, didn't it?"

Leaning in, Andre kissed Trey full on the mouth, tasting his own tang. Trey hummed against his lips, returning the light, tender embrace. Andre withdrew and gave Trey a peck on the cheek. The blush was back, but the look of ecstasy on Trey's face slid away when their eyes met, replaced by panic. He began breathing rapidly again, but it was clearly no longer from pleasure. Fumbling a little, he tucked himself away and zipped his fly.

"You okay?" Andre asked, touching Trey's trembling hand.

Trey shook his head and pulled his arm away. "Shit...I have to go," he mumbled.

He yanked at the latch on the door and finally managed to get it open, nearly banging it into Andre's nose on the way out. Andre hurriedly dragged his jeans back up and rushed after Trey. It was obvious the poor guy didn't know how he felt about what they'd just done, and Andre didn't want to leave things that way. By the time he got out into the hallway, there was no sign of Trey.

Andre leaned against the wall and blew out his breath. His pocket vibrated, and he pulled out his phone. It was a text from Julian asking where he was and how things had gone with "that blond hottie." Andre ran a hand over his face before sending a text back saying, "I'll give you your five dollars in the morning." He shoved his phone back in his pocket and closed his eyes, knowing he would have to endure Julian's questions the entire train ride home. Huffing, he pushed off the wall and walked slowly out of the hallway.

Chapter Four

Julian hovered in the entryway of Andre's new townhouse on Summer Street. "You gonna be okay?"

After church, Julian had joined Andre's family to help him move in. Everyone else had left following the dinner Andre's mother had insisted on making with the groceries she and his Grams had brought along to stock his shelves. The tiny place was still a mess, but at least all the furniture was arranged. Andre scanned the room, looking for anything else he might need help with, but he didn't see anything.

"Yeah. I'll probably just turn in early and clean up tomorrow." He ran a tired hand over his face, pulling on his chin a little.

"You know you can call me, right?" Julian's voice was low and a little hesitant.

"I know."

There didn't seem to be anything else to say. They hadn't talked again about New Year's; Julian knew better than to pry, even if it was obvious he wanted to. Andre hadn't even gotten a phone number from "Trey," so it wasn't as though Julian could make assumptions about how ready Andre was to move on. On nights like this one, he wasn't ready at all, the loneliness setting in even before he was by himself. All Andre could do was hope this new chapter in his life would mean a chance to begin again away from the place where he'd built so many memories with Dahlia.

"You want me to check in tomorrow, maybe help you get this stuff sorted out?" Julian asked.

"Nah." Andre waved him off. "'S cool. You and Elisa need time to do some stuff yourselves." He swallowed heavily. "That baby's gonna be here before you know it."

The pause was uncomfortable. Elisa was now past where Dahlia had been, mere weeks away from her due date. Julian constantly teetered on the edge between clearly wanting to share his impending joy and not wanting to damage the thin link between Andre and the rest of the world. Andre knew it was why he hadn't spoken much about it until the job was final and Andre had already secured a place to live. Julian had been afraid too much gushing would be enough to make Andre back out of their agreement, and if Andre were honest, Julian wasn't entirely wrong.

Eventually, Julian cleared his throat. "I'll see you at the office, then. We have several jobs in the queue, and we'll need an early start."

Snapping out of his haze, Andre replied, "Yeah, you're right. Guess we'll sort out which projects you want me working on when I get there."

Julian stepped back in far enough to clap Andre on the shoulder. "Night," he said.

Just as he was about to turn around, he changed his mind and folded Andre into his arms. He lifted a hand and rested it on the back of Andre's head, drawing it down so his cheek was against Julian's shoulder. For a long time, they stood there, Julian rocking a little and neither of them hiding their raw pain. Eventually he let go and used his thumb to swipe away his tears.

"Hey," he said. "I love you, man. Whatever you need, I'm here."

"I know." Andre pulled off his glasses and drew his wrist across his eyes before replacing them.

"Sure you don't want me to stay?"

"Yeah."

Julian nodded to Andre before he walked out of the house, the door clicking softly behind him. Andre slumped against the wall, closing his eyes and leaning his head back. He didn't want to move. The thought of rearranging his body drained him of all his emotional energy. He reminded himself it would get easier, if not truly better. The change of scenery would do him good someday soon.

Not yet having his television and other components set up and not in the mood to turn on his laptop—which wouldn't have Internet until Tuesday anyway—he pulled out a book. It was a dense technical tome, exactly the sort of thing he needed in order to relax his mind and remove himself from any other thoughts. He dragged himself up the stairs, hauling the book.

Even the routine of undressing, washing up, and turning down the covers set his teeth on edge and made his head throb. There was no way to escape the grief that clung like vines, wrapping themselves around his chest and squeezing until he was sure they would press the life out of him. He'd been convinced moving back to the city was the right thing to do, but now he questioned it all. The ache was deeper, a longing for everything he'd left behind mere hours earlier.

He curled on his side, the book splayed open on the bed beside him. For a few minutes, he stared at it, the words running together on the page. Andre closed it again, intending to sleep, but it was too early and he wasn't tired. He sat up and reached for his phone, where he had a couple of podcasts stored. Plugging in his earbuds, he opened the app and searched for one he wanted. Most of them were on technical issues or gaming, all requiring too much thought. The history of jazz one reminded him too much of Dahlia. He settled on something called Discoveries in Worship, which sometimes had interesting commentary on contemporary church music.

"Hey, this is Trevor Davidson of Harvest Church in Boston. Tonight's topic is bringing fresh perspective on old songs."

Andre had heard Trevor before; he appeared on the podcast about once a month, usually to talk about songwriting or how technology had changed the way church bands led worship. Trevor's mellow voice continued, and Andre frowned. There was something nagging at the back of his mind, like a dream he wasn't remembering clearly, but he couldn't put a finger on it. He ignored it and turned up the volume.

"We've all been in those churches where a choir ruins a gospel song by turning it into something pretty bland, right? We can have a great talk about cultural appropriation—and maybe we should—but tonight I'm turning it around. Up and coming gospel artist Irina Clay-Jones has taken old-school hymns and turned them into everything from R and B anthems to swinging jazz to soul-stirring spirituals. She's here with us tonight to talk about her art."

Feeling more awake, Andre sat up and devoted his full attention to the podcast. He'd been listening to Irina for a couple of years, and her voice was incredible. She performed some of her own songs, of course, but the tag line on her web site was "Re-imagining the classics for a new era." Her rendition of "Amazing Grace," a hymn Andre admitted he'd never especially liked, was haunting and included several of her own verses. As soon as Irina's rich, warm voice joined Trevor's, Andre smiled and settled in to listen to the rest of the hour, pleasantly distracted from his loneliness for the time being.

Andre had been in the office thirty minutes, setting up his workspace before Julian took him on a tour of the small building. A file sailed past his head to land on his desk with a rustle and a thump, and he looked up to see Julian leaning against the door frame with a smirk. Andre grunted and turned away again, reaching into the box on his chair. He wasn't giving Julian the satisfaction of being obnoxious this early in the day. Julian came and sat on the edge of the desk.

"What?" Andre asked, shoving at Julian's leg in a futile attempt to get him to move.

"They're looking for people with your experience as a consultant for this church," he said, crossing his legs at the ankle and folding his arms over his chest. "They're revamping their entire website now that their band, or whatever they call it, is getting popular. They landed some recording contract, so they need to rebrand."

"Yeah?" Andre tilted his head. "That sounds more like your expertise, if it's all design. What's involved?"

"I already told you most of it. It's less the web design and more what they want to be able to do on the site. They want someone to come in and make the whole thing user-friendly and easy to navigate but still look good."

Andre finally swiveled his chair to face Julian. "Where did you say the job is?"

"That big church in Braintree—Harvest Christian Community."

All the blood drained from Andre's face. "Hell no," he replied, picking up the folder and extending it to Julian. "It's one of those megachurches with about three thousand members. I know what they're like." He didn't have the balls to add commentary on privileged white pastors and their conservative expectations, but he knew Julian got what he meant.

Julian shrugged. "That's a little judgmental of you, considering you've never been there. It's a good contract, and they're paying well." He ignored the folder and remained where he was, his eyes boring into Andre.

"So, these people are gonna be okay with me, then? Come on. Seems like they'd be better off dealing with you directly."

"You have a background in this stuff. Besides, you're more religious than I am."

Andre huffed. "I'm not *that* religious, and I already have a church." *Sort of.*

"You have the credentials, and you don't have to go to church there. You can do all your work during the week. They're not expecting you to become a member or some shit. You've worked here less than an hour, and you're already refusing a job? Only reason I'm not firing your ass is our long history. Whatever your personal opinion on Harvest or its people may be, don't you ever pull that shit with me again or I really will fire you, friend or not." He narrowed his eyes. "You gonna tell me what you have against this church?"

Andre fiddled with the corner of the file and set it down then looked up at Julian. "I don't set foot in a church that doesn't plaster its views loud and clear on the front door. The first time I heard I was an abomination was at Dahlia's church. She knew how I felt about hearing it week after week, the Reverend more or less saying I was under Satan's control. She said as long as she and I knew it wasn't true, that's all that mattered." Andre looked down at the file. "She was wrong."

"Damn." Julian shook his head. "Well, like I said, you don't have to go there on Sunday mornings. I doubt you'd want to anyway. It's just a job."

Slamming his hand on top of the file, Andre stood up. "It may just be a job to you, but there are people—thousands of them—who give enough money to that place they can afford to hire us. They're the same ones who throw away the kids my Grams works day in and day out to reach. They spew hateful things about people like me because who they think I am matters as much as who I'm with, thanks to the damn 'one drop' rule for being gay."

Julian's face went red, and Andre realized he'd crossed the line. They both knew what it was like to live somewhere in between one set of expectations and another, and it had always been a sore spot for Julian. Everyone he met made uncomfortable assumptions about his race based on his light skin and green eyes, and he was forever fielding questions such as "What are you?" It didn't help having been raised by his volatile white mother and stepfather—that only fueled questions about where he'd come from. Andre backed down.

"I'm sorry, but you're pushing this awfully hard." Andre leaned back and crossed his arms. "What aren't you telling me?" he asked.

"You caught me." Julian relaxed somewhat. "You should really read the file, but I'll give you some motivation. They're looking to put their music out to a wider audience, so they need someone to organize everything they do and put it into marketable format. This isn't just any job. They have a weekly podcast called Discoveries in Worship, and once a month their music director—"

In surprise, Andre put up a hand. "Wait, wait, wait, now. It's *that* Harvest Church?"

"Uh...yeah. Why?" Julian frowned.

"I listen to the podcast. Trevor Davidson's their music director. Him, I like. Did you know their first guest this year was Irina Clay-Jones?"

Julian's eyes widened. "The gospel singer? Even I like her, and you know how I feel about the shit they put on Jesus radio."

"She's got a great voice," Andre agreed.

"And she's—"

"Oh, no you don't. Do not even say it."

"—hot as Hades," Julian finished, grinning when Andre punched his leg.

"Told you not to say it."

Julian shrugged. "So, you'll take the job, then? They have a growing audience in the Christian contemporary music scene, thanks to Irina and others like her. It has the potential to lead to a lot more work for us beyond bars and clubs."

"Ah, this isn't about the job. It's about making sure your company's name gets out there." Andre nodded. "Why didn't you say so in the first place?"

Julian waved his hand dismissively. "I thought getting a big contract your first day on the job was good enough reason. Would it have helped?"

"Yes." Andre huffed. "Fine. Leave the folder with me, email me the original application, and I'll look through it. I'll take the work, but the minute I have to deal with some homophobic ass, I'm out and you can finish the job."

"Fair enough." Julian crossed to the door and paused before exiting. "Anything you need?"

"No. I'll meet you for the tour as soon as I get my desk in order."

Andre picked a random item out of the box and set it on his desk, keeping his back to Julian to indicate their conversation was done. He didn't look up again until he heard the snick of the door closing behind Julian on his way out.

The day Andre showed up at the church was blustery and cold. He stood in the parking lot, looking up at the massive structure. The building was relatively new—probably built sometime in the mid-nineties—and had been added to at least twice that Andre could see by the slight variation in the color of the bricks and the slope of the roof. One part of it appeared to have been an entirely separate building, now connected to the main part of the structure. In any case, it didn't look like most churches Andre had been in.

He pulled open the door and entered. Pastor Bret Carmichael met him in the front foyer and ushered him into the church office to have a look at the programs they used for their various multimedia.

"We'll ease you in," he said. "I know we sent you all the files, but I wanted the chance to see you in person to show you what we already have, in case any of it is useful to you."

Andre nodded. "All right. Why don't we sit down and you can explain what you had in mind for your redesign?"

Bret led him down a hallway and through a set of doors. Andre thought he'd be lucky to find his way out again without getting lost. Eventually, they entered through a glass door labeled with the church name and logo. The sign on the wall beside the door read, "Church Offices."

Inside, there was a long desk, enclosed with a swinging half-door. Three secretaries, two women and a man, perched on leather swivel chairs, their eyes focused on the screens in front of them. One of the women had a phone pressed to her ear, and she was giving out information which sounded like times and dates. Her businesslike manner reminded Andre of his years at the tech support call center. There was a vague note of impatience in the woman's voice which Andre recognized as a reaction to the person on the other end being especially dense. He wanted to catch her eye and give her a nod of solidarity, but she didn't look in his direction even once.

Bret half-waved to the other two secretaries, who both looked up and nodded before returning to their work. He led Andre into the inner offices to a tiny space cluttered with books and papers. While

Andre hovered in the doorway, trying not to look uncomfortable, Bret removed a stack of books from a chair and pulled it over to the desk. He motioned for Andre to sit and then plunked himself into his desk chair.

"This is the website as we have it now." He made a few clicks. "We're looking to keep the logo, but we need something better for the rest of it. It's informative, but it's not eye-catching."

"Got it." Andre craned his neck to see, and he understood what Bret meant. They had a great logo—a stylized cornucopia and the church's name hand-lettered beneath it—but the site was boring and not intuitive to navigate.

"When we designed this, we had someone on staff who could do it. But back then, we had a third of our current membership. The point was to give an overview of the staff. Since then, we've branched out. It's crucial we get this done and linked to the sister sites for the church band and our multimedia, including recorded sermons and our weekly podcasts. We'll need some help for those, too."

He clicked over, and there was a simple page for the band which listed their few in-house CDs and some information on upcoming performances at the church. It was bland and unhelpful for most of what they probably wanted to do with it.

Andre said, "Well, you'll definitely want to beef this up. I have a few ideas, but I'll need to take this back to my office and play around with it some. Let me come up with a few proposals, and I'll get back to you in about a week. Meanwhile, I'll email you and you can send me a few more files I'll need, like photos of your recent staff additions and some decent pictures or videos of the band."

"Sounds good."

They spent the next forty-five minutes going through some of the features of the old site, deciding what Andre needed and what could be discarded.

Bret sat back and grinned. "Looks like we made a good choice in going to an outside source. We usually just hire from among our congregation, which is easy to do with so many members. I think we needed another set of eyes, though. Julian came highly recommended."

"How did you hear about us, anyway?" Andre asked. As far as he'd seen, most of Julian's work wasn't with the sort of clients who were likely to attend Harvest.

Bret waved a hand. "Oh, just a friend of a friend. Julian did the web site for his…business."

Sensing Bret's discomfort and assuming the man must have had some idea about Julian's usual clientele, Andre bristled. "Right. Well, I'm going to be doing the primary work on this."

"I'm sure you'll be able to put something together that works for us," Bret replied.

"I'll do my best."

They stood, and Bret followed Andre into the outer office. When he asked if Andre needed to be shown out, Andre declined, not wanting to spend more time in Bret's presence at the moment. He was sure he could find his way to the church entrance on his own.

Andre tried to follow the same route they'd taken, but somehow, he managed to get turned around somewhere. Instead of the glass double doors at the front of the church, he was facing a different set of doors, and there was no way around them. He would have to retrace his steps or take a chance and go in. Maybe there was a way through to the front. He pulled open one of the doors and stepped inside.

It was darker in there than in the hallway, and he blinked in the dim light. Once his eyes adjusted, he saw it was the auditorium, a vast room with seating for two thousand. Andre wondered what they would do if the church expanded beyond the maximum capacity. He was distracted from his thought by the sound of someone playing music. He sought the source and spotted a grand piano on the stage at the front of the auditorium. Surprised, he turned toward it, and his gaze stopped on the young man at the keys.

He was a bit too far away for Andre to see clearly, his face half hidden by a music stand. Singing and playing softly, he paused periodically to make notes on the sheet in front of him. His thick, wavy golden hair hung almost to his shoulders, which were hunched in concentration. Each time he stopped, he briefly put the tip of his pencil between his lips and closed his eyes, moving his hand over the keys, nodding, and making a mark.

Andre would happily have continued to watch his creative process, inching his way nearer, but the man stopped playing and glanced up. He slid off the piano bench and hopped down from the stage. When Andre had a closer look, his heart leaped into his throat, and he knew his eyes must be wide as saucers. He recognized the face despite only having seen it once before. *Trey.* It was hard to forget the mouth that had kissed him with such hunger and sucked him off so eagerly. Blood pounded in Andre's ears, and excitement zinged through him at the chance to talk to him again.

For a moment, Andre thought the young man was pleased to see him, too. Trey's lips parted and his eyes opened wider, but then he narrowed them and a deep scowl crossed his face.

"You're not supposed to be in here," he said, dashing Andre's hopes for a happy reunion.

"I-I'm sorry," Andre stammered. "I got turned around after a meeting in the church office."

Trey, or whoever he was, appeared tired—not just physical exhaustion but something else, some kind of emotional strain, and Andre wondered if he was the cause. Concern must have shown on his face because panic flashed across the other man's features briefly. He shrugged and his face relaxed into a half-smile.

"And you are?"

"Andre Cole." Shaking off his disappointment, Andre extended his hand, and the man accepted it.

"Trevor Davidson."

Andre's mouth dropped open. Reality smacked him forcefully and anxiety welled up. *Oh, God...oh, God...I got an anonymous blow job from the voice of my favorite podcast.* "I know who you are."

"Yeah, I get that a lot." Trevor sighed. "Look, can I do anything for you? If not, I'll show you out."

"Just showing me out is plenty." It really, really wasn't, but Andre wasn't sure how to ask if Trevor remembered their encounter as well as he did.

Trevor turned away and led Andre out of the auditorium. He opened a door tucked next to the stage then stepped out into a narrow hallway. At the end, another set of doors opened into the foyer where Andre had come in. Trevor motioned with his hand, and Andre thanked him. As he walked toward the entrance, he heard the door they'd come through thump closed. He turned around and stared at it for a moment, puzzled and disturbed by their exchange.

He exited the building, torn between hoping he wouldn't have to spend much time working with Trevor and hoping he would, if for no other reason than to see if Trevor eventually remembered who he was.

Chapter Five

Days later, Trevor couldn't get the random encounter with Antoine—*no, Andre*, he reminded himself—out of his head. Of all the places they might have seen each other, his own church was the last place he'd imagined. What was he doing there, anyway? It was like something out of a bad movie. It wasn't as though they lived in a tiny town and couldn't avoid each other. Trevor hoped he wouldn't run into him again.

Or maybe he hoped they *would* see each other again. He hadn't been able to let go of their encounter. The few days after New Year's Trevor had off weren't enough to erase the night. He'd hoped he was drunk enough he wouldn't remember, but he hadn't been nearly so lucky. He hated himself for what he'd done—he'd managed to tick off every box on the "Trevor was thinking with the wrong body part" checklist: a bathroom blow job, a complete stranger, no condoms, and a mouthful of come, all while promising he was eventually going back to his girlfriend. The combination wasn't his wisest move to date. One doctor visit later and he counted himself lucky nothing developed other than his own guilt.

After running away from the bathroom, he'd hidden as far in the opposite corner as he could. He'd texted Nate repeatedly until he answered, by which time Nate had collected Mack and Jamie. Trevor and Nate had stayed long enough to help the Creepy Crullers take care of what they needed to then bummed a ride home in Mack's van. The entire trip, Trevor had kept his head down, breathing shallowly and periodically taking a swipe at Nate, who repeatedly asked if he was going to puke.

Trevor shook himself. It wouldn't do any good to dwell on it. Andre had said he was there for a meeting, and he'd had a briefcase with him. He was probably some financial adviser or lawyer or something entirely unrelated to Trevor's job. It was the unknown that was killing Trevor, both the fear they would meet again and the disappointment they wouldn't.

He huffed and set down his portfolio of music then pulled out a fresh sheet. Bret Carmichael, the Pastor of Worship and Communications, was Trevor's immediate supervising minister. He wanted a full new set of songs for their upcoming release, and Trevor had only done a couple. Months of rehearsing and playing the praise and worship sets every Wednesday and Sunday, plus office hours and practice time and the weekly radio spot and podcast in between, left Trevor little time for anything else. Lucky for him, Tom Seltz, the lead guitar player, had also done a few, and they were set to cover a song popular on Christian radio for the last few years. That left Trevor to come up with the remaining tracks.

Unfortunately, his time was limited. Bret wanted most of the new songs introduced during worship in the coming months before recording to test their endurance against crowd-singing. It was a whole different ballgame. Most Sundays, the band played old standbys and a few newer favorites, and they typically introduced only one original song every month or two. They would have to test a new one every week at this point to gauge popular appeal.

Before Trevor was hired, they'd only ever covered other people's songs, and it was typical Sunday morning worship. When Trevor was promoted from his part-time work as their pianist, they played his songs along with those written by other musicians. At Trevor's insistence, this had included their own band members. Tom had been in a semi-popular local band for years in his youth, and he still occasionally played a gig as a fill-in with a few different people. He was a marvelous musician, and he had a knack for songwriting.

It didn't take long before he and Trevor were collaborating on songs. The down side of living in an apartment with three other people was not being able to practice at home—no room for a real piano, and too many people underfoot all the time. Trevor took to using the church's auditorium to play, and he used some of his time to write songs. Not all of them were necessarily on the approved worship set list, but he kept those to himself. Besides, they were mostly unpolished imitations of pop songs anyway, not anything other people would care to hear.

Trevor warmed up by rehearsing a song he'd co-written with Tom. He finished singing the lyrics about longing after God's own heart. It was a little cheesy, but the congregation seemed to like that sort of thing. He set the music aside and sighed. His heart wasn't in it, too full of the upheaval of the past few weeks. Eying the clock, he tilted his head to the side, listening. The senior pastoral staff was in their weekly meeting, so he wasn't likely to be interrupted.

Reaching into his bag, he pulled out a half-written song he'd been working on since he'd run into Andre again. He sang softly, pausing periodically to change a word here and there or to add another line. He began the third verse, his voice trembling as he poured into it everything he was reluctant to speak.

Hold this moment
On my knees, sinking low
Can't describe it
Spilling over, letting go
Heal my spirit,
Make me real, make me whole

A sliver of light and the door thumping shut alerted him to the presence of someone else. His hands stopped moving, hovering over the keyboard. He looked up to see Pastor Bret standing at the back of the aud.

Trevor jumped, his face flaming, and he was glad for the dim light hiding the red flush he was sure marked his cheeks. "Uh...hi?" he squawked out.

"Don't stop on my account," Pastor Bret said. "The song is fantastic. You've been holding out on us, acting like you didn't have anything big for the recording. Where've you been hiding that one?"

Covering his tracks, Trevor joked, "Under my hat." His stomach churned.

"Uh huh. Well, I'd like to see you finish up your new song so we can use it. How long do you think it'll take?"

"It's about done, but—" He coughed, stalling while he worked out what to say to Bret to put him off. "I was thinking about changing some of the words, though. It's not—I mean, it doesn't specifically say God or Jesus, and it probably needs some other fixes. You know, so it sounds more...spiritual." Trevor gritted his teeth in frustration as the inspiration for the song rose to the forefront of his mind.

Bret looked thoughtful. "I don't know. Can you play it for me?"

All the blood which had previously rushed to Trevor's face drained away, and sweat trickled down his neck to his collar. "I—"

"Not sure you want anyone to hear it til it's perfect, eh?" Bret laughed. "Come on. Don't worry that it's not good enough."

Oh, God, help me! Trevor prayed. "Okay," he heard himself say, even though he'd really meant to say, *No way in hell.*

He played the opening chords and began to sing, quietly at first and then with more confidence. "You touch my heart..."

You touch my heart
Where I don't want to be seen
You call my name
I don't know what it means
You shake my soul
And you shatter my dreams

I'm holding back
Hoping you can forgive
Something in me
Longs for what you can give
If I trust you
I'll find freedom to live

You draw me in
You fill me up
Let me hide away in you.
You draw me in
You fill me up
Let me hide away in you.

Hold this moment
On my knees, sinking low
Can't describe it
Spilling over, letting go
Heal my spirit,
Make me real, make me whole

I long for you
It's holy, holy
Lose myself in you

It's holy, holy

He immersed himself in the song and in the memories he'd drawn on to write it. It didn't matter what it was about; he was perfectly capable of making it sound like a love song to his God. He kept his gaze trained on the chord sheet in front of him, not daring to look Bret in the eye just in case. When he was through, he let the note fade away and closed his eyes. He didn't want to see Bret's reaction.

It took a moment, but Bret finally broke the silence. "Wonderful. I wouldn't change a thing. When we have a thousand members all singing this together, they'll all know who they're singing it for."

Trevor's immediate reaction was, *No, they won't.* Out loud, he said, "If you're sure." Meanwhile, he was internally cursing himself for not finding a better place to practice. He sighed.

"What did you say it's called?"

"Um...um..." Trevor hadn't named it. He looked down the lyrics and said, "Uh, 'You Draw Me In.'"

"You say the word, and when that song's finished, you introduce it to the team. It'll be fantastic, and it will go perfectly as an introduction to the sermon series on doubting God's call on our lives." Bret grinned. "I think I know what the title track on our CD is going to be. We'll use the name, unless you object." With that, he turned around and strode out of the auditorium.

Trevor put his head in his hands and groaned. He couldn't think of anything he wanted less than to have the song featured on the CD. So much for putting everything behind him.

Several poor nights' sleep left Trevor irritable, and he couldn't get the whole sorry situation off his mind. Nate tried coaxing it out of him, but Trevor remained stubbornly mum on the subject. He couldn't handle either of Nate's probable reactions—judgment or dismissal. Mack and Jamie weren't much help either. It was almost a relief to escape to work early Sunday morning to prepare for the multiple services.

The congregation loved Trevor's song, much to his annoyance and Bret's delight. The other band members were enthusiastic as well, cementing it as the title track. Trevor, on the other hand, couldn't even look his band mates in the eye after singing it. The first few times they'd played it, he could barely listen to the others as they sang backup to his lead vocals. He wondered if any of them had any idea what they were really singing about.

It was later than usual when he got back to the apartment, and Nate was waiting for him. The minute the door closed behind Trevor, Nate threw aside the trashy magazine he'd been reading and moved to block Trevor's path to the bedroom.

"Oh, no you don't," he said, wagging a finger at Trevor. "Marlie called because she couldn't get you."

"Ah, shit!" Trevor exclaimed, balling his hands into fists. Marlie was the last person he wanted to talk to.

Nate glared at him. "What the fuck is the matter with you? You've been a holy terror to live with since New Year's, and it's gotten worse by the day. I thought you wanted to talk to Marlie after your big, stupid Christmas fight. You're going to tell me *right now* what's going on."

Trevor turned past him into the living room and flopped onto the couch. He put his head in his hands. "I sort of made out with this guy at the bar." He mentally crossed his fingers, praying Nate wouldn't ask for details he wasn't prepared to give.

Nate didn't. He shoved Trevor until he made room then plunked down next to him. "Well, isn't that why we were there? This isn't so bad."

"Yes, it is! I feel like I cheated on her, even though she's the one who wasn't talking to me. She's probably calling because she wants us to try again, but..." He left the sentence hanging.

"You don't want to?"

"I do want to!" Trevor insisted. "But she still doesn't know about...you know."

"She doesn't know you're bi. Come on, Trevor. Just tell her."

"I can't, okay? She won't understand." He looked at Nate, pleading with his eyes.

Nate snorted. "It's not like you have to give her details." He sighed. "You ever think maybe the reason you're so uptight all the time—and let it out in monumentally stupid ways—is 'cause you haven't told anyone but me?"

Trevor rested his head on Nate's shoulder. "No. I lost control the other night, but it doesn't have to mean anything." He closed his eyes. "I'll call Marlie, and we'll get back together. Then everything can be normal again."

He watched Nate's chest rise as he sighed, but neither of them said anything else. Nate pushed Trevor's head off and stood up.

"Deal with it however you want. I've been trying to help you, but

I can see you're going to do what you want regardless."

Trevor looked up at him. "I—"

"Save it. Feel free to destroy your life, but leave me out of it when the shit hits the fan."

Nate stalked into the bedroom and closed the door most of the way. Trevor tipped his head back and blew out his breath with force. Nate didn't understand at all how much Trevor would be risking even if he only told Marlie. Still, he didn't like being at odds, and he would need to find a way later to make it up to Nate. First he had to call Marlie back, though. What happened was in the past, and he needed to move on. He pulled out his phone and hit her number.

She answered on the second ring. "Trevor!" She sounded relieved, if not exactly happy.

"Hey, sweetheart. I...um...Nate said you called."

"Right. I tried your phone, but you didn't pick up. Everything okay?"

"I was at church." He leaned back and stretched his legs, settling in for their conversation.

"Oh, of course," she replied. "Well, um, did you want to meet me for coffee later? I mean, if it's okay. You know, to talk."

"Talk?" Trevor sat back up. The last time Marlie had used the word it was so she could break things off again to "think."

"Well..." There was a long silence. "I want to try to make this work again, but after Christmas, I wasn't sure you'd want to."

"Of course I do!" Trevor was quick to assure her. "When did you want to meet?"

"An hour? We can go to that cute little shop right by your place."

Trevor was grateful it was Nate's day off from working there. He answered, "Sounds good. I'll be there."

They ended the call, and Trevor set his phone on the coffee table. He sighed and scrubbed his face with his palms. Everything would be fine as long as Marlie never found out what really happened on New Year's. He glanced at the partially closed bedroom door. What Nate didn't know wouldn't kill him, either. Trevor rose from the couch and retreated to their room to change, hoping Nate wasn't in the mood to have another crack at him when he found out where Trevor was going.

Trevor's church wasn't one of those ones where every interaction between men and women was policed, but it still made Trevor feel strange whenever he and Marlie went out alone. Staff were expected to hold themselves to a higher standard of behavior, so he was constantly looking over his shoulder to see if one of the elders had followed them. This was mostly because before Christmas, he was at Marlie's apartment—or she was at his—more often than not by the end of the date. There was no way he needed the church to be in on the details of their relationship.

He met Marlie outside the place where Nate worked, and when he saw her, everything else flew out of his mind. She had her springy blond curls pulled into a ponytail stuck through the back of her Sox cap, throwing a shadow over her brown eyes. A smile lit up her heart-shaped face when she saw him, and she rushed forward to throw her arms around him. When they connected, Trevor inhaled, appreciating her scent—a little of the cocoa butter soap she liked combined with the warm smell of her own skin.

While they sat in a cozy booth at the coffee shop, Trevor tried to find the right words to explain everything to Marlie. He made small talk, casually slipping in mention of the CD as a lead-in to a deeper conversation. He told her he was responsible for the title track, hoping to ease into what he wanted to say, but he never got the chance. Instead of smoothly opening the door, Trevor's comments only caused Marlie to gush about the music.

"I can't believe you're actually doing this!" She gripped Trevor's arm. "It could be the big thing you're looking for. Just think—what if someone hears you or sees you wrote your band's big song?"

"Yeah, about that—" Trevor started.

"So, tell me about it." She smiled.

Hand trembling, Trevor got out the lyrics and handed them to her. "Here."

She read them over, her eyes sparkling when she asked him to sing a bit. Softly, he hummed the first verse for her.

Marlie laced her fingers in his across the table. "I love it. The song's a classic 'fall in love with God' anthem, like what's all over in churches and on the radio." She grinned. "I love the idea of seeing God as the perfect soul mate."

"Uh..." Trevor wasn't sure what to do with that information. He didn't quite buy into the idea of Jesus as a lover, so her reaction both puzzled and amused him.

"Well, I mean, human relationships can go wrong, but this is eternal," she continued. "So I love the idea we're not only worshiping but we're loved in a more complete way." She tilted her head. "What?"

"You don't find it kind of...I don't know, weird? Like you're singing something sort of sensual about God?"

She shook her head. "Not at all. Worship is a fully sensory experience, so why not add all the emotions?" She laughed. "It's not like you're actually singing about sex, silly. It's the feelings associated with deep, passionate love. Those are universal."

Trevor wanted to slide under the table. He supposed he should be grateful Marlie hadn't figured it out. He would have a devil of a time explaining to her exactly how he'd come up with those words. Relaxing at the knowledge it had gone over her head, he put his hand on top of hers.

"Absolutely," he assured her. "Great passion."

Her smile slowly descended into a smirk. "I know other ways to express great passion."

The words definitely brought Trevor's mind off his worship song woes. "So...do you mean you want to get back together?"

"Yes," she replied. "My parents are being ridiculous about this. I'm sorry I dragged you into their mess." She sighed. "They expect it, you know? We've been together for so long, in a way, and they want to know what's holding us up."

"I know." Trevor shifted, both his previous amusement and embarrassment long gone. "I'm sorry, too."

"Then let's make it up to each other," Marlie suggested, and her smile returned.

Trevor raised his eyebrows. "Anything in mind?"

Her smile widened, and she hummed. "Maybe. My roommate is out in Springfield for the weekend to visit her sister."

"Meaning?"

"Meaning I have the apartment to myself."

Trevor squeezed her hand and let go. "We should go pay," he suggested.

"Good idea."

Anything, Trevor thought on their way out. *Whatever it takes to get that damn song—and everything that goes with it—out of my head.* He took Marlie's hand in his as soon as they were out the door of the shop, tugging to get her to stop walking. When she turned toward him, he leaned in and kissed her. She smiled against his lips, and the effect of her sweetness gave him a pleasant tightness in his belly. He melted into their kiss, and everything else washed away in its tenderness. He drew back and slipped his arm around her waist, heading for the train station.

He only barely registered, and quickly dismissed, the shadowy figure behind them, watching them as they turned their backs.

Chapter Six

On Valentine's Day, Trevor and Marlie met up with his friends at a crowded bar in Pawtucket. The place wasn't big, and as soon as they were inside he spotted Nate waving to them from the balcony. He led Marlie upstairs, grateful to be farther from the noise.

This might not have been Trevor's idea of a romantic date night, but he liked how Marlie was entirely comfortable listening to live rock music in a bar. He was sure her parents would be less than thrilled, both by the location and the company Trevor kept. More than likely, his church coworkers wouldn't be thrilled either. Then again, Trevor had so far made no effort to get any of his roommates to come to church. At first, he'd dodged questions from the pastoral staff. He'd made noises about living with other musicians, but there didn't seem much more to be said, so they'd let up. Trevor didn't feel responsible for their eternal souls even if he suspected some of the other staff thought he should.

Jamie's cousin, Brandon, was already there, as his fiancée was the keyboard player in the Creepy Crullers. He'd brought a friend, and he'd set Nate up with someone he knew from work. The four of them were seated at a large booth in the corner.

Brandon and his friend were keeping up a steady stream of ASL, only a small part of which Trevor followed. Jamie had been trying to teach all of them, and he was nothing if not patient, but Trevor wasn't quick to pick it up. He watched for a pause in their conversation. When he tapped Brandon on the shoulder, Brandon slid over to make room.

He motioned to the other man, whose hearing aids looked almost like stylish earrings. "C-i-a-n," Brandon spelled. That, at least, Trevor could understand.

"See-an?" Trevor tried. "I'm Trevor, and this is Marlie."

"It's pronounced Kee-an," Cian said. "Pleasure to meet you." He had an accent not attributable solely to being deaf; Irish, Trevor thought, though he was unable to be more specific.

"You too." Cian signed something to Brandon, but it was too quick for Trevor to make sense of what he'd said.

They made polite conversation and ordered drinks and food while they waited for the band to set up. A short while later, they were joined by a petite dark-haired woman. She slid into the booth next to Marlie and stuck out her hand.

"Hi," she said as Marlie accepted it. "I'm Amelia."

"Mack's friend," Trevor clarified, not adding the details of Mack and Amelia's friends-with-benefits arrangement. He also didn't mention how it was usually wise to steer clear of the apartment when Mack was in a mood to call her.

"Ah, okay," Marlie said. "I'm Marlie, Trevor's girlfriend."

"Oh!" Amelia's face lit up. "It's nice to have another woman here. When Mack said he was living with some gay guys, I assumed he meant everyone."

Trevor's heart nearly stopped. He choked out, "No, only Nate and Jamie."

She waved her hand dismissively. "I already knew about Jamie from the band. Speaking of, is The Boyfriend here somewhere?"

Amelia was referring to Jamie's endearingly awful significant other. The Boyfriend—none of them ever called him by his actual name—had been on-and-off with Jamie for at least two years. It was always obvious when they'd had one of their all-too-frequent fights because Jamie would come home looking like hell. All he ever did when questioned about what happened was shrug and say he "should have known better." Once, Trevor tried to ask what he meant, but Mack shushed him and said it was no one's business but Jamie's and The Boyfriend's.

Relieved to have the conversation move on, Trevor replied, "No idea. They broke up *again*."

Amelia threw her hands in the air. "Those two are such a train wreck. I wish they would—"

She never finished telling them what she thought because at that moment, The Boyfriend sauntered up to the table. Amelia groaned, and Marlie looked at all of them in bewilderment. Even though Trevor had lived with the guys for almost two months, he hadn't bothered explaining much to Marlie when they got back together—not The Boyfriend or Mack's seemingly endless string of partners or his own history with Nate. It never occurred to him to wonder why he would rather not share.

To everyone's dismay, The Boyfriend plopped himself at the other end of the booth after Amelia refused to move over. Nate scrunched his nose and went back to his conversation with his date. The Boyfriend helped himself to the appetizer in the middle of the table, and for a moment, Trevor thought Amelia might reach out and slap his hand away. She didn't, though it looked like it was killing her not to.

Eventually, the band started playing, and Trevor had something else to concentrate on. As they listened to a song that seemed to be mostly Mack wailing about what someone had done to ruin him, Trevor stole glances at Marlie. She was making nice with Amelia, and they seemed to have hit it off. Trevor was pleasantly surprised to discover Marlie wasn't any more interested than he was in using their evening to evangelize his heathen friends. He was particularly grateful she wasn't the type to open a conversation with how the Lord had blessed her. That might have been awkward. Instead, she was sharing a story about having been sent from her usual pediatrics unit to a floor with adults in traction following joint surgery. Whatever it was, she had Amelia laughing so hard she snorted.

It was a good thing Trevor didn't have to go anywhere but back to the apartment, and an even better thing he didn't have to drive there. His head was swimming from alcohol and loud music, and he was developing a headache from the ambient noise in the bar. Trevor was about to turn to Nate and ask if he wanted to go outside, but Nate was saying something in his date's ear. Trevor couldn't remember the guy's name; something starting with a P, he thought. He was dressed entirely in black, including his hair, which was short and slicked back, and he'd painted his lips glossy red. He looked more like he belonged in a vintage Robert Palmer video than out at a bar in Pawtucket to hear a friend's band.

Nate motioned to The Boyfriend to let them up, which he did before wandering off. They went downstairs, and Trevor watched them step onto the painfully tiny dance floor. He wondered exactly how they thought they might move to whatever the Creepy Crullers were currently playing. It didn't have a discernible dance beat.

When there was a break in the conversation, he stood up and grabbed his jacket.

"I'm going to get some fresh air," he said, extending a hand to Marlie. "Want to come?"

"Sure," Marlie replied. She stood as well.

Trevor tapped Brandon gently, and he turned around. It was slow, but Trevor managed enough sign to tell Brandon where they were going. Brandon was kind enough not to point out all his mistakes and waved them off, motioning that they would save the seats. Trevor and Marlie descended the stairs and stepped out into the crisp night. They stood just beyond the entrance to the bar, their breath coming in visible puffs against the chill. Once the ringing in his ears stopped, Trevor turned to Marlie.

"Having fun?" he asked.

"Sure," she said. "Your friends are...interesting."

Trevor sighed. He'd known this was coming. "Look, I'm sorry if it bothers you. This is why I don't tell a lot of people who I live with. I thought you were cool, but if it's going to be a problem, we don't have to hang out with them anymore when we're together."

Marlie shook her head. "No, it's not. I mean, I'm not really used to guys like them, and Nate's...boyfriend...person...date weirds me out just a little, but I'm okay with things. I promise. Or at least, I will be. Just give me time. It's not like what we grew up with." She sighed. "This is why it's been so hard to make things work, you know. You're really different from how you were."

Trevor sighed too. He could never be fully honest with her, then. She might learn to appreciate Trevor's roommates, provided they didn't have to interact too often, but there was no way she'd understand Trevor's conflicting feelings. It was fine, he thought; he could deal with that. He'd made a commitment to no one ever finding out, and he intended to keep it.

He reached up to tuck a stray piece of hair behind her ear. She was right about his being different, but she'd changed too. They weren't the same people they had been, and as he looked at her under the glow of the bar's external lights, he realized he hardly knew the woman she'd become. Hell, he hardly knew who he was himself. He wanted to, though—he wanted to learn who they were, preferably together. A host of emotions hit him at once—love born from years of friendship, an urge to discover everything he'd missed in their time apart, and a hot bolt of desire. It all culminated in the need to reach out to her. He leaned in and pressed his lips to hers, trying to tell her everything with one kiss. She slipped her arms around his neck as she kissed him back.

When he pulled away, he searched her face. She smiled, and it gave him a pang of sadness to know there were some things he would have to leave behind. He could, though. There was one simple way to secure their future. On the spot, he made a decision. He'd been planning to wait until they were home, tucked in bed together after their night out, but he was determined to move forward and not back. He moved his hand to cup her cheek. A wave of nervous energy zinged through him, and he used his entire willpower to keep his eyes on her.

"I know it's different, but I've really enjoyed spending time with you again." He swallowed. Why did asking girls important questions never, ever get any easier, even long after junior high?

She stretched up on her tiptoes and kissed his cheek. "Me too."

His heart thumped, and his palms grew clammy. He pulled his hand away from her and wiped it on his jeans. "C-can I...I mean...There's something I want to ask you."

Before Trevor had a chance to finish his thought, the door opened beside him, and out came The Boyfriend. Trevor bit back a growl. He flexed his fingers to keep a straight face and not glare at him for interrupting.

"Have you seen Jamie?" The Boyfriend asked.

"Last I checked, he was on stage," Trevor said, rapidly losing his patience. Any longer and he wouldn't be able to hold off on telling The Boyfriend exactly where he could go.

"Ugh, they're on break." The Boyfriend's voice had a whiny quality that grated on every last one of Trevor's nerves.

"I've been out here, and no one but you has come out."

The Boyfriend nodded. "Well, I need to find him. The one song was about me. I have to find him and tell him I'll take him back. Think he'd go for it?"

Trevor desperately wanted to say no, but it would have been a lie. He replied, "I'm sure he would."

"Great!" The Boyfriend grinned. "So, what are you two up to?"

This was not the time for The Boyfriend to act all warm and fuzzy with Trevor. Gritting his teeth, Trevor told him, "We were having a conversation. An *important* conversation."

"Oh."

At that moment, the door opened again, and two more people came out. Trevor saw them only in his peripheral vision, but the glimpse was enough for him to suck in his breath and do a double take. He shook himself before Marlie or The Boyfriend noticed anything.

No, no, no, he thought. *It can't be.*

The cold air hit Andre's cheeks, and he breathed deeply. It had been hot inside the bar. The only reason he'd gone was that his date lived nearby, and it was more convenient for her. It was the first real date with anyone he'd been on in three years, and already he regretted asking Trinity to set him up with her friend who'd been asking after him. He didn't even like this band—they were the same ones who had played the bar on Boylston on New Year's. Unfortunately for him, his date did like them. Or, at least, she liked the lead singer. She hadn't shut up about him the entire time.

It wasn't that Andre disliked her. She was very sweet, and ordinarily, she would have been the kind of woman he wanted. She had opinions on virtually everything, so she kept her end of the conversation going. On the drive there, he'd enjoyed her company. Once inside the bar, however, it was hard to hear, and she was absorbed in listening to the band. Andre was glad to finally get her out of there when the band took a break.

He was just about to ask if she was ready to go somewhere else where they could talk without shouting, but something caught his eye, and he looked over to where three other people stood by the corner of the building. His heart sped up, and he tensed. The blond man looked up, and their eyes met. Panic was written all over his face, and Andre couldn't blame him. He was sure his own expression matched.

It only took a moment before Trevor steadied himself and stood up straight. He turned toward Andre and clasped hands with the woman at his side. They moved closer, and Trevor dropped her hand to slip his arm around her shoulders.

"Andre, right?" he asked, his tone casual but with a slight tremor underneath. "You were doing some work at my church."

Andre cleared his throat. "Yes. I'm redesigning the website."

Trevor's eyebrows went up then his whole body relaxed. "Ah! I wondered why I hadn't seen you again. I thought maybe you were the financial adviser."

The idea amused Andre, and he laughed. "Not a chance. I'm all right with my own bills, but don't give me anyone else's."

Humor flickered across Trevor's face, but he quickly controlled himself. "Are you going to be around for a while, then?"

"Not really, no. I work remotely from my office. I'll pop in again a time or two, but not until the site's nearly done and we need to test things out."

"Fair enough," Trevor said. He drew himself up and smiled. "I'm being rude. This is Marlie, my girlfriend." He said nothing about the other man with them.

Andre's stomach clenched. That explained everything, though he was more than a little upset at having been Trevor's affair, brief though their encounter had been. He might have assumed their relationship was open or just starting if it hadn't been for Trevor's nerves and the sheer panic afterward. Nodding, Andre put his hand on his date's arm. He didn't think she required a fancy title, but he could at least introduce her.

"This is Nia," he said.

It was Marlie who made the next move. She held out her hand to Nia. "Nice to meet you." Her glaze flicked to Trevor, but she said nothing other than, "You're welcome to join us. It sounds like the guys are already acquainted."

Trevor said, "Marlie! They're probably out on a date. It's Valentine's Day." To Andre, he said, "Sorry, man."

Marlie elbowed him, and Andre almost laughed. The way she kept him in line reminded him of Dahlia, but for the first time, it was in a way that didn't make his chest ache. He looked at Nia, who seemed a little confused but not unhappy. Her calm acceptance of the situation cemented in his mind a desire to ask her out a second time, surprising even himself.

"It's all right. No one's really talking in there anyway," he told Marlie.

"Great!" she said.

Beside her, Trevor stiffened. He turned toward her. "I brought you out here for a reason."

Marlie's eyebrows went up. "Oh?"

"Yeah. Um..." He looked at Andre. "Maybe just give us a moment?"

"Sure."

Andre retreated with Nia to the opposite corner of the building to enjoy a few more minutes of peace before reentering. The man they'd been talking to when Andre and Nia came outside remained where he was. Trevor sneered at him and turned so his back was to everyone but Marlie.

He said to her, "There's something I want to ask you."

Marlie's eyes widened and her lips parted. "All right."

Just as Andre settled against the wall, he saw movement out of the corner of his eye and looked over in time to see Trevor kneeling in front of Marlie, her hand in his. Even though he knew what Trevor was doing, it didn't stop his brain from conjuring the image of Trevor on his knees in front of Andre, touching him. He wondered if Trevor had ever told Marlie that detail. Shaking himself, Andre returned his attention to Nia, only to find her caught in the thrall of watching the romantic moment, a delighted smile on her face.

Trevor took Marlie's hand in one of his and dug around in his pocket with the other. Andre went rigid and sucked in his breath. Beside him, he heard Nia's soft sigh. He peered around her to watch, grateful for the cover of the dim streetlights to hide his face.

Producing what he'd been looking for, Trevor said, "Marlie, I think it's about time I showed you how serious I am about us. Will you marry me?" There was a distinct tremor in his voice, and his hands shook.

A long silence followed. It extended to the point where even Andre began to sweat. He wondered if she was going to say no. Some horrible, tiny part of his brain hoped to find out what would happen if she did. Marlie's expression was unreadable in the low light. She bit her lip and looked into Trevor's eyes, searching, before she set her hand on his cheek.

In a soft voice, she said, "Yes."

Trevor slid the ring into place and stood back up, trembling enough even Andre saw it. He drew Marlie in for a tight embrace, his shaky breaths against her hair echoing off the building wall. Nia slipped her fingers into Andre's hand and pressed lightly. He looked away from Trevor and Marlie to find Nia smiling up at him. He squeezed back and let go to drape his arm around her shoulders.

The spell was broken by the grating sound of the other stranger's voice, whom Andre had nearly forgotten was still there. "Aw, that's so sweet!" He sighed dramatically. "And on Valentine's Day and everything."

There was a wistful look on his face, and Trevor laughed. "I'm sure it will work out for you too."

"Yeah?" the man's eyes lit up. "I'm going to go find Jamie and beg him *so hard*."

Under his breath, Trevor said, "Is that what they're calling it?" prompting muffled laughter from three of the other four people present. Louder, he said, "Wait! Don't tell him, okay? I want to be the one to do it."

The man shrugged. "Whatever. I don't care about that—I just want to make out with him. This shit makes me hot. See you." He waved over his shoulder and ducked back inside.

"He seems like kind of a tool," Nia muttered to Andre, causing him to choke on his own spit.

At the same moment, Marlie commented, "He's obnoxious."

"Yeah. But he's our obnoxious...whatever-he-is. Roommate-in-law?" Trevor snickered.

"That's not even a thing," Marlie told him.

"Wait, you know him?" Andre interjected.

"Unfortunately," Trevor said. "He's my roommate's...boyfriendish-person-thing."

"Wow," Andre replied. He wanted to ask what that meant, but he didn't think he knew any of the others well enough to fish for the whole story.

"Why does Jamie keep him around?" Marlie asked.

"We've all been asking the same thing," Trevor answered. "Maybe now that you're going to be a permanent part of our lives, you can help us figure it out. Let's not dwell on him. Ready to go back in and hang out with the others?"

"Sure," she said, sliding her hand into his.

Andre glanced at the place where their hands were joined and saw Trevor caress her knuckles with his thumb. He bit back the rush of jealousy, unsure whether it was aimed at Trevor or Marlie. He looked up to find Trevor watching him, and his stomach tightened. Nia looked like she'd enjoyed the whole thing, but Andre couldn't muster a convincing smile.

Running a hand through his hair, Trevor asked, "Joining us?"

Andre opened his mouth, but nothing came out, so Nia answered. "Sure." She sidled up to Marlie and said, "Lemme see?"

Marlie held out her hand to show off the ring, and Nia gave the obligatory *ooh* over it. Trevor caught Andre's eye behind the women's backs, and for the first time, Andre's lips curved into a smile. Trevor rolled his eyes, earning a soft chuckle. Together, the four of them stepped back inside.

CHAPTER SEVEN

Trevor's roommates insisted on a more private celebration. Much to Trevor's dismay, that involved inviting Amelia and The Boyfriend over. Mack had asked whether Trevor wanted any of their other friends there, including Andre and the woman he'd been with. Trevor declined; he didn't know Andre well enough—it had been one awkward evening in a bar, much like their first meeting only with less dick. The whole time, Trevor had sat in such a way that he wouldn't brush against Andre even accidentally. His date hadn't seemed to notice a thing, happily keeping up a conversation with the other women.

For an indiscernible reason, Nate had ignored everyone after they returned to their table, including his own date. The poor guy had left early, visibly upset. Consequently, Nate had no one to invite to their private engagement celebration. Nate had been in a mood ever since, but he was mum on what was going on in his head. Trevor left it alone, knowing eventually he'd be out with it.

In a rare fit of generosity, Mack offered to cook. He made a surprisingly good meal, and the whole group spent the evening in relaxed conversation. Amelia gushed appropriately over the ring, and the guys needled him about not making Marlie wait too long to set a date. The Boyfriend wasn't kidding when he said it made him hot; by the end of the evening, he had his tongue nearly down Jamie's throat, right next to Marlie. She smirked at Trevor and stuck her elbow in The Boyfriend's ribs. He pulled off Jamie's lips with a slurp.

"Sorry," he said, not sounding sorry at all.

He and Jamie disappeared into the bedroom, and Mack rolled his eyes. "Couch for me tonight," he muttered.

"Nah," Amelia told him. "You can come over later. I'm alone tonight."

Mack grinned. "You're a lifesaver."

On that happy note, everyone not currently having sex cheerfully cleaned the dishes and tidied the living room before Mack and Amelia bid them goodnight and slipped out into the early summer night. Marlie had work, and a very present roommate, so she tugged Trevor outside the apartment for a more private goodbye before leaving him alone to choose between listening to Jamie's bed banging or attempting conversation with Nate. When she was gone, he sank onto the couch, his mind still reeling from the whole situation. It still seemed surreal being engaged to Marlie after all this time. He wasn't sure what he'd expected to feel, but somehow, this wasn't it. He couldn't even identify whatever it was settling in his chest—he felt hollow and drained.

Nate dropped onto the couch beside him. "Thank God that's done. You okay?" he asked.

"Yeah. It's just going to take some getting used to. This is a big change."

"Well, yes." Nate snorted. "You've been dragging it out forever. I really didn't expect this. Had you been planning for a while?"

"Uh...sort of," Trevor admitted. "I mean, I've had the ring, but I wasn't really going to do it at the bar. It just...slipped out."

Angling himself toward Trevor, Nate frowned. "That kind of thing doesn't just 'slip out.' What's up?"

"Nothing," Trevor said. "We've been talking about it, and I thought now was as good a time as any. I was going to wait until we were alone, but it seemed right." He wasn't about to tell Nate it felt right because he had something to prove to Andre—chiefly that he was not available for another round of awkward bathroom sex, ever. Not that Andre had been asking; his date might have been an indication he was in the same position.

Nate pursed his lips and exhaled forcefully through his nose. "You ever tell her about what happened with us?"

"Hell, no. I already told you, it's behind me. Why would I change my mind?"

"Because I think you probably need to deal with it before you can marry her. I tried to tell you this before you got back together with her, and now you've gone one step further."

Trevor looked away. "Yeah, okay. I just...it wasn't like it was while she and I were together, though. Why does she need to know?" He kept his eyes focused straight ahead, praying his body language wouldn't give anything away. Nate could go right on assuming he was the only man Trevor had ever touched.

"The fact that you're even asking says a lot," Nate said.

Silence hung between them for a moment before Trevor said, "Why is this so important to you?"

Nate frowned and pursed his lips, letting another long silence grow before answering. "Because I'm sick of you being ashamed of yourself." He swallowed visibly. "I'm sick of you being ashamed of me."

"I'm not—"

Nate put his hand up. "Yeah, you are. I told you before, it wasn't an experiment for me when we were in high school. I liked you, and I wanted you to like me, too. Then you got with Marlie, and you said you weren't gay. I was crushed."

"I'm sorry," Trevor said. "It's the truth, though."

"Yeah, well, I know now. At the time, I thought you were lying. I was miserable for like a year after, but then..." A slow smile spread across his face.

"Rocco Alesi," they said at the same time.

Trevor laughed. "I remember him. I thought he was hot."

"You never told me that!" Nate exclaimed. "And he *was* hot. He was my first full-on, get-naked sex. We fucked in his parents rec room with the Sox game in the background and his mom making lasagna upstairs in the kitchen."

"What?" Trevor almost choked.

"Wait, I never told you the story?" Nate leaned back and stretched out his long legs. "Okay, well, we'd been working up to it for a while, but that day, we were down there and out of the blue, he goes, 'You wanna?' I'm like, 'Yeah, whatever, but what about your mom?'"

"What did he say?"

"He says, 'When Pop and his friends are watching the game, they make these sounds like they're screwing. So we put on the game and turn it up, and if Ma hears us, she'll just think it's that.'"

"Oh, my god. You believed him?" Trevor gaped at him and burst out laughing.

"Well, yeah. I mean, horny seventeen-year-old, right? Anyway, so he puts on the game, and we just kind of take our clothes off and start doing it. Then, while he's pounding me and I'm just about to blow, his mom calls down, 'You boys want something to eat?' I was too close, Rocco kept moving, and I let go, groaning real loud. A second later, his mom says, 'You all right?' And Rocco, still without stopping, goes, 'Yeah, Ramirez just struck out. Looks like they're gonna lose.'"

Trevor snorted. "Did he just pick a random player?"

Nate elbowed Trevor. "Well, of course. It had probably been several years since Rocco actually cared about baseball. I'll get to it."

"There's more?"

"Oh, yeah. Rocco's mom just yells something else, and he looks down at me, gives me this shit-eating grin, and leans in for a kiss just as he comes. It was fucking fantastic." Nate shook his head. "Later on, Rocco's dad comes back home after watching the game with his friends. We're standing in the kitchen, eating the lasagna his mom made, when he shows up. She doesn't know any more about baseball than we do, so she says, 'Sorry about the Sox game' and repeats what Rocco told her. His dad gives her a real weird look and says, 'The Sox played a great game. I think Rocco was messing with you.' Then he walks off. She looks at us, and she pretty much catches on—she'd suspected for a while—goes beet red, and says she has things to do so we need to get out of her kitchen. You know, she never, ever offered us food again when we hung out."

Trevor laughed until his eyes watered and his stomach hurt. When he finally calmed down, he said, "I can't believe you never shared that with me. Whatever happened to him, anyway?"

Nate sobered. "I don't know. We decided to come out to our parents at the same time, since we were dating. Well, and having sex by then. My parents were cool about it, but his weren't. He eventually just told them he'd been confused, and we broke up." He sighed. "I haven't seen him since. Last I heard, he got married and has a kid. Found out from the guy he's been having an affair with for the last two years."

Nodding, Trevor said, "You don't want Marlie and me to end up like him."

"I guess." Nate shrugged.

They sat quietly for another minute before Trevor said, "Marlie was my first, you know. I mean, other than what you and I did.

Summer before college."

Nate glanced at him. "No, I didn't know. Guess I should have assumed, though."

"I'm not going to be like Rocco. This is different. I won't cheat on her." He tilted his head. "Huh."

"What?" Nate asked.

"That's it. I said it out loud—I won't cheat on her because I love her." Saying it gave him a rush. He laughed and ducked his head, knowing his cheeks were turning red. In all the years he'd been doing this dance, he'd never said the words to Nate's face. "I love her," he repeated.

Nate relaxed, though his smile was sad. "You'll be happy with Marlie. Think how much happier you'll be if you tell her the truth." Nate patted Trevor's knee and stood up. "Congratulations again," he said.

As Trevor watched Nate retreat to their room, he thought, *He's wrong. It's all behind me now.*

Valentine's Day at the bar, listening to the same crappy band he'd endured on New Year's and sitting next to Trevor without giving anything away, was beyond draining. Andre had sat next to him all evening, doing everything in his power to avoid even a random touch. He'd witnessed the man proposing to his girlfriend, which explained a whole lot of everything, from the fake name to the bad case of nerves to the way Trevor folded in on himself whenever they saw each other. Andre had always been more careful about choosing his partners, even for casual sex. He never wanted to be with anyone who was ashamed of him. It was one thing he'd learned growing up—be proud of who you are, no matter what. He would not allow himself to become Trevor's dirty little secret.

Afterward, Andre returned to work with renewed vigor, taking on several new clients for projects he enjoyed immensely. Julian left him in charge the following week while Elisa was having the baby. Andre took all the jobs Julian hadn't put on hold and threw himself into them, grateful he was single and not coping with sleep deprivation and diaper duty then feeling guilty for having those thoughts. He knew it was hard on Elisa, and only a few years before, it would have been him.

Andre spent extra hours in the office, avoiding both alone time at home and any thoughts of his repeated meetings with Trevor. He was in the habit of listening to contemporary praise and worship music during his after-hours work sessions. There was a host out of Boston who liked to feature local bands. He was on three evenings a week from eight to ten. On that particular night, he was featuring music from Harvest Community, who were due to have their first professionally-mixed CD out in the spring. Andre's stomach tightened at the mention of the name.

They'd sent the title track, a song called "You Draw Me In." The show's host played the song, and Andre turned up the volume. Trevor's mellow tenor soared over the thrum of the bass and the rich piano notes. The melody was full of longing and a touch of sadness as he wove words about his world being shaken. Andre could relate. Something in it made him think about the way he'd resisted letting even God in after losing Dahlia. He closed his eyes, pausing in his work to listen. It wasn't until the third verse that it clicked.

Hold this moment
On my knees, sinking low
Can't describe it
Spilling over, letting go
Heal my spirit,
Make me real, make me whole

There was no possible way the song was about Jesus. Andre's eyes flew open, and his jaw dropped. How did he get that song past whoever was in charge at his church? There was no question Trevor had written it—no other musician would have dared—and it was glaringly obvious what the song was about. It occurred to Andre that in a church like Harvest, there were probably codes to obey, and as such, none but a few would even notice what the words meant.

Andre's emotions rode the roller coaster from horrified to angry to a spark of pleasure that what he and Trevor had done meant something to both of them, even though they'd been strangers. The spark turned into full-blown joy, and a chuckle worked its way out from deep in Andre's chest. By the time the song had reached its peak, Andre was almost doubled over in laughter. His whole body shook through the rest of the song, and he didn't begin to calm down until the last chorus faded. He wiped his eyes and sat back in his chair, still snickering.

The radio host came back on. "That was 'You Draw Me In,' from Harvest Community's upcoming CD. Wasn't it fantastic, folks? I'll play it again at the top of the next hour. In the meantime, how about another great uninterrupted set, starting with this classic from Irina Clay-Jones."

Andre glanced at the clock. Another forty minutes until the song came on again. He looked down at his phone, contemplating, then sent Julian a text.

Turn on WKXN around 8:55.

He knew Julian was probably exhausted from caring for a newborn, but Andre wanted his reaction. He'd never given Julian the details, but he had to know if the song sounded as suggestive from an outside perspective. From within the church, he could see how most people wouldn't notice a thing—a lot of what played on WKXN had at least vaguely romantic tones to it. Still, he wondered how many listeners picked up on it. The thought made him sweat despite knowing they wouldn't be able to trace it directly to him.

A few minutes later, Julian's reply came through: *You know I don't listen to that shit.*

Andre sent back: *Trust me. You need to hear the song playing at 9.*

Julian didn't answer, so Andre returned to his work, sneaking peeks at the clock every few minutes. He wasn't accomplishing much other than making himself jumpy, so he eventually put his work aside and listened to the typical cycle of songs. At five minutes to nine, his phone rang. He grinned when he saw the number.

"You turn the radio on?"

"Yeah, yeah." Something sounding like a yawn followed. "Why?"

"You gotta trust me." Andre couldn't help laughing.

"Mind telling me what's so damn funny?"

Andre said, "Mm-mm. I wish I could share the joke, but that would spoil it for you. It was a song I listened to. They're gonna play it again at nine."

"Was it a parody?"

Laughter welled out of Andre again. "I wish! No, they were entirely serious."

"Come on," Julian whined. "Just tell me."

"No way. The ads are over. Listen to it then call me back." He ended the call.

At last the song came back on, and he listened to it, this time allowing himself to think about Trevor. He wondered if he was going to hell for getting turned on by praise music. The humor he'd felt when talking to Julian drained away, replaced by a wash of frustrated sadness. No matter how significant the moment had been to Trevor, that's all it was and all it ever would be. Trevor was engaged and heading toward being one of the future stars of contemporary Christian radio. There was no place in his life for someone like Andre, on multiple levels.

The song ended and his phone rang again. Without waiting for Andre to greet him, Julian said, "What the hell did I just listen to?"

"I guess you heard the song."

"No shit, I heard it. Please tell me I'm imagining things. I thought those Jesus types weren't allowed to have sex."

Andre rolled his eyes. "I'm a 'Jesus type,' asshole. And no, you weren't making it up. I have no idea how he managed it, but the whole song is about giving a blow job."

"You don't sound as amused as the last time I called."

There was a long pause before Andre could answer. "No."

"Give it up, man. What's going on?"

Andre sighed. "The song was about me."

"You? But you just said he was singing about—*oh*." The light had clearly gone on. "Oh, boy."

"I know!" Andre took off his glasses and rubbed his eyes.

"When were you planning on telling me this?" Julian demanded.

"I wasn't. I already paid up for New Year's. You didn't need to know kissing a man at midnight turned into—well, *that*."

"Fuck, Andre. That's—that's messed up." He paused. "Wait. How do you know it's about you? Maybe this guy gives a lot of random blow jobs."

"No way. He said I was his first." Andre grabbed a paper off his desk and tried to fan away his embarrassment. "I keep running into him because of the church job, and it's hella awkward. I don't know what to do."

"Ask him out, you fool."

"No!" Andre huffed. "Sorry. I can't. He's engaged—to a woman. I have no idea what's up with why he hooked up with me, but I'm not gonna take her man away from her."

"Shit, man. That's rough. You want me to take the job back so you don't have to deal?"

"Naw. I'm okay, I guess. It's only a couple more months, and then I can be rid of them. They want anything else after that and you can have 'em."

"Fair. Gotta go—baby's awake. I'll call you tomorrow."

The call ended, and Andre sat there staring at his phone while the radio continued to play in the background. He'd told Julian he could manage, but just how he was to accomplish it was a mystery even to himself.

Chapter Eight

The first week of March, Trevor brought home the early release copy of the CD. The song had already been circulating courtesy of WKXN broadcasting it during their evening show. Trevor was grateful his roommates didn't listen to Christian radio because he wasn't sure how he was going to explain the song to them. The minute he walked through the door, Nate and Jamie were all over him to get a look.

"Let me see!" Nate grabbed the CD out of Trevor's hands and opened it, pulling out the insert.

Jamie leaned over his shoulder, reading the lyrics. His face lit up and his mouth dropped open in an O of surprised pleasure. He recovered and looked over at Trevor, grinning. "You didn't."

"Didn't what?" Trevor tried to sound innocent even as heat crept up his neck.

Nate read the words to his signature song out loud. "This song isn't at all about Jesus, is it?" he asked.

"Don't know what you're talking about." Trevor crossed his arms in a futile effort to hold in the rising embarrassment.

Jamie laughed and took the insert from Nate. "You're good," he said. "You had your entire congregation singing an ode to men blowing each other? And they thought it was a worship song?"

"Uh..."

Scanning the lyrics of the other songs, Jamie's smile widened.

"This one is about BDSM, and here's one about fucking. How did you get them past the censors?"

"It's not about sex!" Trevor tried to take back the lyrics sheet so he could figure out which song Jamie meant. There was no way any of the other songwriters had penned anything like what Jamie was suggesting.

Jamie held it out of his reach. "Oh, come on. The part about the beating drums is obviously about a pounding heart, and this here—" He stopped and read through it again. "Yeah, this part seriously reads like thrusting."

Trevor snorted. "First of all, just because you all are reading other meanings into it doesn't mean anything. Second, I didn't write anything that hasn't been done before." He grabbed the insert back from Jamie and put it in the CD case, tucking the whole thing away. "The theme is on intimacy with God."

Jamie shrugged. "I really have no stake in this." He turned away from the others and retreated back to his room.

Nate rounded on Trevor. "I can't believe you." His expression darkened, all traces of the fun they'd had erased.

"What?" Trevor frowned.

"This song," he said. "I should've realized when you were working on it. Have fun explaining it to Marlie."

"Shut up," Trevor snapped. "Just shut the hell up. You've been a complete ass about the whole thing, ever since I got back together with her. You mind telling me what's going on?"

Nate's eyes flashed. "If you were going to go public with everything, you might have told her first like I said you should. You could have talked to me, too. Instead, you turned it into a damn worship song—or several, from the looks of it. "

"I wasn't intending to make this into anything," Trevor snapped. "My boss heard it and insisted I make it officially part of our set. I still work for him, and there's no way I was going to tell him what it's about. I did what I had to in order to keep my job."

Nate snorted. "Ah, right. Like lying about who you are. You know, I'm a lot less pissed at you for writing a song about sucking a guy off than at how you lied to me. You kept telling me everything was about Marlie and your goddamn image, and you made me think I was the only one. Your holier-than-thou attitude about saving it all for her was just an act. For once, Trevor, be honest with yourself. You might be able to convince someone else you went through a phase, but that song proves you're still thinking about having your mouth around some guy's cock. Since it wasn't me, it must have been someone else you were sucking behind her back. And mine, apparently."

Trevor balled his hand into a fist. At first, he wanted to reach out and smack Nate, but the urge was replaced with the same burning shame that had kept him from telling Nate the truth the night he'd met Andre. They stood there staring at each other, tension rising between them. The moment was broken by Jamie reentering the kitchen. He took one look at the two of them, and his eyebrows rose nearly to his hairline.

"Jesus, you two," he remarked. "How long has this been going on?"

Snapping out of the moment, Trevor turned to look at Jamie. "How long has what been going on?"

"This." He gestured between them. "Heard you two yelling and came to see what was going on. I have no idea what it was all about, but damn." Jamie shook his head.

Trevor sighed. "There's nothing going on."

"Not anymore," Nate said, an edge still in his voice.

Jamie crossed his arms and leaned on the counter. "What do you mean, 'anymore'? Were you two a thing?"

"No," Trevor said; "Yes," Nate said.

"Which is it?" a voice asked from the hallway. A moment later, Mack came around the corner. "You three should keep it down. Don't want to wake Mrs. Crotchety in two-B."

Trevor scrubbed his chin. "We were never a couple, no." He huffed. "Nate's right, though. We kind of had a thing."

"You two were having sex?" Mack asked. He blinked a couple of times. "Didn't see that one coming."

Jamie raised his hand. "I did."

"We weren't having sex!" Trevor insisted. "God, this is humiliating. All we did was fool around a little, okay? Something we did when we were both between relationships. It wasn't a big deal, and it doesn't mean anything now because I'm engaged."

Nate glared at him. "Maybe you should also clue them in on the blow job you never told me about."

"Whoa." Mack leaned away. "I definitely don't need to know the specifics, and I don't know why you think I do."

Nate's jaw twitched. He turned to Mack and said, "Jamie was right about the song. Trevor wrote an anthem to blow jobs, inspired by real life and not involving me."

"Does Marlie know?" Jamie asked.

"No, and none of you are going to tell her. It's not like we filled each other in on the details of our other previous partners." Trevor glared around at them to make sure they understood.

Jamie crossed his arms. "You can't marry her if you're gay. She's going to get hurt."

"I'm not gay!" Trevor roared at him, causing Jamie to flatten himself against the counter.

"Right," Mack said slowly. "But if you've been with guys, she probably should know. That's gonna come up at some point if you're going to keep hooking up with men."

Nate threw his hands up. "That's what I keep telling him!"

"No." Trevor was adamant. "She doesn't need to know because I am *not* planning to do anything with anyone else—ever. That was history. "

Nate's face contorted with anger. "It's not history if you're writing songs about it. You can pretend all you want, but eventually, she'll find out the truth."

"What truth?" Trevor snapped. "Seems to me like you're seeing what you want to see. Jealous because someone else got what you wanted from me?"

A shocked, hurt look replaced Nate's anger. His jaw dropped, and for a moment, he stood rooted to the spot, staring at Trevor. He opened and closed his mouth a time or two then turned on his heel and stalked into the bedroom, slamming the door behind him.

Mack watched him go then turned to Trevor. "You're an asshole," he pointed out.

Trevor clenched his teeth together. His stomach hurt; he hadn't wanted to cause problems between himself and his roommates. Ignoring Mack, he turned to the sink and gripped it tightly, closing his eyes. The silence behind him was deafening. He knew both Mack and Jamie were still in the room, waiting for him to say or do something. He steadied himself before slowly turning around to face them. He locked eyes with both of them in turn then started toward the bedroom.

"Don't even think about it," Jamie said, moving so he blocked the hallway. "Give him time to cool off before you try to talk to him."

"Whatever," Trevor said through gritted teeth. He retreated to the living room and flopped onto the couch to wait for Nate to emerge.

Mack stalked over and stood in front of Trevor, glaring down at him. "I'll say what Jamie wouldn't. Don't talk to Nate until you have your head out of your ass. At least try to understand what you did wrong first, or you'll end up fighting again. I'd like to live here in peace. Just so you know, if it's a choice between the two of you, I'm leaning toward replacing you with The Boyfriend." He didn't wait for Trevor to reply, walking away without another look back.

Trevor heard the second bedroom door slam and glanced over his shoulder at Jamie, who had gone about his business in the kitchen, ignoring everyone else. Trevor didn't doubt Mack was serious about kicking him out if he didn't sort the mess he'd made with Nate. With Jamie otherwise occupied and Mack in his room, Trevor decided to take a chance and sneak in to talk to Nate.

The minute he stood up, Jamie turned around. "Not a chance," he said. "Mack's not kidding." He snorted. "Even I would rather not have to cope with the alternative, so give it time and talk to Nate when you're both calm."

Trevor nodded. "Fine."

He waited a moment longer, hoping Nate might emerge and they could talk about it, but the door remained firmly shut. They wouldn't have time to talk before Nate went to work, so Trevor grabbed his coat and headed for the door. He glanced back once, noting that Jamie was still ignoring him and the bedroom doors were still shut. Trevor stepped out of the apartment, not sure where he was headed but knowing he needed to be away.

As he walked toward the train station, he realized there was no one left he could talk to. His thoughts drifted to Andre, and the intense shame threatened to overcome him again. He stopped walking as an idea occurred to him, and he reached into his pocket for his phone.

Pastor Bret answered on the second ring. "Hey, Trev."

"Uh...hey. Listen, can you give me the phone number for the guy who does our web site? I, uh, wanted to check on something for the band. I had an idea." Trevor's hand trembled in sync with his voice, and he was glad Bret couldn't see him and spot his lie.

"Sure. Hang on." There was a pause. "Ready?"

"Any time."

Andre heard Julian's phone ring and was surprised when a minute later, he was handing it off saying the person had specifically asked for Andre. He took the phone from Julian.

"This is Andre Cole. What can I do for you?"

"Uh..." There was a long silence and the sound of throat-clearing. "Um. This—this is Trevor Davidson."

Oh, Lord, help me, Andre prayed silently. He tried to keep his tone casual as he said, "From Harvest, right?"

There was a nervous chuckle on the other end then Trevor said, "Yeah, sure. Among other places."

Andre let out a small snort. This was the first time either of them had mentioned knowing each other beyond work. Between the acknowledgment and the song, it couldn't be a coincidence Trevor was calling, but Andre figured he'd play along.

"Right. Well, what can I help you with?" he asked.

"Oh. Um, well, I wanted to ask...about...the web site for the band. So, uh, maybe we can meet up? Should I come to your office?" He sounded both eager and hesitant.

This had to be good. Andre couldn't stop the tiny thrill that ran up his spine. "Are you at the church?"

"No, I'm still close to home. I'm in Weymouth."

Andre did his best to keep his voice calm. "Didn't know you lived there too. I can meet you near your place, actually. I was going to finish up for the day and head home."

"Well, um, good. There's a nice coffee shop around the corner from—wait, never mind. Can't go there. Any place you like?"

Andre wondered why Trevor had backtracked on the place he was about to suggest, but he didn't question Trevor on it. Instead, he gave the name of a diner a few streets over from his house. Trevor agreed, and they ended the call.

"Hey, Julian?" Andre called.

Julian poked his head out of his door. "Yeah?"

"Tre—someone from the church wants to meet with me to go over the web site. Gonna take off early, meet with him, and head home after. Cool?"

Julian's eyebrows rose, and a smile played on his lips. "Yeah, cool. I hope you can work things out with the 'web site.'" He made air quotes.

"I pretty much hate you." Andre scowled at him.

"No, you don't. Count yourself lucky I didn't decide to take the call." He turned around and walked back into his office.

Andre shoved everything he needed into the bag with his laptop and straightened up his office space. He couldn't help the combination of excitement and nerves at seeing Trevor outside the church and away from his friends. With one last hurried goodbye to Julian, he dashed out the door and ran to catch the train so he wouldn't keep Trevor waiting too long.

When Andre reached the diner, Trevor was already there, hands in his pockets and shoulders hunched against the early March chill. His nose was red from the cold, and his lips were chapped, but Andre was struck with how good he looked. His thick blond hair had grown a bit since the last time Andre had seen him, brushing his shoulders in soft waves. He stamped a little and blew on his hands.

"Hey," Andre said.

Trevor jumped. "Hey." He smiled, but it quavered.

"Wanna go in?"

They stepped inside. The warmth hit Andre. He breathed in the scent of coffee and cooking food as he led Trevor to a table near the back. He sat facing the rear wall, allowing Trevor the privilege of looking at the door. Trevor took off his coat, and Andre almost sighed. Trevor looked like he'd lost some weight, and it disappointed Andre to see his masculine curves reduced to undernourished leanness. Andre tried not to remember the way his body fit so comfortably against Trevor's. It was a single night, and no matter how much it meant, this was someone else's man he was talking to.

Trevor sat down and picked up his menu, staring at it even as it shook in his hands. Andre wanted to reach out and put a hand on his wrist. Instead he sat back with his own menu and pretended to look at it while stealing glances over the top.

"Why did you ask to meet me?" he asked.

"Told you," Trevor replied. "The web site."

The server appeared, and Trevor ordered coffee while Andre ordered a cup of tea. Trevor's face morphed into an amused expression, and Andre rolled his eyes.

"What?"

"Guess I'm just surprised," Trevor replied. This time, the quiver in his voice was a thinly-veiled attempt at not laughing. "I don't know a lot of guys who drink tea."

Andre snorted. "That's my Grams' influence right there."

Trevor set his menu down. "You're different than what I thought."

"You wanna explain that? 'Cause I'm lost." Andre frowned.

"I guess...I don't know." Trevor's shoulders slumped. "I don't know why I called you."

"I think I do." This time, Andre did reach out, but he only rested his fingers for a moment on Trevor's wrist before withdrawing his hand. "I heard the song on the radio. You needed someone who knew what happened."

"Yeah." Trevor leaned back and closed his eyes. "I'm so, so sorry," he said.

Before Andre could respond, the server returned with their drinks and took their orders. Trevor looked up briefly but didn't make a move to pick up his cup. Andre took two packets of sugar and dumped them into his tea.

"What're you sorry for?" he asked. "For what we did?"

"No. The song." He tilted his head up and opened his eyes. "I'm not sorry we—you know. I couldn't process it. I didn't mean to hurt you."

Andre shook his head. "'S cool. You did what you had to. I get it."

"No, you don't." He pressed forward, leaning his chest against the table. "I'm not—" He glanced around before whispering, "gay."

"Fine. Never said you were."

"But other people might. My fiancée doesn't know. Like everyone else, she thinks the song was about God." He rubbed his forehead. "My roommates found out. Jamie took one look at the lyrics and knew. He told Nate, who...crap." He put his head in his hands.

"Relax. Just tell me what happened."

"I can't!" He was loud enough several people glanced over. That seemed to shock him out of his panic for a moment. When he looked back at Andre, Trevor's eyes were wide, fear reflected in them. "What if someone else finds out? Oh, God, oh, God." Trevor was breathing hard as though he were on the verge of crying or vomiting.

"Hey. Hey." Andre gripped Trevor's forearm. "Stop. Breathe."

Trevor nodded and took several slow breaths. "I shouldn't have let my boss hear that song."

"Look, I'm not going around telling people, if that's what you're worried about."

Shaking his head, Trevor replied, "Not you. Nate—one of my roommates—has been pushing me to tell Marlie because he and I were...I guess sort of friends with benefits, but it was more just messing around. Never went anywhere much. When he found out what I'd done, he went apeshit on me."

Andre sat back. "Are you gonna tell her?"

"I don't know. I wanted to see you first."

"Nate's not completely wrong, and neither are you, but you gotta decide why you're telling her, if you do."

Trevor groaned and slumped down in his seat. "Not you too."

Andre said the only thing he could think of to make Trevor understand. "My wife knew."

There was a long pause while Trevor absorbed that. Then he said, "Knew? Did she leave you because of it?"

"No." Andre took a deep breath. "She...died."

"Oh, God. I'm sorry." Trevor straightened up. "What happened?"

"Car wreck. Look, that's not my point." Andre leaned in. "She knew I was bisexual when we got married. Now, maybe you got a whole 'nother reason for not telling Marlie, but if that's all it is, you better say something before she finds out a different way. Like maybe your roommates letting something slip or someone else clues her in about the song."

"You—you're bi, not gay?" Trevor tilted his head.

"Yeah." Andre drew his brows together. Of all the things he'd said, that was the one Trevor was fixated on. "Why?"

"Well, I mean, you seem so...okay with that."

Andre couldn't hold back a laugh. "Why shouldn't I be?"

"I—" Trevor stopped, his face turning red. "I thought—"

"Oh, Lord Almighty. Is it because I'm black or because I'm a Christian?"

"Um. Well...damn. Both?" Trevor cringed visibly.

"You need to know a few things," Andre said in a ferocious whisper. "First of all, whatever you've been led to believe doesn't apply to all of us. Maybe I got lucky, but my Grams didn't raise my dad like that. She was an out and proud activist back in the sixties, and she still runs a shelter and health clinic for homeless youth. My sister's a married gay woman. You got it right that it's rough, but maybe when you're having your fancy-ass, lily-white wedding to a woman who you have the privilege of staying in the closet for, you'll remember that there are kids—*our* siblings, yours and mine—out there on the street or taking their own lives because they didn't have that. Some of us don't want to see more of them die. I'm damn proud of two things." He held up one finger and then another. "I'm proud to be a black man, and I'm proud to be bisexual. I want them to love who they are too."

"I'm sorry," Trevor said. His face had gone pale.

"Good." Andre sat back and studied Trevor, trying to pick up on his thoughts. "You too," he said, angling his chin at Trevor. "Be proud of who you are. Own it. If the woman you're about to marry can't handle it, she's not the one. If you love her, and she loves you, it shouldn't make a damn bit of difference."

"You don't understand." Trevor shifted in his seat. "There are expectations."

"There always are. Question is, what's more important to you?"

The server brought their food, which Trevor pushed around on his plate like a child. They ate—more or less—in silence for some time before Trevor set his fork down.

"It meant something, you know," he said.

"I know." Andre waited several heartbeats before adding, "Meant something for me, too." Andre thought about telling him it was the first time he hadn't had to push thoughts of Dahlia out of his mind, but he kept it to himself.

They finished their meal, and Andre paid, despite Trevor's protests. Outside the diner, Trevor put his hand on Andre's shoulder before he turned to head home.

"Thanks," he said.

"No problem."

Trevor was too close, and his breath was warm against Andre's ear. There was a look of longing on his face, something so sad and almost desperate that Andre's heart ached. If Trevor wasn't going to say it, neither was he. There wasn't any chance Andre was going to be an accomplice to a cheating boyfriend. He took a step back, nodded at Trevor, and turned his back on him, walking away for what might be the last time.

Chapter Nine

Trevor stayed away until after dinner, spending most of the time hiding in a Dunkin' Donuts about a mile from the apartment. He felt disloyal, eating a muffin and drinking a decaf somewhere other than where Nate worked, but he couldn't bring himself to go there. Eventually, he returned to the apartment, knowing Nate had rehearsal and wouldn't be in until late.

When Nate did get home, Trevor was waiting for him. He was lying in bed, but he was wide awake. Despite how angry he'd been earlier, Nate still made the effort to be quiet when he entered the room. Trevor took it as a good sign Nate still cared as much as Trevor did. The damage wasn't irreparable.

"Hey," Trevor said.

Nate twitched, startled. "I didn't mean to wake you." His tone was clipped.

"You didn't. I was waiting for you." Trevor sat up.

With a soft sigh, Nate turned around. "Why?"

"I think we need to talk about this. I'm—I'm sorry for what I said earlier." Trevor didn't break eye contact, though he felt uncomfortable under Nate's gaze.

"Which part? I think for once you didn't hold back with me," Nate replied. He sat down on the bed. "I'm sorry too."

"For what? I was the one being a dick."

Nate looked down at his hands. "I didn't tell you the whole

truth either."

"Sorry—what?" Trevor frowned. "Tell me what's really going on."

Nate flopped backward, his feet still on the floor. "I was jealous of Marlie. Then when I read those lyrics and knew you didn't mean me, I was so pissed. You said I was the only one you'd been with. I thought it meant something. You were right, you know. I...I wanted what you gave a random guy in a club."

"I didn't know," Trevor said. "You always told me what we were doing was just letting off tension."

Nate sat partway up and propped himself on his elbows. "After Rocco, when we were in college, I wanted more, but I told myself it was out of desperation." He gnawed on his lip. "Maybe part of me hoped moving in with you here would make you change your mind. All it did was prove there's no chance at all, and whatever we had is over."

"Yeah. I've tried to tell you," Trevor said.

"No." Nate shook his head. "That isn't what you tried to tell me. You've been saying you were going to end up with Marlie regardless of any other feelings. I think I'd always hoped you were one of those guys who says he's bi but really means he's not ready to come out. You know how the song sounds?"

"I—"

Nate cut him off. "It sounds like you're still feeling confused about it. I don't want to make you admit you're secretly gay, and I don't want to break you and Marlie up. All I want is for you to acknowledge it meant—*I* meant—more to you than some experiment. It hurts that you needed a stranger to prove something to yourself. You wrote about him the way I once wanted you to write about me."

Trevor sighed. "You're right. It wasn't a phase. You've been my best friend for years. Of course you mean more to me!" Trevor drew up his knees. "I don't know how to deal with any of this."

Nate got up and moved to Trevor's bed, causing Trevor to tense. Nate huffed. "I'm not over here to grope you. Listen, I know you love Marlie. Why do you think I keep pushing you on this? I'm honest with the people I date. You need to give yourself permission to feel these things."

Trevor's heart thundered. Nate deserved the truth after all his pushing. Trevor swallowed. "The guy the song was about? He meant more too, even if I was drunk and didn't get his real name."

Nate's jaw dropped. "Who—" He stopped, and his eyes widened.

"New Year's. The great-looking guy you were dancing with."

"Yeah. The problem is, it turned out not to be as random a hook-up as I thought. I wrote the song because I couldn't wrap my mind around sucking dick in a filthy bar bathroom—it wasn't something I planned on doing, ever. And then..." He wiped his sweating palms on his shorts. "He started working for the church. He's doing our web redesign."

Nate whistled. "So that really is what the song is about."

"Oh, yeah. Jamie called it right. It was never supposed to make it this far, but my boss walked in when I was singing it. He loved it and wanted to put it on the CD. The other songs are about God, as far as I know. I wrote three of them, including the one Jamie insisted was about fucking, but 'Drumbeat' honestly isn't about sex, no matter what he says."

Nate said, "Not consciously, maybe. You need to let this out. If you don't, it's going to keep bleeding into your work. Someone's going to figure it out."

Trevor scoffed. "I doubt it. Do you have any idea how much erotic worship music there is out there? People get paid a ton of money to write these Jesus Is My Boyfriend songs, and everyone sings them without really thinking about it. There's one where you sing about Jesus coming like forty thousand times. No one even bats an eye." He nudged Nate's knee.

Nate gave him a piercing stare. "They pick up on it a lot more quickly when you use metaphors. 'Spilling over'? Really? You think no one's going to know you don't mean you're so full of the Lord's love?"

"They'll see what they want to see," Trevor said. "A lot like Jamie did. Even the Bible uses similar language—'my cup overflows' and all. I mean, ever read Song of Solomon? It's these two people going at it for eight chapters, but it got included in the Bible because everyone was convinced it was a metaphor for God and His people. I watched some documentary on it once where this scholar said the part about filling the woman's navel with wine was a reference to eating pussy."

"Uh..."

Nate's eyebrows were nearly at his hairline, and his lips twitched. A moment later, he was laughing, and Trevor joined in. As they calmed down, he leaned against Nate and rested a hand on his leg. Nate dropped his head to Trevor's shoulder.

"It still hurts a little," Nate said.

"What?"

"That someone else got to be your first. So it was good?"

"Yeah," Trevor said, tracing his thumb in slow circles on Nate's leg. "It was...different, I guess. I didn't have any idea what I was doing. It freaked me out when sucking him got me so hot, and I still don't know what I think." He closed his eyes, not sure how much to tell Nate. It seemed too personal to explain how the taste and feel of Andre on his tongue gave him the same rush he had when Marlie's hips bucked under him. For Trevor, it all centered on the excitement of giving someone else pleasure more than the body he was touching, as though their joy transferred to him and his to them. It exhilarated and terrified him at once. He opened his eyes again. The best he could do was say, "I'm—I'm not gay."

"I know."

"Sometimes, I go through phases where I miss it," Trevor admitted. "Not only you, but..." He cleared his throat. "What we had."

"Me too," Nate said.

Trevor withdrew his hand and sat back up. "I made it clear I'm with Marlie. I won't be cheating on her with strangers or people working for my church or anyone else. You and I can't be like we were before. There are no breaks in between this time—she and I are getting married."

"I know." Nate sighed. "I need some time, okay? Give me a while to process, please."

"Yeah. All right."

Trevor stood up and made for the door, knowing he wouldn't be able to sleep yet. As he turned the knob, he glanced back at Nate in time to see him curl up, his knees to his chest. Trevor slipped out, shutting the door gently behind him.

They were in Marlie's apartment, making love. Everything was heat and need and desperation as Trevor lost himself in her and in the moment, full of her scent and her taste. His breath came in ragged pants as he and Marlie moved together. Her legs were wrapped around his back, and her head was tilted so her neck was exposed to his lips. As she ground her hips up against him, he mouthed along her pulse point and palmed her breast, making her arch her back. He thrust almost frantically, a slight whine escaping with every exhale. Just before he erupted, he grasped the back of her head and drew her into a messy, eager kiss. He gasped as his orgasm hit, twisting his fingers in her hair and moaning as he descended from his high.

He clung to her, trying to burn the moment into his brain. When he was calmer, he pulled out, grunting as he slipped free. He hurried to shed the condom and toss it out. Reaching for Marlie, he slid his hand between her legs, his fingers alongside hers as together they brought her to her peak. She whimpered and shivered, leaning into Trevor and turning as the last waves washed over her. The tremors transferred to him, and he groaned, enjoying the sensation. She sighed in contentment as her body relaxed, and it made Trevor smile into her hair. That, too, was a memory he wanted to capture. He kissed the top of her head then her forehead, cheeks, nose, and finally lips.

"Mm," she murmured. "So good."

"Yeah."

As they lay in each other's arms, Trevor's sleepy mind wandered to his conversations with Nate. Trevor wasn't pleased at the intrusive thoughts, and he attempted to banish them in favor of sleep. They wouldn't let him go, however. He'd meant to tell Marlie everything over dinner. All through the meal, he'd started to say something then stopped when the conversation redirected. Afterward, they'd watched a movie, and there hadn't seemed to be a good time to bring it up—especially once the movie was forgotten in favor of making out. Now there was nothing stopping him other than his own stubborn refusal.

He thought about what Andre and his roommates had all said. Maybe Andre was right—she'd been one of his two best friends for as long as he could remember. If she really was the one he was meant to be with, she would listen and accept whatever he shared with her. He'd lived too long without being able to fully trust anyone else with the deepest part of his soul. He brushed the hair away from her face and sighed.

"What is it?" Marlie turned so she was looking up at him. She rested her hand on his chest.

Trevor looked at her, his lovely fiancée, her face so open and inviting. This hadn't been when he'd planned to do it, but he figured he might as well take a chance. He'd been doing that a lot lately, jumping into things without a plan.

"I need to tell you something." His neck prickled, and he clenched and unclenched his hands.

"All right." She adjusted so she didn't have to crane her neck.

"The thing is...you knew I'd gone out with other people, right? When we weren't together, I mean."

"Sure," Marlie replied. "You knew about my exes, too. So what? I don't think it's been a problem." She smiled. "Having a bit of experience was a good thing."

"Yes," Trevor said, "but there's more you don't know."

Marlie rolled over on her stomach and laid her arm across Trevor's chest. She rested her chin on it. "Okay. Tell me."

"Nate and I—" He stopped and looked at her before trying again. "Nate and I used to fool around some. Kissing and stuff. Not much."

"Like, experimenting?" Marlie frowned.

"Not—not really," Trevor said. He cringed. "I mean, yeah, in the sense we weren't in a relationship. Mostly...jerking each other. You know how guys are." His forehead broke out in beads of sweat.

Marlie scrunched her nose. "Yeah. I have four younger brothers. So that's it? It didn't mean anything, right?"

"Um. Well, after Christmas, when you said you needed a break to think, I—" Trevor stopped when his gut tightened, and he had to take several deep breaths. "I sort of hooked up with a different guy and sucked him off."

"You did what?" Marlie blinked.

"I wanted to know what it felt like." Trevor's face flamed, and his whole body was tense.

"Oh, my God." Marlie sat up and pulled the sheet around herself. "Wait. Are you saying you've messed around with other guys besides Nate?"

It felt like Trevor had swallowed a rock. "Yes. More or less."

"Like, sex?"

He shook his head. "Not like you're thinking. A couple of times making out, a couple of hand jobs. This was..." He twisted the sheet in his fingers. "It was my first time giving a blow job."

Marlie had moved farther away from him, putting a hand on his chest to keep him away. "But...what about you and Nate? You live together! Have you been fooling around with him this whole time too, even after we got back together?"

"No, I—"

"You've been cheating on me! That's what this is about. Are you looking for my approval so you can mess around with him until we get married or continue after? Is that why you were practicing your new oral skills, to keep Nate around as your—what, part-time boyfriend?" Her expression had gone from puzzled to angry, a deep scowl lining her face.

"No! Will you listen to me?" Trevor sat up, pushing her arm out of the way.

Marlie was shaking, and Trevor tried to pull her in to reassure her, but she stiffened and moved to the edge of the bed.

"Don't touch me," she snapped.

"I'm sorry," he said. "It was just the one guy while we were apart, and it wasn't planned. As for Nate, he and I are friends, which is all it's ever going to be. I wasn't trying to hurt you."

"Hurt me? Trevor, you should have told me you were gay. I said I didn't have a problem with it when I met Jamie, and I've known Nate for years."

He sat up too. "First of all, you did have a problem with it. You always have. You said it would take some getting used to. Second, you wouldn't have liked it any better than the truth, which is I'm *not gay*."

"You gave a guy a blow job. Sounds pretty gay to me, unless you didn't like it." She crossed her arms.

Trevor huffed. "I don't actually know how I felt about it." He cleared his throat. "Yeah, I liked it. That doesn't mean—"

Marlie stopped him. "I don't know what you're even saying here. I've seen those shows. Those documentaries about guys who marry women so they can act like they're straight. Are you using me as a cover?"

"Of course not. Did you hear what I said?" he snapped. "There are more than two options, you know."

"You're lying to yourself. What happens when this isn't enough and you decide to mess around with other men? Am I supposed to approve and let you go suck whoever when you get an itch?"

"No. I'm marrying you, which pretty much means I only want to be with you. But even if it did mean something else, we'd work through it together, right?"

She glared at him. "You waited until now to tell me. Why? Because you were still trying to figure yourself out? Or because you were still doing whatever-it-was with Nate?"

Trevor sighed. "I wasn't still doing anything with Nate except sharing an apartment. This was something we did when we were between partners, let off a little steam. I already told you it's over. Same with the other guy. I have no plans to do anything with anyone but you. "

Marlie got up and began sorting out her clothes. "I wish I believed you," she said. "But the last guy I was with who stuck his thing where it didn't belong left me for someone else."

"'Stuck his thing where it didn't belong'? For real? Geez, Marlie. I had mine in you a few minutes ago, and you're still wondering if I'm interested?"

"I think you're confused," she said. "Since I'm not inside your head, I have no idea what you were fantasizing about while you were with me. I'm not prepared to have a gay man faking it with me because he can't be honest with himself."

"The hell?" Trevor asked.

Marlie's eyes flashed. "You heard me." She threw his pants at him, and they smacked him in the face. "Get dressed," she snapped.

Trevor got up and pulled on his clothes. "You're being damned unreasonable," he said. "I only told you because everyone else said I should. They were afraid someone would figure it out eventually because the church insisted on putting the song I wrote on the CD."

Her mouth dropped open. "So your big song *was* about sex. And all your friends except me knew you wrote an ode to putting your mouth on a stranger?" When he didn't say anything, she continued. "What the hell are you going to do when the church finds out? People are going to be pretty pissed! The song's been played everywhere." She yanked on her shirt. "It's going to change everything."

"It won't change anything other than you knowing more about my past, unless you plan to broadcast this to the world. No one has any intention of making it a public spectacle." He held his hands out to her. "Please," he begged. "All I'm doing is telling you something about myself. I'm trusting you with something here. Let's sit down and talk about it so we can work things out."

Marlie stood at the foot of the bed, facing him. "I need you to leave," she said. "I can't deal with this."

Trevor pulled on his shoes. "I'm not in any way confused about who I am. I'm with you because I want to be. I hope you'll figure that out." He straightened up and headed for the door. "I understand if you need time to process this, but don't take too long. Please?"

"It's over, Trevor. This time it's for good. Get out."

Her deep frown and pursed lips were etched into his memory as he turned around and walked out of the bedroom and then the apartment.

CHAPTER TEN

The early spring wind stung Andre's cheeks as he and Julian made their way to the bar on Boylston. He hadn't been back since New Year's, and he wasn't exactly feeling enthusiastic. Not to mention he still wasn't sure why Julian of all people kept dragging him to gay bars. He would need to ask what was up with that. Of course, he also hadn't called Nia despite his plan to do so. He hadn't seen her since Valentine's Day, and he hadn't made much effort to see anyone else either. He reasoned Julian was probably trying to give him options.

When they arrived at the door, they were surprised to see a burly, bald man with a small black beard hovering there, stamping his feet against the cold. He looked up as Andre and Julian came to a stop in front of him.

"Evening, fellas," he said. "You here for the event?"

"Uh, no," Andre replied. "What's going on?"

"Charity fundraiser—Covers for Covers."

Andre's curiosity was piqued. "What is that?"

"Bunch of local acts doing covers of other bands' songs to donate blankets and books for local homeless youth shelters."

"Hey, that's pretty cool," Andre said.

"Do we need tickets or something?" Julian asked.

"Nah," the bouncer said. "Price of admission is a new blanket or a book, or you can make a donation."

"You have a list?" Andre wanted to know.

The bouncer reached into his pocket and drew out a folded piece of paper. "Here you go."

Julian leaned over Andre's shoulder and they browsed the list. "Is it on there?" he asked.

"Yep, right here." Andre pointed to his grandmother's shelter. He pulled out his wallet and withdrew some cash. "My Grams operates the Lighthouse over in Quincy."

"No kidding!" The bouncer's face lit up. "That place helped me and my brother."

"Yeah?"

"Went there after our folks died. My brother ain't gay, but 'cause of me, they wanted to take him away from me. They helped us so we could stay together. Now he's all fancy and shit, even went to college. Me and him, we never thought that would happen. That was more'n twenty years ago."

He was tearing up a little, and Andre put a hand on his arm. "Well, this is a great thing you're doing. The owner here must be a real good guy."

"He is." The bouncer ducked his head.

Andre grinned. "He's your man, huh?"

The bouncer's lips twitched, and he looked back up. "Yep. And his wife—she's at the bar—is our woman."

"Oh!" Andre's grin widened. "No wonder I like this place. Well, Mr.—"

"Curtis. My name's Curtis."

"—Curtis, you must be a real good guy, too." Andre handed him the money.

"You don't have to," Curtis said. "Your grandmother and all."

"Nope. It's for other places too, right? Make sure this gets into the fund."

"Will do. Have a good time, boys. Gonna be quite the night— couple of bands, a drag show, and a hot Irish dancer with his back-up fiddles."

Curtis held open the door for them, and they stepped in. Andre blinked in the dim light until his vision cleared and he could have a look around. He nearly groaned at the first two things he noticed. One, the band on stage was the same one that had been playing on New Year's. If Andre remembered right, they were also the same ones he'd taken Nia to see on Valentine's Day. The second thing he saw was that Trevor was there, sitting at a round table near the back.

His companion looked familiar. Andre thought he recognized him from among Trevor's group of friends. Even sitting, Andre could see he was a big man—well over six feet tall, broad shouldered and muscular.

Julian took in the look on Andre's face and said, "What?"

In order to avoid telling Julian he'd seen Trevor, Andre replied, "I really, really hate this band."

"They're not so bad."

"They sound like teenagers messing around. At least they're not doing their own shit this time." He couldn't help the tiny flick of his gaze back to Trevor when he remembered they were supposedly friends of his.

Julian noticed and turned his head in the same direction. "Isn't that—"

"Yes. And no, I'm not going to go talk to him. He's engaged and therefore unavailable."

"Guy with him isn't bad, though." Julian shrugged.

"How do you know he's into men? Besides, he's not my type."

"We're in a gay bar. But I'd forgotten you prefer curvy, blond, and broody."

Andre growled. "*You're* not gay *or* bi, and you're here. Wait. Did you really just call Trevor curvy?" Never mind that Andre had used the same word himself, or the fact that it was an apt—and very sexy—description of Trevor's body type.

"I knew you were still interested." Julian smirked.

"Up yours."

"You wish. I want to meet him, that's all," Julian replied, earning him a hard glare.

"Fine. We can ask to sit with them. If they say no, you will not push it."

Julian held up his hands. "Hey, I'm only trying to help. I'll be good. Sort of."

Andre jabbed him in the ribs, but he relaxed. Nothing was going to happen. They were all just a bunch of guys, there to enjoy their night of terrible rock bands, drag queens, and—had Curtis really said Irish dancing? Andre shook his head. At least he wasn't alone in this thoroughly bizarre experience. He glanced around then back at Trevor's table. If things went south, either with the entertainment or the company, they were near enough to the door for him to make a hasty escape.

Just as he and Julian headed for the table, Trevor looked up. His eyes opened wide for a moment, and his lips parted. His evident shock passed as quickly as it had arrived, and his expression settled into something that wasn't welcoming but wasn't unfriendly, either. Julian nudged Andre, and he involuntarily took a step forward. Now committed, he had no choice but to make it look like he'd been heading that direction anyway.

He approached Trevor and the huge guy with him. "Hey."

"Hey." No warmth there, but he didn't sound hostile, either. Trevor put a hand on the shoulder of the other man. "Nate, this is Andre."

Nate's eyebrows shot up. "Nice to meet you." His gaze drifted past Andre to Julian, and he smiled. "And you?"

"Julian."

He accepted Nate's hand, holding it for what Andre decided was just slightly too long. He rolled his eyes behind Julian's back, and to his surprise, Trevor choked back a laugh, covering it as a cough into his elbow. Andre grinned and sat down next to him. Trevor leaned in so only Andre could hear.

"Julian's straight, right?"

"Yes, and married. Don't mind him. He's an ass and a flirt, but he's not going to break poor Nate's heart. He'll let him down easy."

Trevor chuckled. "Good thing. I need some entertainment other than this horrible shit trying to pass for music."

Andre laughed. "Aren't they your friends?"

"My roommates, actually. I'm sure they'll improve...eventually." He sighed. "This was Nate's way of making me not sit home and mope."

"Trouble at work? Or..." Andre wanted to ask if it was about their last conversation, but he refrained.

"I took Nate's advice. Well, and yours." He snorted. "Didn't go so well."

"Oh." Andre knew he shouldn't get involved, shouldn't want anything to do with the situation at all. Except he was already in it. He blew out his breath and said the last thing he wanted to say. "She'll come around."

Trevor shook his head. "We're done." He sighed. "I'm not sure we ever started, to be honest."

Nate interrupted them. "Trev, you want anything? I'm going to grab a drink." His eyes flicked to Andre, but he said nothing, and his expression was hard.

"Yeah, just a beer." Trevor turned to Andre. "You?"

"I didn't offer him anything."

Nate spun around and stalked off. Julian shot Andre a look, but Andre just shrugged. He had no idea why Nate was being hostile. Julian nodded and stood up.

"I'll get us something."

He headed for the bar without asking Andre's opinion. Andre glanced at Trevor, but the other man's shoulders were hunched and he had his head in his hands. There was obviously something Andre was missing.

"We can go if it's making you uncomfortable."

Trevor looked up and shook his head. "Not me. It's Nate, and there's nothing you can do." He sighed dramatically, and Andre almost laughed. He had the good sense to keep quiet as Trevor continued, "He wants something I can't do for him. My life is one giant, fucked up ball of...something."

The band switched to something slower, and Andre almost groaned again. He stole another glance at Trevor. All the color had gone out of his cheeks, and he turned his head slowly to stare at Andre for a long moment before dropping his head onto his arms. He mumbled something into his sleeve that Andre didn't catch.

"This song—" Andre started.

Trevor lifted his head. "I know."

It was the one that had sent Andre and Trevor to find the nearest place with some amount of privacy. The memory of their encounter made him too warm as he recalled the feel of their bodies pressed together, the scent of Trevor's skin, and the pulsing of the music all around them.

"It's not even a good song," Trevor muttered.

This time Andre did laugh. A moment later, Nate and Julian returned and set drinks down on the table. From the looks of it, they'd gotten chummy while up at the bar, and they both settled in to ignore Andre and Trevor. The band concluded with an upbeat tune that had an 80s throwback feel to it and left the stage. The emcee announced the next act, and Andre sat back in his chair. Nate and Julian had their heads together, talking about something. Andre elbowed Trevor.

"You want to get out of here?"

Trevor eyed him for a moment then tilted his head at the others. "What about them?"

"They'll be fine. Julian will keep Nate occupied."

Nodding, Trevor turned his eyes to the stage. The performer, a drag queen with a full beard, was doing an excellent version of Annie Lennox. When Trevor looked back at Nate, Andre followed his gaze. He was amused to see Nate was transfixed, his eyes hardly blinking and his lips parted, leaning forward in his seat.

"I don't think it will be a problem after all. Can Julian look after him?"

"Absolutely," Andre said.

He tapped Julian on the shoulder and motioned to Trevor. Leaning in, he said, "We're going to find somewhere else to go for a bit. We'll be back."

Julian raised an eyebrow. "Of course you are. You'll be careful?"

"I'm not gonna hurt him."

"I wasn't worried about Trevor."

Andre shrugged, and Julian nodded. They both looked to Trevor, who was trying to get Nate's attention. Nate only waved him away after giving him another frown. Something about the way they were interacting bothered Andre, but he couldn't put his finger on what. He chalked it up to Nate's earlier rudeness and his present distraction.

Trevor led the way to the door, Andre close behind. When they stepped out into the windy night, Curtis grinned at them and waved. Andre's neck heated up, knowing what Curtis had assumed, but he said nothing and waved back.

They made their way up Boylston. There were several other gay bars along that stretch of road, but Andre had something else in mind. Out of the way, tucked between two other buildings, was a small place with good coffee and better jazz. What seemed like an eternity ago, he and Julian had once played there on a similar night. There had been a group of women, celebrating a birthday. Andre had only had eyes for the one he thought was the most beautiful, vibrant woman he'd ever seen. He counted himself lucky she'd waited around for him afterward.

He turned to Trevor. "Am I remembering right that you like jazz?"

They stood outside the tiny place, Andre's question hanging between them until Trevor realized he hadn't answered. He held open the door for Andre.

"Yes, I do," he said before they entered.

Inside, it was warm and smelled like cinnamon and sugar and fresh coffee. Trevor liked the place immediately, even more than he'd liked the little diner on Summer Street. There was a low stage at the back, and the band was playing something with a 1940s-style swing. Andre led Trevor past the tables in the middle to one on the far side of the room. Once they'd removed their jackets, Andre offered to get something for Trevor and disappeared to the counter.

He was back in a few minutes with two steaming mugs and a plate with several different desserts, none of which looked familiar to Trevor. He took one of the cups and began doctoring his coffee. For several minutes, they were quiet, enjoying the music and the food.

"Oh, you've got to try this," Andre said, waving his spoon at his plate.

It looked like some kind of pie, but Trevor wasn't sure. He picked up his own spoon, about to take a bite, when Andre held out his own. Without thinking, Trevor leaned in and closed his lips around the spoon. Cool sweetness burst on his tongue, and he couldn't hold back the sound of surprised delight. Andre laughed.

"Good?" he asked, his dark eyes twinkling.

Trevor swallowed his bite. "Yeah. What is it?"

"Pecan custard pie."

"It's amazing."

He was about to simply go back to drinking his coffee and listening to the band, when Andre put a hand on his arm. Trevor looked up to see the concern written there.

"You want to talk about it?" Andre asked.

Trevor shook his head. So this hadn't been about escaping the club; Andre wanted details on where things had gone wrong with Marlie. Trevor withdrew his arm.

"I don't know. Is that why we're here?" he asked.

"Partly. I'm sure the guys meant well, but neither of us was in the mood for it. If you don't want to be here, it's cool. I get it."

Trevor drew in a deep breath and let it out slowly through his nose. "It was...bad. I mean, I guess I could have had better timing, but the way she reacted made no sense."

"Better timing?" Andre's eyebrows rose.

"Um." Trevor's face was hot. "I told her while we were in bed. After."

"Oh, my God. Yeah, you're an ass."

Trevor snorted. "Probably, but it didn't mean she had to let loose on me. All the drama." He looked down at his plate. "Everyone said I should tell her. Well, now I have, and there's no way to fix what got broken. She says it's over for good this time."

"This time?" Andre blinked.

"Yeah." Trevor propped his cheek on his fist. "We've known each other from diapers. We've been breaking up and getting back together since we were in middle school."

"That's a hell of a long time."

"I know. I think..." Trevor ran his hand through his hair, tugging on the ends. "I'm not sure why we stayed together. I guess most people just expected us to." He closed his eyes briefly. "I did love her."

"But?"

Trevor was silent for a long time before voicing what he knew was the truth. "But we're not the same people we were as kids. I don't think we know each other anymore."

Andre's eyes were fixed on him. "And Nate?"

"I was never in love with him, but he says he wanted more. He was glad when she and I broke up and hurt when I didn't want to go right back to fooling around with him. We had the third fight in as many weeks over it. Since our roommates were playing, I agreed to go to the club tonight to avoid both of us sitting home in misery."

Resting his forearms on the table, Andre leaned closer. His expression was neutral, but he kept his eyes locked on Trevor. "Why are you here with me?"

Trevor had to swallow several times before he could answer. His throat was clogged, and his heart thundered. If he were honest, he didn't know why he'd left Nate and Julian for a cup of coffee with Andre, any more than he'd been sure why he took a chance when Andre was a stranger. He tapped his fingers on the table while he searched for a response that would capture the unidentified feeling in his gut that it just plain fit. It sounded too ridiculous in his head to tell Andre the truth, so he evaded.

"This was your idea," he said at last. "You asked, and I agreed."

Andre shook his head and sighed. "You and I both know that's not what I meant."

Trevor leaned in and said, "I'm here because this is where I want to be right now." He let a few seconds pass then slumped back in his chair. "Sometimes, it's good to be with someone who gets it, you know? Someone who isn't trying to figure me out or make me fit a category."

Andre's shoulders relaxed. "I hear you." He pursed his lips as though he was thinking hard about what to say next. After a minute he said, "It was easier sometimes when I was with Dahlia. I didn't have to worry what anyone would think or about keeping secrets from her. She knew everything already." He reached out and put two fingers on Trevor's wrist. "I'm sorry Marlie didn't feel that way."

"It's not your fault." Trevor laced his fingers together on top of the table, and Andre removed his hand. "You never told me what happened with Dahlia."

Andre tensed visibly, his face turning stony. "Why do you want to know?"

"I just wondered. You don't have to tell me."

After a pause, Andre said, "We hadn't been married long—a couple of years. She was...she was pregnant, with twins." His hands, still resting on the table, shook. "Drunk driver took out her car on the way to visit her parents. It was quick, and she was already gone by the time anyone got to her."

"God, I'm so sorry." Trevor wanted to reach out for him, but he wasn't sure what the proper response was in the middle of a coffee shop with a live jazz band. So he simply sat there in silent solidarity.

The band stopped, and there was a smattering of polite applause. The trombone player announced they were taking a quick break, and Andre stood up to collect their dishes. When he returned, Trevor offered him something for his part of the bill, but Andre refused.

"Next time," he said.

Trevor's stomach jumped at the idea there might be a next time, and he mentally berated himself for entertaining the thought. It was a bad idea, getting ahead of himself. To counter the surge of both excitement and anxiety, he said, "Maybe we should go back to the club and see if Julian and Nate are still there. Judging by Nate's reaction to Annie Lennox, they won't have left yet."

Andre laughed. "Does Nate have a thing for Annie Lennox? Or bearded drag queens?"

"No idea," Trevor admitted. "He was staring pretty hard, though."

"Yeah, all right," Andre said. "We can go back. Besides, Curtis—the bouncer—promised there would be Irish dancing. I do not want to miss my first experience watching that at a gay bar."

Trevor couldn't help the grin spreading across his face. "Let's go then. With a bit of luck, we'll be just in time."

CHAPTER ELEVEN

Andre entered the clinic, briefcase in hand. There were spring flowers everywhere—artificial, of course, but a welcome splash of color all the same. The on-again, off-again chill had finally given way to warmth, and the cheerful decor was a welcoming and bright match for the blooms outdoors. Inside, volunteers and paid staff went about their business, all with the same professional yet unhurried presence his grandmother herself exuded.

She had asked Andre to sort through some of her files and update both her laptop and the computer in her office as well as giving the clinic's website a spring cleaning. He typically volunteered there a few times a month, but with work for Julian picking up, it had been several weeks. Both Phyllice and Trinity frequently stopped in as well, but neither of them were there. Andre suspected Trinity was busy preparing for the baby, but she'd reduced her hours due to fatigue anyway. It hadn't been a problem; Joyce Bridges was nothing if not sensitive to the needs of both her volunteers and the people she served.

Waving to the person at the front desk, Andre was about to step into Joyce's office when he paused and turned around. The young woman was new, which wasn't noteworthy, as there were several people rotating through different positions. He recognized her, though. He approached the desk.

She smiled and ducked her head. "I remember you," she said.

Andre flashed her a grin. "That was months ago. Didn't think I was memorable. Tell me your name again?"

"Lina," she said, holding out her hand. "Almost five months, and trust me, you and your sisters aren't people I would forget any time soon."

"Trin and Phyllice are definitely unforgettable." Andre nodded then asked, "Been working here long?"

"A couple of weeks. I had to get back on my feet, and I needed some help with all the legal stuff. Your grandma insists on having everything just so." Lina laughed.

"That's Grams," Andre agreed. "I'm glad to see you're doing well, though."

"As well as I can." Her smile turned sad.

"I understand."

Andre gave her one last reassuring glance before rounding the desk and entering his grandmother's office at the back. She looked up from her desk and smiled, but it didn't reach her eyes. Joyce looked worn out, and guilt settled in his stomach for not having been by to visit her sooner.

"Hey, baby," she said as she stood up, reaching out to give him a hug across her desk. "Everything's all ready for you."

She stepped out from behind the desk, trading places with Andre. He set to work, and she retreated from the office. Half an hour later, she was back with a cup of tea, which she set to the side before standing in front of Andre with her arms crossed. He looked up.

"Well?" she asked.

Andre shook his head. "Grams, why didn't you tell me you were in trouble?"

Joyce sighed. "What would you have done that I haven't already tried? My accountant took care of this year's taxes, and I'm trying to squeeze as much as I can out of each month's budget."

"You've been over budget for a couple of months. What's going on?"

She sank into a chair. "Funding is scarce these days. Donations come in the form of things we need for the shelter, but the clinic is hurting. Everything is so expensive, even with the changes we made so we could accept insurance plans. I don't want to turn this into one of those places that offers luxury services to support the free ones. That will turn away the very people I want here." She reached across to take Andre's hand. "I'm working on it. I promise."

Andre nodded. "I know. You always do. I just wish I could help you."

"Oh, baby. You've done enough for me all these years—you and Phyllice and Trinity and your parents, too. You all still believed in my work."

It was strange hearing those words come out of his confident grandmother's mouth. Andre had never known she was insecure about the value of what she did. To his mind, nothing could be a better use of her time and skills. When he looked at her again, he was struck with the fact that she was in her late seventies and still doing this. What was she going to do when she couldn't run the clinic or the shelter anymore?

"Grams, we'll figure it out," he promised. "We'll make sure you get what you need."

Joyce smiled and let go of Andre's hand to rest her palm against his cheek. "That's my boy," she said. Abruptly, she changed the subject. "I have something for you, now that you're back home."

"What is it?"

"My old piano. The thing is sitting around collecting dust, and it's high time you took it off my hands."

Andre laughed. "I don't play!" He sobered quickly. He hadn't even touched his saxophone since Dahlia died.

"Well, you can learn, then." She patted his arm. "Come by some Sunday for dinner and to pick it up." She raised an eyebrow. "Or you might think about coming to church with me first."

"We'll see about that." He huffed, catching on to her ulterior motives. "But I'll at least get the piano." He'd have to find someone who could help transport it, but he didn't tell her so.

"Good. I'm going back to work. Let me know when you're finished." Joyce stood up and walked back out of her office.

After another hour, Andre finished going through all the files his grandmother wanted cleaned up and had everything he needed to make adjustments to the web site. He packed up his things, said goodbye to Joyce with another reassurance he'd be there on Sunday, and headed out. Just as he was about to leave, he spotted a vaguely familiar woman emerging from the exam rooms in the back.

She turned his direction, and he stiffened. It was Marlie. He'd only met her the one time, but he was certain it was her. She met his gaze, and her lips formed an O of surprise. Snapping to her senses, she whirled around and rushed to the desk, where she talked for a few minutes with Lina. She gathered everything she had with her, scrambling to shove it all into a bag. Keeping her back to Andre, she whisked her bag off the desk, not noticing she'd forgotten to put her wallet away. The bag brushed against it, and it fell to the floor. Marlie must not have realized because she left it there and hurried to the door.

Andre picked up the forgotten wallet and chased after Marlie, running outside and blinking in the bright sunshine. He spotted her about half a block from the clinic and followed, calling, "Wait! Marlie!"

At first she sped up, but eventually, she gave in and turned around. "What do you want?" she demanded.

"This," he said, holding out the wallet. "You left it inside."

"Oh." Marlie put out her hand, but she didn't take the wallet. Instead, she stared at Andre for a long moment. "You're Trevor's friend." She said his name like it was poison.

"I guess," Andre said. He wasn't sure exactly what they were to each other. His stomach twisted with guilt; he hadn't tried to call Trevor since their night out with Nate and Julian, mostly because Andre hadn't gotten his number and had been too stubborn to ask Julian for it. "I mean, yes."

Marlie scoffed. "Right. That sounds like him. Can't figure out what kind of relationship he has with people."

Andre couldn't help chuckling. "Actually, yeah. 'Bout right."

Startled, Marlie's eyes widened. After a few seconds, she relaxed and gave a half-amused snort. "I'm sorry. This has just been a really crappy day, and I didn't mean to take it out on you."

"No problem. I do understand."

"Do you?" Marlie tilted her head.

"About Trevor, at least." It was as close as he was willing to get to telling Marlie anything. He had no idea whether Trevor had told her or not.

Marlie sighed. "I'm sure you mean well, but you don't know the half of it. Did he tell you we're not together anymore?"

"Yes, he mentioned it."

"Right. And did he tell you why?"

Andre fidgeted. Of course he knew exactly why, but he wasn't sure how much to say. Marlie read his silence and rolled her eyes.

"Obviously he did, or you wouldn't be acting all..." Her voice died on the last part. "Oh, my God."

Andre's heart rate picked up. Surely she hadn't guessed the truth. Trevor wouldn't have given her enough detail. "What?"

"It was you," she said. "You're the one he wrote his song for."

"I—" He faltered. "How do you know?"

"I mean, I guess I don't for sure, but I think so. Something in the way he acted around you when we were all together the one night. Like he was holding back, but he needed you to know he'd moved on. And now, the way you reacted...well, it's my best guess."

Andre couldn't look her in the eye. "Yeah. It was about me."

Marlie shook her head. "I wish he'd written like that about me," she said. "Hell, I wish he'd ever felt like that about me."

Andre's head snapped up. "He did. At least, at some point."

"Maybe, but he hasn't in a long time, or at least he hasn't seemed like it." She sighed. "Neither have I, for that matter, but I thought we could work everything out because we both needed the same things. Shouldn't it be enough?"

"I don't know," Andre replied. He wasn't sure who she was trying to convince. "Did he—did he ever feel that way about anyone else?" An image of Nate popped into Andre's mind.

"Not that I know of. Trevor gets kind of attached, but I don't think he knows what he wants. The only other time I've heard him write songs with so much emotion was for church." She gave a huffy laugh. "Apparently, he's passionate about two things—Jesus and you." She smiled, but it was faint and sad.

Andre was quiet for a minute, watching Marlie as she shifted on her feet. He knew he had no right to ask, but he wondered what had brought her to his grandmother's clinic. He supposed she might be thinking the same thing about him. Meaning to say goodbye, he held out her wallet again. She accepted it, but she hesitated rather than turning away.

"Everything okay?" he asked.

She shrugged. "It will be. I'm...I need to make some choices, and no matter what I decide, at least one person will be unhappy with me."

Andre put his hand on her upper arm. "Then make the one that's right for you, and don't listen to everyone else."

"Easier said than done." The corner of her mouth lifted. "Maybe I won't choose at all."

"Not choosing is a kind of choice itself," Andre answered.

"Right," she agreed. She pulled away and turned to go. She'd only gotten a few steps when she looked back over her shoulder and said, "Take care of him, please."

Andre opened his mouth to respond, but no sound came out. By the time he'd thought of telling her he didn't know what she meant and it wasn't up to him anyway, she was gone.

After his trip to the clinic, Andre decided he would at least return to church, even if he was avoiding the piano. He'd sold Dahlia's, and he couldn't imagine having another one. Who would play it? Andre wasn't interested in learning, and he didn't understand why Joyce hadn't offered it to Phyllice for her family or even Trinity and Krista. Since Joyce rarely did anything without a reason, Andre understood what she meant him to get out of it. That didn't mean he had to like it.

Returning to church was an easier change. He'd always liked the one his mother and grandmother attended, and it was comforting to sing hymns and read the Psalms. For several weeks, he kept it up, always ducking out afterward to avoid uncomfortable questions about when he was coming by for the piano. Eventually, however, Joyce refused to accept no for an answer and demanded he find a way to get it out of her space. He conceded to keep the peace and prevent his sisters from tag-team calling him repeatedly to remind him after Joyce put them up to it. There was no alternative but to take it home with him after dinner the next Sunday.

As the week came to a close, Andre was feeling desperate. He had no idea how he was going to get it out of his grandmother's house. He tried asking Julian for help, but Julian and Elisa already had plans. Julian unhelpfully suggested renting a van, which Andre had been planning to do if he couldn't think of a better option for hauling the thing. He sat at his desk, drumming his fingers and trying to figure out what he was going to do when an idea struck him. He picked up his cell phone.

"Julian!" he hollered.

Julian stuck his head out of his office door. "Yo."

"You got Trevor's phone number somewhere?"

A huge grin split Julian's face. "Knew you'd get around to calling him. Why didn't you get his number when we were out at the bar? Or any of the other times you've seen him?"

"Shut the hell up. I'm not asking for the reason you think. Since you ditched me for moving the piano, I don't know too many local people, and he lives in my neighborhood—sort of—I'm asking him and his roommates for help. They're in a band, so they must have a way to transport their shit. Are you gonna give it or not?" Andre glared at him, hoping to avoid the uncomfortable feeling Julian was right and it was about more than the piano.

"Yeah, yeah. Hang on." Julian ducked back into his office. He emerged with his phone. "I'll text it to you."

Andre created a new contact and hit send. Trevor answered on the second ring.

"Hello?"

"Hey, Trevor. It's Andre."

"Oh! Um. Did you need something? You know, for the church web site."

Andre smiled at how nervous Trevor sounded. "Nah. That's pretty much wrapped up."

"I'm sorry to hear—I mean, it's great the job is done," Trevor said. "So...if it's not work, then what can I do for you?"

"Well..." Andre hesitated. "See, there's this piano—"

"A piano?" Trevor interrupted.

"Right, yes. And it's technically mine, I guess—"

"You play the piano?" Trevor sounded incredulous.

"No. Will you stop interrupting? My Grams needs me to get it out of her house this Sunday."

"And you want some help."

"Yeah."

"How are you planning to get it home?" Trevor wanted to know.

"Um. Well, see, I haven't figured that out exactly. I was hoping maybe your roommates would be able to help."

There was a pause then Trevor said, "Mack has a van, but he and Jamie are working their other jobs Sunday night. I could ask if he'll let me borrow it, though. You have any other help?"

"My family will be there. Might be able to recruit a couple of them."

"Yeah, okay. What time? I have to work Sunday morning, obviously."

Andre considered. His family would eat dinner around two, after everyone was home from church. Or, in the case of Phyllice's husband, out of bed. He wasn't the church type. Andre wondered if Trevor would feel uncomfortable having dinner with them.

"Well, uh, if you like, we're having everyone in for dinner at two. You can come if you want."

"Oh. Um." Silence. "Yeah, okay."

"If it bothers you—" Andre started.

"No! It's not that. I know it's only dinner, but it feels weird after—after. You know?"

He didn't have to spell it out: after what had happened between them. Andre gave a small sigh. The whole situation was already awkward; no reason why they shouldn't make it even more so.

"No one knows anything," he reassured Trevor. "It really is nothing but dinner. Watch out for my sisters, though. They can be a bit enthusiastic with new people."

"I have no idea what that means." Trevor laughed, and the sound warmed and relaxed Andre.

"It means you'd better be prepared to get the third degree from them."

"Fair enough," Trevor replied. "I've been warned. See you Sunday at two, then. Should I bring anything? And can you give me directions?"

"Something to drink, maybe," Andre suggested. "I'll text you the address—it's not too far, just over in Arlington."

He ended the call and looked up to see Julian grinning. Andre frowned at him and returned to staring at his computer screen, hoping to send the message he was not available to discuss anything. He could still feel Julian's eyes on him, so he looked up again.

"What?"

"You invited him to meet your family and you're not even seeing each other."

"Oh, don't even start with me." Andre glowered at him.

It didn't deter Julian. "I haven't seen you like this in a long time, man. I'm happy for you."

"It's not like you're thinking!" Andre insisted. "Just friends, that's all."

"Friends who you bring home like a lost puppy."

"That's exactly it," Andre said. "He has a lot to work through right now."

Julian's smile widened. "And you're just the one to help him."

Andre shook his head. "Uh-uh. No. I'm not getting involved with someone who hasn't figured himself out yet."

"No one said you can't take your time. Looks to me like you think he might be worth it."

Julian didn't wait for an answer but retreated into his office and closed the door. Andre gave a long, drawn-out sigh and slumped down in his chair. The horrible feeling Julian was right stirred back up in him, and he closed his eyes.

He would need to be careful not to let things go too far, or he and Trevor would both be left broken-hearted. Telling himself it was only a piano, Andre opened his eyes again and distracted himself by working on a web site for a private-practice therapist.

CHAPTER TWELVE

Andre's mother had put something in the oven to slow-cook before taking off for church that morning, and now the whole house smelled good. She still refused to use an actual slow-cooker for some reason known only to her. Almost the minute Andre was through the door, she and three other women were all over him, taking things out of his hands. He shook his head. This was the one way his nowhere-near-traditional family still fell into their roles. Not one of the women, his sister's wife included, trusted any of the men with food. It made no difference that Andre had lived on his own for years or that Joyce had taught him to cook before he even reached middle school; they still all shooed him out of the kitchen every time.

Phyllice's husband, Henri, was in the living room, lounging on the couch and watching the Sox play Baltimore. It was his one indulgence. He and Phyllice were both college professors, and Andre sometimes thought Henri felt guilty about his love for sports of every kind. Phyllice never said a negative word about it, but Andre sensed Henri's wariness of judgment for failing in the Progressive Man department because he'd rather sit around watching guys pound each other's asses than read heavy philosophy texts or learn to crochet.

Five minutes later, they were joined by Trinity's wife, who had no doubt been booted from the kitchen. Andre shook his head; he was more capable around appliances than Krista, who was apt to burn water in the microwave. She had no guilt at all about plopping herself next to Henri and yelling at whoever had just struck out. Andre cared very little about baseball, so he merely pretended to be paying attention while warring internally over whether he wanted Trevor to hurry up or stay away until he figured out how to protect him from his sisters' wiles.

Before he had a solution, the doorbell rang. He sprang to his feet, but his grandmother reached it first on her way out from the back bedroom. Andre was at her side the moment she opened the door. Trevor stood there with a bottle of red wine in one hand and a carton of some kind of juice in the other. He held them up to Andre.

"Wasn't sure what would be better," he said, his grin sheepish.

"Andre?" Joyce turned toward him.

"Uh, sorry. Grams, this is my...friend, Trevor Davidson. He's here to help me move the piano. Trev, this is my Grams, Joyce Bridges."

"Pleased to meet you, ma'am," Trevor said.

Joyce turned to Andre and arched one eyebrow. "Polite young man."

"He is," Andre agreed, relieved she hadn't asked any further questions. The admonishing look had said it all about her view of his own manners. To Trevor, he said, "Come on in."

Trevor stepped inside, and Andre led him to the kitchen to deposit the drinks with his mother and sisters. He considered whether it would have been better to ease him in by leaving him with Henri and Krista instead, but he decided he might as well get it over with.

As soon as they were in the kitchen, whatever echolocation Trinity and Phyllice possessed for guests kicked in, and they turned around simultaneously. Trinity's eyes traveled up and down Trevor's body, and Andre tensed, waiting for her assessment. It could go any direction. She snatched the wine out of his hand and gave a sly look to Andre.

"Oh, he is yummy, baby brother," she said. "Like a big scoop of vanilla ice cream."

Trevor's jaw dropped, and his cheeks turned bright red. Andre groaned. "Trin, do you have to do that?"

"Uh..." Trevor had almost found his voice.

"Don't mind her," Phyllice said before Andre could step in.

"Trinity's harmless. She's also married and not remotely interested in men."

"That's not any better!" Andre snapped. "Trevor's here to help move the piano."

Phyllice gave him the exact same look Joyce had done not five minutes earlier. "Oh, really?"

"More or less," Trevor muttered, causing everyone's attention to snap to him.

Andre sighed. "I did warn you," he said. "Trevor, meet my sisters, Phyllice and Trinity. That's my mom, Belinda, at the sink." He indicated his mother, who was dutifully ignoring her children in favor of draining a pot of vegetables. She glanced over her shoulder and smiled.

"You're Andre's friend? He said you'd be coming."

Andre gritted his teeth. At least she hadn't implied anything directly the way Trinity had. "Right. Well, I'm going to take Trevor to meet Henri and Krista before you all eat him alive in here. Where's Dad at?"

"Probably out back with Phyllice's littles," Belinda replied. "Would you call them in? Dinner's going on the table."

"Sure."

Andre led Trevor into the living room and made introductions there. Henri and Krista knew better than to say anything. They shoved over to give Trevor room and invited him to watch the game. Trevor looked much more interested in it than Andre was, and he seemed more comfortable than he had a few minutes before. Andre relaxed and went to find his father, the sounds of Henri's soft Creole accent echoing behind him as he said something not to Trevor but to the television.

It took another fifteen minutes to round everyone up and play a game of "convince the kids to wash up." Phyllice's bunch were hardly rowdy, but there were three of them, and they all shared their mother and auntie's handy verbal skills. They were all lucky the kids closed their mouths long enough for Joyce to say grace. Andre noticed Phyllice's youngest, barely three, had hold of Trevor's right hand. Her middle child squeezed in between Andre and Trevor, gripping both of them with still slightly damp fingers. Trevor looked down at her then up at Andre, a grin spreading across his face. Andre was too surprised to reprimand his niece for being rude.

After they prayed, they all sat around the big table, the little ones tucked in between the adults. Five-year-old Theodora looked up at

Trevor and blinked.

"Who're you?" she asked.

"Thea!" her mother chided.

"It's okay," Trevor said. "I'm your Uncle Andre's friend Trevor."

"Oh." Theodora poked her peas one at a time. "Friend like how?" she wanted to know. "Like Uncle Julian or like Aunt Krista?"

Trevor looked at Andre, his expression reflecting helplessness. "What?" he asked.

Andre had never been more grateful that he could hide a blush so well. "Like Uncle Julian," he told Theodora.

"I'm sorry," Trevor said. "I'm still confused."

Zion, the oldest, picked up where his sister left off. "She means are you Uncle Andre's boyfriend." It was a statement, not a question.

"Oh, my God!" Andre put his fork down and buried his head in his hands.

"Zion!" chorused several voices, while Belinda's rose above the rest to say, "Andre!" Leave it to her to be more concerned about his taking the Lord's name in vain.

"What?" Zion demanded. "I just wanted to know."

To Andre's surprise, Trevor laughed. "I have a feeling you *all* wanted to know," he said. "And no, I'm not, but I do like spending time with him."

That broke the tension. The rest of the meal passed the way most Sunday dinners did, with multiple simultaneous conversations interspersed with "please pass the potatoes" and a muffled yell any time Henri got up to check the score of the game. Every so often, Andre sneaked a peak at Trevor, and every time, Trevor looked right at home. It should have felt wrong or awkward, but instead, it was just about perfect. Andre let the food and conversation fill all the empty places in him, leaving aside the question of where Trevor fit into all of it.

Andre coasted into the garage. Trevor parked the van in the narrow driveway, and the others pulled in behind him. Together, Andre, Trevor, Phyllice, and Henri lifted the piano and carried it into the house. Andre wasn't sure what he was going to do when it came time to move again, but at least for now he'd taken the instrument off his grandmother's hands. He half suspected that was the reason why—so he could figure out what to do with it instead of her. He hoped that didn't mean she or his parents were thinking of moving, but he couldn't be sure.

He offered Phyllice and Henri drinks, but they declined on the grounds they'd left the kids in Trinity's care too long already. They said goodnight, and Phyllice gave Andre a meaningful glance which he pointedly ignored. He turned to Trevor, who had stepped closer to the door as well. Andre hid his disappointment and contemplated returning to his parents' house for the rest of the evening.

Trevor said, "Maybe I should go?"

It was his hesitation that broke Andre down. "You don't have to, you know. You can stay." He held his breath.

"I—" Trevor started, but he cut himself off, looking past Andre's shoulder. Raising his hand, he gestured at the instrument case in the corner right beside where they'd put the piano. "What do you play?"

Andre took a moment before answering. He hadn't touched it other than to keep it in good repair since Dahlia died, and he wasn't sure he could share that part of himself with anyone again. It was one thing to move a piano he was never going to play; it was far different to acknowledge his own musicianship.

"Saxophone," he said. "I play saxophone." He scrubbed his chin. "Or at least, I used to."

"Used to?" Trevor stepped closer, his head tilted and his eyes soft.

"Yeah. Before Dahlia—my wife—died. We met because the same night Julian and I were playing with our band, she was having a birthday party in the jazz club I took you to."

"Oh."

The word hung gently between them, and Trevor didn't seem to feel the need to press for more details, much to Andre's relief. He was about to offer Trevor something to drink, just to change the subject, when Trevor put a hand on his upper arm.

"Can—would you play now?"

The question took Andre by surprise. He started to shake his head, but something in Trevor's earnest expression made him reconsider. It was a strange request. No one had ever asked him in the years since Dahlia's death. It was as though they'd all thought it would be too *something*: too painful or too sad or too hard. Andre wondered if it might be the opposite—giving in to the one thing that had always been a source of joy and pride might bring him the kind of peace he needed to honor her memory and let go of the choke hold his past had on him. He realized he'd wanted them to ask, wanted them to stop tiptoeing around him like he might break if anyone brought it up.

Trevor's voice interrupted Andre's thoughts. "I could accompany you on the piano."

Once again, Andre hesitated, remembering how he and Dahlia had often spent their evenings. He stalled by saying, "Not sure how the neighbors would feel."

"We won't play loudly."

Andre chuckled and it steadied his nerves. "Okay, then. Give me a minute. I'm not sure I still have any reeds."

He did, though. Andre had made sure to keep everything in working order. He might not have made the kinds of melodies he had before, but he insisted on periodically cleaning, oiling, and repairing his instrument. As he opened the case, he considered how it was his one tiny seed of hope. It felt right to be taking it out again, even if he didn't want to examine too closely what it meant. He didn't dare look up at Trevor while he kept the reed in his mouth, wetting it and making it pliable while he drew the pieces of his instrument out and fitted them together. Soon enough, he was ready.

He warmed up by running up and down blues scales, first as they were and then with an improvised flare. He finally looked at Trevor, who sat on the piano bench facing out, his eyes fixed on Andre. A warm burst of amusement rushed to Andre's belly, and he laughed softly around his mouthpiece. Trevor's cheeks reddened, and he glanced away before straightening his back and making eye contact again.

When Andre felt he'd warmed up enough, he twitched an eyebrow at Trevor. "See if you can keep up, big man," he said and began a hot-tempo piece from back in his days playing with Julian's band.

Trevor jumped a little then spun on the bench to face the keys. He cocked his head, listening for a few minutes then began to play just with his left hand—a steady bass rhythm. As they got comfortable, he picked out notes with his right hand, fitting them alongside Andre's melody. Up and down they played, fingers moving and bodies swaying and hearts pounding with the effort to keep up with each other. When at last Andre played a long, sweet note, Trevor offered a few last, playful plunks of the keys, and they both almost collapsed, laughing and gasping a little from chasing each other through the song.

After they'd calmed down, Andre began to play again, this time a soft, lilting tune. For several minutes, Trevor sat with his hands hovering over the keys, his head turned toward Andre, watching. Eventually he joined in, but he played low and quiet. It was lost to Andre as he fell into the rhythm and the notes. *Like riding a bike*, he thought, pleased he could still do it. The song ended, and Andre set down his saxophone. Trevor swiveled on the piano bench to look at him. His face was flushed, and blood rushed to Andre's head, making him hot. His heart drummed against his ribs, and he was sure it had nothing to do with the music.

Trevor spoke into the silence between them. "My God," he said. "You can really play."

Andre let out a breathy laugh. "Yeah, I really can." He stretched and yawned.

"I've stayed too late. I'm sorry," Trevor said, standing up. "I should go."

Andre wanted to tell him he didn't have to; they could find something else to do. He opened his mouth, but the only words that would come out were, "All right."

He walked Trevor to the door, but before he opened it, Trevor turned around to face him. His lips moved like he wanted to say something, but all he did was stand there. He reached out his hand and put it on Andre's arm, and Andre felt the slight tension and tremor. Making the decision for both of them, he leaned in. Trevor's eyes drifted closed, and in the next minute, they were kissing. A bone-deep thrill raced through Andre's whole body.

Trevor pushed gently until Andre's back hit the wall behind him, and then he pressed against Andre, transferring his nervous excitement to Andre by way of his shaking. Andre wanted to soothe and settle him. He ran his hands up underneath the back of Trevor's t-shirt and mapped slow circles along the muscles. Under his touch, Trevor relaxed, and their kisses progressed from hesitant to heated.

The memory of the last time they'd been in this position—Andre against the cold metal of the bathroom stall and Trevor rocking slowly against him—flooded his mind, and he gasped with a flash of arousal. He trailed his hands down to Trevor's hips, dragging him closer. Trevor let out a moan and then a sharp intake of breath before pulling away.

"I-I'm sorry," he mumbled.

Andre tried to reach for him. "Don't be."

Trevor flinched. "I can't. I don't want—"

Frowning, Andre dropped his hand. "You don't want to do this?"

Trevor nodded then shook his head. "You have no idea how much I want to, but I can't."

Without waiting for an answer, Trevor spun around and took off through the front door, leaving it hanging open and Andre staring at his back. When he heard Trevor's van start, he shoved the door closed with his foot and leaned back against the wall, running his hand over his closely cropped hair. He should have known better than to think either of them was ready for anything. They were both bound to be hurt—again.

Andre closed his eyes. *No,* he thought. *It doesn't have to end like this.*

Maybe the problem for both of them was they were expecting the wrong things. It had been so long since Andre had been with anyone he cared about as more than the comfort of another warm body. That had worked fine for a season, but he wanted more now, and Trevor deserved someone who didn't treat him as a throwaway. If he was worth it—and Andre was starting to feel he was—then Andre wasn't going to let him go without a fight.

He returned to the living room and picked up his phone, typed a text, and hit send. For a moment, he held the phone in his hand, staring at it and wondering if he'd done the right thing.

CHAPTER THIRTEEN

Trevor waited until the following morning to check the text he'd gotten just after pulling the van out of Andre's driveway. He hadn't cared who it was from; he was in no mood to respond to anyone or anything. He'd been grateful Mack and Jamie were still at work when he arrived home, and Nate was sleeping off his weekend of shows. Despite it being only eight when he got back to the apartment, Trevor had gone straight to bed.

Naturally, that meant he was up before the sun. He tiptoed out of the bedroom, not in a hurry to wake Nate and have another strained conversation. Nate hadn't exactly been supportive when Trevor and Marlie broke up, though the tension had eased between them as time passed. He had implied Trevor should move on already, and Trevor was well aware of what he meant. Trevor had carefully avoided the subject with their other roommates so as not to let on he and Nate were at odds; he took Mack's threat to move The Boyfriend in very seriously.

Trevor remembered the text and plopped down on the couch to read it. He was surprised to see it was from Andre.

Hey. Sorry for the way things ended. Think we're going too fast. How about dinner instead?

Trevor's heart sped up, and his hands were clammy. Andre still wanted to see him, even after the crappy way he'd behaved when he left the previous night. Trevor had been sure Andre would write him off, yet here he was, asking for a date. A *real* date, not a blow job in a bathroom or an awkward reunion or a semi-emotional diner conversation or a favor requiring heavy lifting. Trevor felt like he was sixteen again and being asked to the prom. He'd have thought he was well past the stage where a first date made him nervous and giddy, but the very idea of being with Andre was enough to light a fire deep in his gut while making him lightheaded and anxious.

Hands shaking, Trevor could barely type out, *Sure. Where and when?*

Friday, and I know the perfect place. Do you like real Mexican food?

Trevor was surprised Andre had replied already. He glanced at the clock and saw it wasn't even six. Grinning, he texted back.

Trevor: *You're up early.*

Andre: *So are you, and you didn't answer my question.*

Trevor: *Mexican is fine. What time?*

Andre: *I work til 4. How about 6?*

Trevor: *Perfect.* He waited a moment before texting, *Why are you up at this hour?*

Work.

There was a pause, then another text.

And couldn't sleep. Was thinking about you.

Trevor sucked in his breath. He wondered what specifically Andre had been thinking about, but he wasn't bold enough to ask directly. Instead, he texted, *Me too.*

There was a long wait, but eventually, Andre texted again. *I'm glad it wasn't just me.*

Grinning, Trevor texted a thumbs up and rose from the couch to get ready for his day. A pang of guilt hit that he wasn't immediately going to Nate to tell him what had happened. He convinced himself it was because he didn't want to wake him, but he knew it wasn't true. Looking back, this had been his pattern forever—willing to talk to Nate about every woman he went out with, including Marlie, but hiding every single man. Instead of asking himself why, he detoured to the shower and replaced thoughts of Nate with visions of his first official date with Andre.

One dinner turned into another evening of coffee and jazz at what was quickly becoming Trevor's new favorite spot. Those dates gave way to two more lunch dates and plans to meet up again over the weekend. By the time they arrived at plans for a sixth date,

Trevor dared to let himself hope there was something more under the surface, even if they were still dancing around the newness of it all and the fact that neither of them had brought up any prior aspect of their history. Andre hadn't even so much as tried to kiss him goodnight.

It had taken a few weeks of seeing as much of each other as often as they could before Trevor was finally willing to admit he was more than merely smitten with Andre and was no longer satisfied with the snail's pace of their "just friends" relationship. Even so, he carefully hid as much evidence from his roommates and the church staff as possible. He couldn't afford to have everything come crashing back down right as he was beginning to feel like he'd started to mend whatever part of him had been broken by too many years of stuffing himself into the role of soon-to-be ideal family man. He'd given as few details as he could manage when explaining the painful break-up to Pastor Bret, who had lent a sympathetic ear and a pat on the back. Outside of that, Trevor made it a habit not to discuss any aspect of his personal life at work.

He couldn't keep the warmth out of his conversations or the aura of contentment out of his posture, though. When he arrived at the church one scorching day, he was already exhausted from the heat and his trek from the train station. Somehow, none of it bothered him, and he whistled while he set up the stage and opened his laptop to work on the flow for Sunday's service.

Midway through creating the draft, Trevor was interrupted when Bret opened one of the auditorium doors and stuck his head in. When Trevor looked up, Bret pounced.

"Busy?" he asked. Not bothering to wait for a reply, he approached the stage. "You seem to be doing well these days," he commented.

Trevor shrugged, and his face flamed. "Getting my life back in order," he replied. "Thought maybe it was time."

"I'm glad. I've got some big news." Bret grinned.

"Oh?" Trevor hopped down off the stage and plopped into one of the seats. "What's up?"

"Do you want the good or the better?"

Trevor laughed. "Either."

Bret looked like he might explode any second if he didn't get it out. He nearly tripped on his words when he said, "You're going to play at the King's Creation music festival!"

For a moment, Trevor stared, his mouth open and his eyes wide.

"You're kidding," he said when he could speak again.

"Nope." He handed Trevor a hard copy of a schedule.

Harvest's band, which had been renamed Harvest Praise, had booked two Christian music festivals, the first of which was a new one near Amherst over Labor Day weekend. They were opening for a far more popular band with a much more clever name. Trevor was pleased, however, to see Irina Clay-Jones would be performing too, opening for a singer he didn't recognize. He didn't know Irina well, but traveling in the same circles, they ran into one another on occasion.

After reading through the document, Trevor looked up at Bret. "So, what's the other news?"

"Irina's asked us to back her up on a song for her next release." Bret gripped Trevor's arm and gave him a conspiratorial wink. "Turns out she wanted you specifically."

Once again, Trevor was rendered speechless. He hadn't thought he'd made much of an impression on her when they'd spoken for the podcast, but he'd enjoyed working with her. He found his words and said, "That's great!"

"It is," Bret agreed. "She loved that song of yours and wants a similar sound for one of her upcoming songs."

Trevor's smile slid away, along with some of his joy. Irina wasn't the only one who had latched onto his song. Both the congregation and the radio public had reacted exactly as Bret had predicted. "You Draw Me In" had quickly become the go-to favorite during the local show, and it had been played a handful of times to a wider audience as well. Singing it for other people's consumption had never appealed to Trevor in the first place, but it had risen to the level of feeling sick every time he saw it on the schedule for a Sunday service. Hearing about Irina's adoration was enough to douse most of his thrill over the upcoming opportunities.

He masked his disappointment with what he hoped was a cheery smile. "I'm glad she enjoyed it," he said.

Bret tilted his head, and a flicker of concern passed across his face before he smiled again. "You'll be spending a lot of time working with her in the next couple of weeks," he said.

"Guess I'd better go down—uh—get down to work, then," Trevor replied.

Bret lingered for a moment, looking like he wanted to say more. With a look somewhere between puzzled and amused, he left Trevor to it, and Trevor returned his attention to his spreadsheet. When he was through, he shut down the laptop, stretched, and began packing up his belongings. His pocket vibrated, and he pulled out his phone. It was a text from Andre, and Trevor's heart rate spiked. A thrill ran through him at the unexpected message. Andre was asking Trevor to meet him later on at the address he texted for a bite to eat and an evening of blues.

Trevor spent the rest of the day in a daze, torn between excitement and anxiety. It spilled over into getting ready to meet Andre, and Nate and Jamie—who both had the evening off—demanded to know who he was meeting. Until that evening, Trevor had been making excuses to his roommates for his whereabouts, passing off his dates with Andre as more practice time for the church band. He suspected they didn't always believe him, but the guys didn't press him on it. Trevor felt guilty hiding someone who was rapidly becoming important to him, and he wasn't sure why he didn't want to tell them.

"Back off," Trevor told them. "I'm just meeting a colleague." It was true, in a sense. They didn't need to know his next statement was unrelated. "Bret told me today we're going to play a couple of music festivals, and we're scheduled to begin rehearsing with Irina Clay-Jones to record on her new release."

"The gospel singer?" Nate asked.

"She's the one."

They left him alone after that. Nate, complaining of a sore throat, holed himself up in the bedroom with a cup of tea, a bag of natural cough drops, and a vaporizer. Trevor brought him a stack of books, including one of Jamie's favorite erotic novels—all the good parts dog-eared—and left him alone to wallow. Jamie was camped out on the couch, watching a dramatic movie for which he apparently required two boxes of tissues. Trevor tried to sneak past him on his way out, but Jamie caught him.

"Hey," he said, pausing the movie. "Hang on."

He reached down and fished around at his feet then turned around and chucked something at Trevor. Startled, Trevor put out his hand to catch the box of condoms. He rolled his eyes.

"I'm not going to have sex," Trevor said.

"Uh huh," Jamie replied. He shrugged, and somehow he managed to make it look condescending. "You might have fooled Nate, who is probably too sick to care, but I can tell you have a date."

"Whatever," Trevor muttered. Louder, he said, "Enjoy your

movie."

With that, he left the condoms on the table by the door and stepped out, leaving his roommates to themselves.

Trevor and Andre took their seats outdoors at the Boston Harbor Hotel and began by ordering coffee. Trevor's nerves were back full-force. He wanted to confess how he'd been feeling and find out where they stood, but the pathway from his brain to his mouth wasn't functioning. Trevor stalled by taking his time with his drink. He slowly added cream and sugar, stirring it and stirring it until Andre finally put a hand on his wrist and pressed his fingers lightly into Trevor's skin.

"I think it's mixed up enough. Kind of like me right now. What's going on?"

Trevor sighed and set his spoon aside. He thought if he started with something good, it might soften the blow. "The last few weeks have been...good. Really good." Trevor flushed. "I know we haven't said anything, but–" He stopped, rubbed the back of his neck and chuckled nervously. "We're more than a couple of friends spending time together."

A slow smile crept across Andre's face. "I was hoping you'd say it. I didn't want to push you before you were ready."

Trevor relaxed, blowing out his breath. "Right." He tried to process how to follow up his previous statement, knowing there was more he had to tell Andre.

Before he could come up with anything, Andre said, "Then we're agreed." He reached across the table and took Trevor's hand.

Trevor looked down at where they were joined then back up at Andre. "You get me," he blurted. That hadn't been exactly what he'd meant to say next, but it was something.

Andre's eyes crinkled, and he laughed quietly. "Okay. Expand on that."

Sliding down in his chair, Trevor groaned. "Sorry. I'm really bad at this. So...Marlie always got the church part of me, but she never quite understood the music. Nate..." He swallowed, still feeling raw from the way they'd drifted apart after the last night at the club. "He understood the music, but he always thought the church stuff was sort of pathetic. You get both."

Andre tilted his head. "Not sure where you're going with this."

Trevor leaned forward and put his head in his hands. He looked up at Andre. "You get *both sides* of me," he emphasized, and Andre nodded as the meaning sank in. Trevor begged, "I need you to understand other stuff, too."

"What other stuff?" Andre frowned.

"Why I still can't tell anyone about us. I could lose my job. My church is...different. They don't have an official policy about who I can date, but they prefer those of us in the public eye to be single or straight. It's the music, you know? We're already starting to gain some ground. If anyone ever finds out I wrote my signature song about you and not God, that's it. It'll be everywhere, and I won't be able to stop it." He closed his eyes, trying to stop shaking.

When he opened them, Andre wasn't looking at him. He was playing with his napkin. "I know. I've always known." He raised his head and met Trevor's eyes. "I won't be your dirty little secret. I obviously don't have a problem with a one-shot deal in a bar, but I'm not gonna play happy couple with you on Friday night while keeping my distance the rest of the week so you don't have to cope with reality."

"It's not what you think." Trevor sighed. "I need this job, and not because I need work. Once we have some standing, then maybe it won't be so bad. It's worked okay for some people. I don't want to risk it before we've even gotten started."

Andre rubbed his temples, remaining quiet for a few minutes. Trevor began to stir his coffee again, but Andre scowled at him and he stopped. The whole scene was eerily familiar, like the one at the diner when Andre had urged him to be honest with Marlie. The result of that experiment had been terrible, leaving Trevor no choice but to reroute his five-year plan's GPS. He pleaded silently for Andre to have some words of wisdom this time, too.

At last Andre caught Trevor by surprise by saying, "Is this what you really want?"

Unsure how to answer the question in a single sentence, Trevor tried to put him off. "I don't know what you mean."

"You said the job isn't about needing work. What is it you want? Because I've been there, thinking the job I had was going to eventually be something more, different, or better, and it never was."

The server returned with their orders, and Trevor distracted himself by enjoying the food. Andre had been right; this place was perfect. They ate without speaking for a while, until Trevor remembered—to his dismay—he had never properly answered Andre's question.

"No," he said. "This isn't what I thought I'd be doing."

Andre nodded as though he had known all along. "Then how do you know you'd be killing your career?"

"I—" Trevor started, but Andre put up a hand.

"You don't have to make a decision now, but maybe think about what you want to do. Like with Marlie, who you are is going to come up at some point. Tell people on your terms before someone else delivers the punchline."

Trevor wanted to ask if Andre would be there for him when everything went south, but it seemed too soon. Instead, he nodded. "Give me some time to figure out how I'm going to do it. Last time didn't go so well, and I need a better plan." He held still for a moment. "Can we keep seeing each other, find out where this goes?"

For a moment, it looked like Andre might say no. His brow creased briefly, but then he relaxed. "All right," he said. "I'd like that."

Even though Trevor was still anxious, he wanted Andre to trust him. He reached out one finger and rested it on the back of Andre's hand, willing him to understand. Andre's dark eyes softened, and Trevor knew they were clear. He relaxed back into his seat, determined not to let this mar the rest of their night.

When they were through eating, they walked away from the courtyard in the deepening evening rather than staying for the rest of the concert. Conversation remained light, mostly exchanging stories about work. It hardly mattered what they talked about; Trevor was glad for the company and still feeling warm from dinner, drinks, and the growing closeness between them. They didn't hold hands on their way back to the train station, but their fingers brushed on occasion, once again giving Trevor the pleasant thrill of possibilities and new beginnings.

They rode the train back together this time, and the good feelings lasted all the way through their commute home. When at last they reached their stop, they disembarked together. Andre was parked in the commuter lot, and Trevor walked him to his car. Andre paused with his hand on his door; it seemed he was as reluctant as Trevor to let it end yet.

"Do you want a ride home?" he asked.

Trevor considered telling him the drive would be less than five minutes but decided against it. Five minutes was still more than he would get if he walked home alone. "All right. Thanks."

Too soon, they pulled up to Trevor's building. Andre got out when Trevor did, rounding the car to stand next to him. They were as close as they'd been the night Trevor helped him move the piano, and Trevor's heart thumped. He swallowed, knowing Andre was going to kiss him good night this time. Trevor wiped his clammy hands on his pants, wondering what was wrong with him. He'd kissed men before. He'd kissed *Andre* before. Yet somehow, this was different. Neither of the previous times had gone the way Trevor had planned, and both had ended badly, to his way of thinking.

Andre maneuvered them so Trevor's back was against the car. He leaned in and said, "Is this all right?"

"Yes," Trevor said, controlling his nerves by breathing slowly.

Andre rested his hand on Trevor's cheek and closed the distance between them. When their lips touched, all the nervous energy inside Trevor exploded, sending sparks radiating down his spine and out to his arms and legs. Instead of trying to take control as he'd done before, Trevor let Andre hold the reins this time. The kiss was gentle and soft, but it left Trevor's knees so weak he was grateful for the support of the car behind him. At last Trevor kissed him back, matching the pressure and movement of Andre's mouth on his. Long before Trevor was ready for it to stop, Andre pulled away. He left fingers against Trevor's skin for a moment longer then withdrew them.

"Good night," he said.

It wasn't until Andre was back behind the wheel and pulling away that Trevor realized he'd never responded. "Good night," he murmured to the tail lights on Andre's car as it sped away. His legs were still like jelly as he climbed the stairs to his apartment.

Chapter Fourteen

From that point on, a good night kiss was always on the table, by which they really meant parking in the lot behind Trevor's building and making out like teenagers. It was embarrassing. They were both adults, and even if Trevor's roommates were underfoot at his place, Andre lived alone in his townhouse—they could have gone there. On instinct, Trevor understood Andre was doing his best to hold the line and not push Trevor before he was ready for anything else. As ridiculous as it may have been, there was something exciting about the semi-public setting and the hearkening back to adolescence. Mrs. Crotchety in 2B only ever surprised them once, and instead of giving them her usual evil eye, she smirked and winked, rapping on the window with her cane before heading back inside. The next morning, Trevor found an envelope under the door containing a photocopy of a love letter her late husband must have sent her when they were young. It was full of poetic language, the subtext of which was enough to make Trevor blush.

The next time Trevor and Andre met up, another Friday evening at the jazz cafe, Trevor couldn't remember why they'd ever set a limit on their physical contact. Andre not only looked good, when leaned in to kiss Trevor's cheek, he smelled good, too. Trevor breathed in deeply, wanting to memorize it. He must have failed the subtlety test because Andre chuckled and pulled away, causing heat to rush to Trevor's face.

Just as they finished their coffee, the band started a string of slower songs. Andre held out his hand to Trevor, who remained seated, looking up at Andre. He'd seen couples dance there before, including women dancing with other women, but he'd never seen two men. When he thought about it, outside of his few excursions to bars, he'd never been in a space where men were openly affectionate. His stomach knotted.

"We're safe here," Andre said, breaking into this thoughts.

"You're sure?"

"Absolutely." He sat down again. "Other than the job I took at your church, I don't purposefully go anywhere I'm not sure about. If anything, the good folks here are more shocked I brought a white person than that I brought a man."

Trevor chuckled. "I do stand out a bit."

"Just a little, blondie," Andre agreed, reaching out to tug a lock of Trevor's hair. He rose to his feet once more. "Now, are you gonna dance with me, or what?"

The *or what* lodged itself in Trevor's brain and turned into a whole host of things he wanted to do besides dance. He kept them to himself and got up, accepting Andre's hand. They earned a few glances from other patrons, but by the time Andre had Trevor in his arms, they'd mostly gone back to whatever they'd been doing. Three or four other couples joined them on the dance floor. A dapper older gentleman with a thin mustache put his arm around his beautiful gray-haired date's waist and pulled her closer.

Trevor imagined they were celebrating something, maybe the anniversary of their first date or their wedding day. Perhaps they'd raised a family and worked hard for a lifetime, and now they were enjoying the rewards of their endurance. A tiny sigh escaped Trevor's lips. Andre caught it and followed Trevor's gaze to the elderly couple. When he looked at Trevor again, there was sadness reflected back at him. It hit Trevor how they'd both had dreams of being like the man and his companion with their previous partners, but those dreams had been obliterated by circumstance and choice. He closed his eyes.

A warm hand on his cheek made Trevor open them again. What he saw made him suck in a breath. The sorrow in Andre's eyes was gone, replaced by affection and longing. Andre wanted him—not the part Trevor had given in to the first time they met or the part willing to endure a family dinner and move a piano or the part with an appreciation for the same music. No, Andre wanted what they'd been working up to all those months. For the first time since he was sixteen years old, Trevor entertained the possibility he could love someone other than Marlie.

He had nothing to lose. Marlie was gone, and with the success of Harvest's band, what he did in his private life might not be much of a complication after all. Trevor pulled Andre closer, surprising a soft gasp out of him. He raised his eyebrows, and a charming smile spread across his face. Trevor almost laughed. Instead, he fitted himself close against Andre and let his experienced dance partner take the lead.

Once again, he glanced at the elderly couple, and this time, he caught the man's eye. He gave Trevor a wink, startling him. Trevor grinned back, and the man offered a tiny nod. They moved with the music, the low, sweet sound of the singer's voice weaving a melody all around them. Caught up in it, Trevor relaxed into the soft, romantic mood.

The song ended and another began, but Trevor hardly noticed. His attention was taken up by Andre's warmth and sensual movement in rhythm with the music. They held each other, unconcerned with the ebb and flow of other couples joining in. Trevor knew the song—"Dream a Little Dream of Me"—and he crooned the lyrics softly in Andre's ear. Somehow, the words seemed fitting. It wasn't until one final, poignant note that they separated, though Andre kept his hand in Trevor's.

"What do you say we finish up here and go make our own music?" Andre asked.

Reading into it exactly what he suspected Andre meant, Trevor didn't hesitate to say, "Absolutely."

The train and car rides back were much too long. When they reached Andre's house, they were barely inside the door before Andre had Trevor pinned against the wall, their positions reversed from the previous time they'd been there. Trevor's heart hammered, and his palms grew clammy, but he didn't stop Andre when he leaned in to kiss him. He continued not objecting when Andre's cool hands snaked up under his t-shirt, instead groaning at the contact. Andre's lips traveled to the juncture of Trevor's neck just below his left ear. He mouthed the spot, his breath hot against Trevor's skin. Trevor's head fell back, and he struggled to maintain awareness of his surroundings.

When Andre's fingers grazed his nipple and their hips pressed together, Trevor gasped and opened his eyes. Andre must have sensed the shift because he let up a bit, removing the weight of his body but keeping his hands where they were.

"Okay?" he asked.

"I—" Trevor swallowed and breathed through his nose. He didn't know how to explain his embarrassment at his lack of experience. Andre was so comfortable with himself, while Trevor was busy fighting his nerves.

Andre slipped his hand out to rest his palm on Trevor's jaw. "We don't have to do this if you don't want to. I'm in no hurry."

"I want to," Trevor said. "God, I want to. I've never—I mean—except for that time in the club and messing around with Nate and making out in your car...wait, that's kind of a lot. But I haven't—"

"Oh." Andre didn't sound either disappointed or surprised. He backed off completely and stood in front of Trevor. "I think the entryway to my house isn't the best place. Come with me?" It was a question, not a command.

"All right," Trevor agreed.

He followed Andre into the back, to the first floor bedroom. Andre turned on a small bedside lamp and sat down on the bed, beckoning Trevor to join him. After a moment's hesitation, Trevor crossed the room and sat. The initial fire had been doused, but the mood wasn't entirely broken. There was something about the way Andre was taking care with him that kept Trevor's pulse pounding.

Andre angled toward him and put a hand on his trembling knee. "Is this what you want? To be here, making love with me?"

Trevor let out a shaky breath. "Very much."

"But?" Andre prompted.

"I've only ever been with one other person this way," Trevor admitted. "It was good with Marlie because we'd been friends—and then going out—for a long time. When Marlie and I weren't together, I went out with a few others, but I was supposed to be saving everything for her. I never went further than a couple of hand jobs with *anyone*. It wasn't much more with Nate. We always kept most of our clothes on." He put his head in his hands, face burning and throat tight, waiting for Andre to deliver some mocking words about being a prude.

Those words never arrived. Instead, Andre toed off his shoes and shifted on the bed so he was lying down then moved over to give Trevor room. When Trevor copied his actions and stretched out beside him, Andre rolled onto his side to face him. Trevor remained on his back but turned his head to look at Andre, who rested his palm in the middle of Trevor's chest.

Andre said, "You expected to wait until you were married?"

"No. That's what our church taught us, but we both knew most people don't. My parents were more realistic than hers—they're pretty open-minded, and I'm fairly sure they knew. We chose not to feel guilty, but we didn't make it public we were sleeping together."

Nodding, Andre said, "So this isn't about being ashamed."

"Not at all." Trevor finally rolled onto his side so he could look directly at Andre. "I'm not ashamed of who I am. Please believe me. It's other people who put that on us. Limiting who I'm intimate with is about me, not about some moral code. When I—when we—in the bar, I was upset with myself for weeks."

Andre rested a hand on Trevor's side. "Can you tell me why?"

It was easier there, alone in the semi-dark, the way it always had been with Marlie until he bared everything to her. Trevor swallowed his nerves, relaxing into Andre's touch and his calming presence, feeling grounded in a way he hadn't in a long time. He turned the words over in his mind, piecing together how he wanted to answer.

"I need more than a single moment of connection. I've known for as long as I can remember that I'm bi. As I got older, though, I used to pray for God to change me." Trevor took a deep breath. "I didn't care how I liked the way it felt when Nate put his hands in my pajamas, or the way I felt when I did the same to him. It was easy—we were best friends, no more, and it felt good. What I couldn't admit was I could love someone who wasn't a girl."

Andre shifted closer, but he frowned. "I'm not sure I understand."

"I don't think I'm explaining this well," Trevor said. "I never went any further with the few people I dated or even Nate because I was keeping my distance. If I give my entire body, it means more. It was fine with Marlie because I thought we were going to get married. That's what I want, Andre. I want the whole thing—marriage, kids, the white picket fence. I could have had a life with her."

"You could build a life with anyone you choose," Andre said.

"No!" Trevor flipped onto his back again and put space between them. "I saw what happened to my mom's brother and his husband. They got married as soon as the law changed, but to be dads? It was almost impossible. Everyone makes it sound so simple, like you can just go buy your gay self a kid. It doesn't even work that way for straight couples. With Marlie, I had this promise it would magically happen. We'd be like all the other families. God, Andre. I've wanted to be a dad since I was eleven years old and decided I'd be exactly like *my* dad. I knew three things for sure—he loved Jesus, he loved my mom, and he loved my sister and me. It was good enough to want it all for myself, too."

When Trevor looked back at Andre, he sucked in his breath, shocked at what he saw. Andre's eyes were streaming, and he was silently shaking. He turned his face into the pillow, but now Trevor could hear the soft gasps as he tried to bring himself under control. Trevor reached out, hesitated, and then rested his hand on Andre's back.

"What is it?"

It was a long time before Andre answered. When he finally calmed down enough to turn his head and speak, his eyes were wet and swollen. He cleared his throat a few times.

"Me too. And I had it," he said. "I had it, but then...it was gone."

"Your wife?"

"Yeah. My wife and our baby girls." He squeezed his eyes shut. "I've wanted the same thing you did since I was a little boy."

Trevor drew Andre in, and they remained close for a long time, both lost in everything the night had dredged up for them. Neither one moved, soaking in each other's warmth. Trevor let his mind and body relax, his eyes drifting closed and the room around them fading out.

The weight on his chest and the chill air on his arms brought Trevor back to awareness. He had no idea how long they'd slept, but he was stiff from immobility and cold from the air conditioning unit in the window. He tried to adjust his position, but Andre was still draped over him, and he couldn't move. He nudged gently, and Andre stirred.

"Hm?" Andre shivered. "Sorry."

"It's okay. I'm a little cold, though."

"Here, let me."

Andre got up and turned down the AC. Once he was back in bed, he dragged down the blankets, and they squirmed until they could crawl underneath. They lay on their sides, facing each other with a small gap between them. It was both strange and not, sleeping in someone else's bed again.

Trevor looked into Andre's dark eyes. "Didn't mean to fall

asleep," he said.

"Don't worry about it." Andre tilted his chin up.

"You all right?"

Andre sighed. "More or less."

"Tell me about the less," Trevor suggested.

"Besides the fact that I haven't had anyone in my bed in a long time, I also hate night." He frowned. "I'm not sure why I told you."

"Because I asked?" Trevor wanted to reach out, but something stopped him.

"I guess."

The fluid motion of Andre's shoulder against the sheet made Trevor shudder with something other than cold. "Want to tell me about it?"

Andre closed his eyes. "This is when I miss my wife."

"You never did tell me what happened, other than it was a car accident."

"We'd had a fight. It was an old argument, based on stupid shit we'd said to each other. She stormed out, intent on going to her parents' place. I didn't hear from her for the rest of the night, but I hadn't expected to. I was just going to go to bed, hoping to call her in the morning and make things right, when her mother called to tell me to get to the hospital because she'd been hit."

"Oh, my God," Trevor murmured. "I am...I don't really have words. I'm sorry."

Andre shifted so he was on his side as well. "It's not your fault."

"I know."

"This is the first time I haven't been alone at night since she died," Andre remarked.

"Is it okay?" Hesitantly, Trevor reached for him, laying a hand on Andre's shoulder.

"I'll let you know."

They both shivered, causing them to laugh. "It's still fricking cold in here," Trevor complained.

Andre was still for a moment then said, "Come closer and turn on your other side."

Trevor obeyed, sliding so he fit into Andre's arms. His breathing sped up at the contact. With Andre's warmth seeping into his back, his breath tickling and warming Trevor's neck, it was hard to remember his vow not to let anyone else in. He sucked in a breath.

Behind him, Andre trembled. "I'm sorry," he said quietly.

It took Trevor a minute to figure out what Andre was

apologizing for, but when he did, his lips parted and his breath came in shallow pants. "Don't be," he managed. "Me too."

He took Andre's hand in his and slid it lower so Andre could feel how wanted he was. Andre groaned softly against Trevor's neck then pressed his lips there, brushing them against the skin. He left his hand on the front of Trevor's pants, moving it in slow circles until Trevor let out a moan. At the sound, Andre flicked the button and drew down the zip so he could slide his hand inside. Trevor thrust shallowly against Andre's hand, both wanting him to continue and craving more contact.

He turned in Andre's arms, and they lay pressed together from shoulder to thigh. They were so close, only a hairbreadth between them. Trevor tilted his head a little in invitation. After a heartbeat, Andre accepted it and leaned in to press his lips to Trevor's. They gave in to each other, kissing and grinding until Trevor thought he might combust. He fiddled with Andre's pants, trying to get them unfastened without success. Andre put a hand on top of his.

"You sure you want to do this?" he asked.

Trevor paused. He hadn't asked himself why this felt all right; he simply knew it did. "Yes."

"Tell me what you want."

The words stopped him. "I-I don't know," Trevor admitted. "I told you, I've never done it before—not like this, with another man."

Andre drew back far enough to say, "Why don't I start by returning the favor you did at the bar?"

Trevor wanted to respond, to say, *yes, please,* but his mouth didn't seem to be working properly. He managed a weak, "Uh huh," before Andre was on him again, turning him onto his back and brushing their lips together.

At Trevor's shaky inhalation, Andre paused. "Are you nervous?"

"A little," Trevor admitted.

"That's all right. I promise, I'm going to make you feel as good as I did." Andre ran his hand over Trevor's chest then slipped up under his t-shirt, his fingers brushing Trevor's nipples. "I'll go slow. You can stop me if you need to."

He leaned in and kissed Trevor again, long and slow, keeping his hand still except for the thumb circling Trevor's nipple lightly. Trevor groaned; the anticipation left him breathless. Andre kissed his way across Trevor's jaw and down his neck, pausing to suck a little on the hollow above his collarbone. He drew back and sat up a little, tugging on the hem of Trevor's shirt. Trevor sat up long enough to pull off his shirt then lay back against the pillows.

Andre ran his hands and lips over Trevor's chest, which moved up and down rapidly. Andre looked up at him and said, "All right?"

"Yes," Trevor said, gritting his teeth against the pleasurable sensations. "It feels too good."

"And I haven't even touched your dick." Andre chuckled and lowered his mouth again.

He used his tongue to trail a path down Trevor's chest and stomach, hovering over his navel. He swirled his tongue, making Trevor squirm from the ticklish sensation. With agonizingly slow pace, Andre pulled Trevor's pants off. He palmed the bulge through Trevor's underwear then dragged them down as well, setting him free from the confining fabric. He teased with his fingers, dipping them in the crease of Trevor's thigh and following them with his nose and then his lips. He kissed his way closer to Trevor's erection, and Trevor groaned in anticipation.

Expecting Andre to take in his length, Trevor was surprised when all he did was lick from the tip to the base. Instead of going back the other way, Andre's tongue trailed farther down, his lips grazing Trevor's balls. Andre pulled his underwear so it was only around one ankle and shifted smoothly so he was between Trevor's legs, encouraging him to spread them wider. Gently, he pushed at the back of Trevor's thighs until he bent and lifted them.

When Andre's tongue breached his hole, Trevor gasped and lifted his ass off the bed. "Shit. Oh, holy shit," he moaned. "I've never—oh, God—I—" He tried to catch his breath.

He was torn between wanting to watch, to see what Andre was doing to him, and needing to close his eyes because the sight was so erotic he was afraid he would come without either of them touching his cock. It was a close thing. Andre sensed what Trevor needed and moved back up to swallow his erection, keeping one finger swirling against his hole. The wet heat all around him and the gentle pressure were too much. Trevor cried out, the only warning he was able to give before exploding in Andre's mouth. He panted, still feeling on edge and desperate despite release. Andre pulled off, wiping his mouth, and Trevor immediately replaced him with his hand, pressing firmly on his overly sensitive penis.

When he was finally able to open his eyes, he saw Andre's expression was amused rather than upset. "That was...direct," Andre remarked.

"I'm sorry!" Trevor lay back on the pillow and covered his face with his hands. "It was a bit much." The suddenness of his orgasm had left him a bit achy, and he shifted against the sensation. Gradually, it subsided.

"Hey," Andre said, pulling on his hand to uncover one eye. "It's fine. It'll be easier to take it slowly next time."

"Yeah." Trevor dropped both hands to the bed. After a moment, he opened his eyes and looked at Andre. "Did you want me to—"

"Only if you want to. If it would be more comfortable for you, I'm fine with your hand." He entwined his fingers with Trevor's.

"I want to," Trevor replied. He chuckled. "Though I'm not sure I'll be as good at it as you were."

"What are you talking about?" Andre propped himself up on his elbow. "You gave a hell of a blow job last time. Where did you learn to do that, anyway?"

Trevor flushed. "Marlie," he said. "I liked being inside her, don't get me wrong, but both of us enjoyed this more. She used to suck me like it was her favorite thing, and I loved..." He let his words die away, not sure how appropriate it was to talk about a former lover with a current one. "I'm sorry."

"I don't expect you not to think about her, you know." Andre put a hand on Trevor's belly. "Are you going to ask me not to think about my wife?"

"No." He cringed. "So I can confess how much I enjoyed going down on her?"

"Absolutely." Andre gave him a wicked grin. "Eating a woman out is hot, and the best part of dating another bisexual guy is being able to say it in the open."

Trevor's laughter rang out, and Andre stopped it with a kiss. They fell easily back into it, all other conversation on hold while they tasted each other again. Trevor ran his fingers up underneath Andre's shirt, following the same pattern Andre had with him. He touched Andre's nipples, liking the way they felt like little pebbles and the way twisting them made Andre squirm against him. Eagerly, he continued to kiss Andre while exploring his smooth skin and the coarse, dark hair on his chest. Hesitantly, Trevor dragged his hand down to cup Andre through his jeans. Trevor's breath hitched at the feel, and he needed more. He tugged at the button, and Andre reached down to help him out. He lifted his hips to shed his pants and underwear.

Trevor explored the length of Andre's erection, reveling in the soft skin and the weight of it against his palm. He drew his hand down slowly, eliciting a long groan from Andre. Spurred on, Trevor experimented with the foreskin, retracting it to fully expose the tip then drawing it back up and rolling it a little. Andre writhed and began to thrust his hips. Trevor bent over him and descended with his mouth, closing his eyes and trying to remember everything he liked having done. He encircled Andre's cock with his fingers just below his mouth.

Within moments, Andre was panting, and Trevor's dick had taken renewed interest. He shifted so he could coordinate wrapping one hand around himself while still giving Andre pleasure. He increased the speed and pressure of his motion until at last Andre cried out, filling Trevor's mouth at almost exactly the same moment Trevor came all over his own fingers. He remembered to swallow this time then withdrew and flopped next to Andre, still breathing hard. They lay together for a few minutes, Trevor's hand still gently moving against Andre's cock. Eventually he stopped, and Andre got up to retrieve a damp washcloth from the bathroom. When they were clean, he tossed the cloth aside and lay back down beside Trevor.

They kissed softly for a few minutes. Trevor slid his hand between Andre's legs again, running his finger through his rough pubic hair and touching the space where his thigh and hip met. He was now far too sensitive to want much, and he assumed Andre felt the same way.

"So good," Andre commented. "You're a fast learner."

"Yeah?" Trevor smiled. "Guess I had the right teacher."

Andre laughed quietly and rested his hand on top of Trevor's. "Mm. If you keep this up, I'll be ready again."

"I don't think I can yet," Trevor replied.

"It's all right," Andre assured him. "I'm in no hurry. We can sleep first." He kissed Trevor's forehead before settling down again.

Trevor withdrew his hand and wrapped Andre in his arms. Eventually, they drifted off, keeping each other warm through the night.

CHAPTER FIFTEEN

Trevor woke up with a pain in his neck. He groaned and rolled onto his back. His arm landed on the bed beside him, in the cool spot where the covers were thrown back from the sheet. Awareness of the rest of his surroundings kicked in, and he realized two things: he wasn't in his own apartment, and he was completely naked. He lifted the covers just to be sure then peered over the side of the bed where his pants and underwear still lay, inside out.

He sat straight up and whimpered in pain then groaned again when he remembered why his neck hurt. He'd slept with Andre. Not just slept, exchanged a couple of the best blow jobs he'd ever had and capped them with two more rounds of waking each other up to relieve their mutual need in other ways. Panic set in as he wondered how he was going to get home and what he was going to tell his roommates when he arrived. A quick glance at the clock alleviated his worry; it wasn't even six yet. He flopped back down on the bed and almost yelped in agony. How was he supposed to work later with his neck so stiff?

Sadly, his neck wasn't the only stiff part of him. His usual morning semi had taken notice of his stray thoughts about sleeping with Andre and decided to react like a disobedient child. He glared down at himself and tried to think about unsexy things, like old mashed potatoes and spoiled milk. It worked to get rid of the arousal but not the anxiety. Now what was he supposed to do? He wished he could ask Nate for advice, but he had a feeling talking about another man would prove detrimental to their already-strained friendship—especially given that Trevor had been hiding his relationship with Andre in the first place. Trevor wasn't so naive as to think Mack wouldn't make good on his threats if things spiraled downward.

Trevor rubbed the side of his neck in a poor attempt at relieving the pain. When he thought he could sit up, he swung his legs over the side of the bed. He sat there for a full five minutes, gathering the strength to get up. Before he had the chance to make any decisions, the bed beside him dipped, and Andre's cool hand was on his arm. Trevor jumped then inhaled sharply at the burning pain in his neck.

"What's wrong?" Andre asked.

"My neck," Trevor whimpered. "I must've fallen asleep at an angle."

"Probably just a spasm. You want some aspirin or something?"

"God, yes. And then I need to go home. I didn't tell anyone I wasn't going to be back last night." Trevor massaged his neck gingerly.

"No problem. I'll drive you." Andre stood up. "Wait here, and I'll bring you the aspirin."

After a glass of water and some medication, Trevor dragged his clothes back on and followed Andre out to his car. They were silent for the short ride, but despite the circumstances and Trevor's aching neck, it wasn't awkward. In fact, just being side by side for the drive felt good; it fit.

When they pulled up at Trevor's building, Andre left the car with the hazards on and walked him to the door. He leaned in and gave Trevor a tender kiss, something that felt like *I'm glad you stayed* and *Let's do this again.* Trevor let his eyes fall shut as he kissed back, hoping he was conveying the same thoughts. From the soft smile on Andre's face when he withdrew, Trevor had communicated successfully. He brushed his hand against Andre's and went inside.

No one was up. Trevor slipped into his room and shed his pants before he slid under the covers, breathing a sigh of relief. At least it was his day off and he didn't have to be at church until late afternoon to set up for the service the following day. Grateful for roommates with night-owl hours, he closed his eyes and drifted off, letting the medication take effect on his sore muscles.

He woke to the sound of voices outside the bedroom. He sat bolt upright then stifled a moan at the ache, which had only partly receded. While he was trying to figure out how he could manage to play later, there was a knock on the door.

"Uh, be right there!" he called then muttered, "Shit."

He reached down for his pants, wincing as the pain in his neck increased again, then changed his mind and crawled out of bed. He dragged his pants on, gritting his teeth. As he hauled open the door, Jamie nearly tumbled inside with a mug of coffee. Trevor stepped back before Jamie could knock into him.

"Brought you something," Jamie said cheerfully.

By the smug look on his face, he was aware of where Trevor had been, at least in some sense. Trevor had known he wouldn't be able to keep Andre a secret from them forever, but he'd hoped not to have a conversation about it so soon. Jamie handed Trevor the coffee and shut the door, sealing them in the room. Flopping onto Nate's bed—which Trevor now noticed was unused—Jamie grinned up at him.

"What?" Trevor asked irritably.

"You know what. How long have you been seeing the sexy guy you were kissing outside earlier?"

Trevor scrubbed his face with his free hand. "What the hell are you talking about?"

"Don't even try to play that game. I saw you out the window when I got up to piss. Just now, I caught the 'oh shit' look on your face when I asked about him. Plus, you're still wearing last night's clothes—they're all wrinkly and slept in. And you're walking like you're in serious pain. You look like hell. Either your ass is sore or you're having second thoughts because you can't cope with your real feelings."

"What are you, a psychic hotline? None of the above." Trevor sat back down on his bed and took a long sip of coffee. It was hot enough it burned a little going down, but he didn't care.

"Try again." Jamie crossed one leg over the other and folded his arms. He gave Trevor a pointed look.

Trevor stared into the coffee cup. When he looked up, Jamie was still waiting. "Fine. You win. We were together, but not like you're thinking. We didn't have ass sex. It's my neck, which hurts because I was stupid and slept at some weird angle. I'm not coping because I don't even know how I feel." He sighed. "No, that's wrong. I know how I feel, but I can't wrap my head around it right now."

"Uh huh." Jamie smirked, but it quickly faded. "Does Nate know?"

"Not yet. Until yesterday, I wasn't sure there was anything for him to know."

"Your private life is yours to own," Jamie said. "I can't make you tell him, but I see how he looks at you. He's waiting for you to notice him now Marlie's out of the picture."

Trevor tried to shake his head, but his neck spasmed and he grunted. "He knows I'm not in love with him."

Jamie's eyebrows went up. "Does he? Don't mess things up around here. I don't want to have to go looking for a fourth roommate when the two of you have an epic break-up."

"We can't have an epic break-up. We're not dating and we never were, or I wouldn't have been with Andre. Besides, you should be happy if I get kicked out. Mack says he's going to replace me with—ow. Oh, God." Trevor shifted then ground his teeth against the pain that shot down his back. He used the pads of his fingers to press on the sore spot.

"Here," Jamie said. "Let me." He moved to sit behind Trevor and began massaging his neck and shoulders.

"Oh," Trevor moaned. "So good." He leaned into the touch, reveling in the way his muscles loosened.

Jamie snickered. "Bet you say that to all the boys."

"Please shut up and just rub."

"Bet you say that, too."

"Oh, my God." Trevor nearly reached around to smack Jamie, but the massage felt too good, and he didn't want to interrupt.

"Explain a bit more about you and Nate," Jamie said. "You're not dating, even though you have this sexual energy between you. Now you've got someone else tied up in it. What gives?"

"Fine. We've been friends since Nate dropped out of his Catholic high school and started going to the public school in tenth grade. We went to college together. There's a huge history there of our being each other's go-to whenever we were between partners and needed a little something. We're friends, but we've never been more." He grunted as Jamie pressed harder.

"Because it's what he wants? Or what you want?" Jamie asked.

"I thought it was both," Trevor replied. "I've always known I wanted a family, something more settled. A house with a yard and a swing set. Nate wants to live right in the city—he needs the people and the noise. We've always looked out for each other, especially when we're both single. What we did was another way we took care of each other. We weren't having sex, just relieving tension now and again." Trevor sighed. "When we moved in, I said we needed to stop, which we did. I'd gotten the job at the church, and they kind of have some rules about the people they hire."

"Can I ask you why the hell you want a job at a church with rules for your love life?"

Trevor growled. "I get so damn sick of that question. I took the job because it's what I want to do. There aren't too many churches creating their own music where there aren't restrictions of some kind. I'm lucky they don't care if I'm not as hot as headliners for other labels."

"Fine. Whatever. And seriously, Trev? Look in a mirror the next time you're tempted to think you're nothing special." Jamie finished the massage and moved to sit next to Trevor. "Go on."

"I figured it would be easy enough to settle down and get married." Trevor shrugged, and it didn't hurt as much as before. "I've been on and off with Marlie since we were kids, and she was a natural choice. It didn't matter anyway, since Nate was seeing whoever-it-was at the time. I've forgotten."

"And now?" Jamie prompted.

"I don't know," Trevor said. "I'm not with Marlie, but I'm not interested in running to Nate to make it better anymore. Last night was...good. Really good." He knew his face was red by the wave of heat. At the thought of the way he and Andre had fit their bodies together, the way they'd kissed and moved and come together, his pants tightened. He knew he was in trouble when the only thing he could think of was how much he wanted to do it again. "I'm so screwed," he told Jamie. "I'm falling for Andre, and I think Nate's going to be upset."

"Thought so. Which is why I told you not to make any messes."

Trevor snorted. "You know, you're not exactly the person I thought I'd be talking about this with."

"No doubt." Jamie was silent for a few minutes. He looked down at his hands then stole a glance sideways at Trevor. "I know you hate him," he said quietly. "You all do."

Guilt crept over Trevor. He knew Jamie was right; none of them had so much as bothered to learn The Boyfriend's name. Still, he had to try. "We don't hate him, exactly."

"Don't lie." Jamie drew his knees up. "We've been together for years, on and off, like you and Marlie. He doesn't really want to commit, but he won't end it, either. We've been through a lot together, and most of what's wrong is my own damn fault. I can't be the boyfriend he wants. He and I both know he deserves better than someone like me."

"Jamie—" Trevor started.

"Save it, okay? I've had enough lectures from Mack on the subject."

Jamie rested his cheek on his knee, and Trevor wanted to put a hand out to him. He'd never asked Jamie anything about The Boyfriend, but now he wished he had. Jamie's words alarmed him. It didn't feel right letting it go, but in the interest of hearing what else Jamie had to say, he backed off.

"All right," he said. "But if you need anything, I'm here."

"You're right, I'm probably not the best person to give you advice." Jamie shrugged one shoulder.

"But you're going to anyway."

Jamie shook his head. "Nope. I don't want to see either of you hurt, though. You're still a mess, and Nate—well, I honestly don't know. You said you two didn't have sex?"

"No, I suppose we sort of did, but not...you know. Not much. Jerking each other, mostly."

"Ah, okay. Sounds like there was more to it, though?"

"Yeah. It was intimate. I saw it as an extension of our friendship. I'm not in love with him, and I never was." Trevor put his head in his hands. "He said he was, but then he got over it. Maybe he lied, too."

"Fuck," Jamie commented. "You really had better talk to him." He stood up. "If he thinks you're yanking him around, he won't take it well if he hears it from someone else."

"He won't take it well even coming from me." Trevor looked up at Jamie. "I think we're all screwed."

Jamie gave him a last, pitying look as he exited the room and closed the door. Trevor sighed and scooted backward on the bed. Regardless of what he needed to say to Nate, Trevor was sure about one thing. He wanted to see Andre again, as much and as often as possible. Hoping he hadn't upset Andre with his standoffish behavior, he fished in his pocket for his phone to send a quick text. *Hey—sorry about earlier. I'm glad I stayed last night. Can't wait to see you again.* He followed it with a smiley face.

When he was done, he rose from the bed to get ready for work. Only as he was pulling the door shut on his way to the shower did it occur to Trevor to wonder where Nate was and why he hadn't noticed the empty bed when he'd first come home.

Chapter Sixteen

It was early enough one morning when Andre left Trevor at his apartment there was plenty of time for a run before it got too hot. Now that he knew the route and most of the residents, Andre preferred circling the neighborhood over a hurried trip to the gym after work. He hoped the physical exertion would clear his head and help him make sense of everything.

As the summer wore on, they'd continued their complicated dance. Trevor rarely stayed all night, but when he did, it was always worth the wait. This time, they'd spent the night before making music again, of more than one kind. Trevor had played a new song for Andre, different from the ones he usually wrote. He called it a "lament," an outpouring of grief and anger toward God, and he'd said Andre had inspired it. Afterward, they'd made love, pressing in close and sliding their bodies against each other, chasing away their histories and making new memories together as they'd done often in the weeks since the first time Trevor had stayed. Trevor was still often reserved with him, and they were taking everything with caution. It was better this way, Andre thought, given where they had both come from.

Andre had expected to feel disappointed in himself for giving in with Trevor and for allowing the nothing between them to become something. It went against every promise he'd made to himself that after Dahlia he would never again put himself in a situation where he had to hide who he was. He'd done it for the sake of her family and her church, but he was through with presenting one face in private and another in public.

Instead of being frustrated with the current situation, all he could think about was the way Trevor never backed off when Andre's grief overtook him. Trevor probed into places Andre's family and friends hadn't dared to go. His careful calculations of his personal risk were different too. Trevor wasn't expecting Andre to hide anything. He wasn't insisting Andre sit beside him in church every Sunday pretending they were "just friends," and he wasn't asking Andre to be anyone other than himself. If what he needed was time until he could be open too, Andre would give him as much as he wanted.

By the time Andre returned from his run, he was invigorated and ready for the day. A quick shower and bite to eat later, he was on his way to work, whistling and feeling more refreshed than he had in a long time. A text message mid-morning assured Andre that Trevor was in the same frame of mind.

Hope the boss-man doesn't ask why I'm in a good mood. Pretty sure "I got laid" wouldn't go over well.

Andre laughed out loud. A moment later, he regretted it when Julian poked his head out of his office and grinned. Andre gritted his teeth.

"Do not even go there," he warned Julian.

His words only made Julian's smile bigger. "Your face says it all. I don't need to say a word." He made a rude gesture, implying he knew what was up.

Andre growled. "I don't call that keeping it to yourself."

Julian laughed and ducked back into his office, shutting his door on the paper wad Andre threw at him. Despite Julian's commentary, it was hard to be truly angry with him. After all, if he hadn't dragged Andre to the club on Boylston, Trevor wouldn't be texting him. The thought that Trevor could have been happily planning a wedding with Marlie instead sobered Andre, and he turned to his work before he could chase it any further.

He pulled up a web site whose owner had recently contacted them to do an overhaul. It belonged to Kurt Vinton, the author of a popular local blog with several thousand loyal followers. He was looking to redesign since he was getting more freelance work and had monetized his writing. Kurt was an independent editor with a popular syndicated column on word history. On his personal web site, he was well-known for his scathing commentary on what he called the Moralizing Majority—any group he felt held all the chips and used them to oppress subgroups. That included religion, especially pointing out uncomfortable aspects of popular church culture.

Andre had no idea whether Kurt had ever been religious or raised in a church himself. He only knew the man was often rude and resorted to mocking people rather than practice. Kurt was generally disregarded by Christians of all types, including liberals and progressives, for simply being an unfunny jerk. Andre wasn't keen on the sarcastic tone of the entries either, but it wasn't his job to evaluate the man's content any more than it had been with Harvest Church. He opened the files with Kurt's requests regarding colors and themes then shot a quick text to Trevor saying, *I'm stuck doing a job for Kurt Vinton, jerk of the blogging world. Wish me luck.*

Trevor replied. *He's an ass. No, wait. That's an insult to asses, which are pretty awesome. Yours especially.*

Andre laughed. *Almost as awesome as yours.* His face heated up as he was reminded of his mouth being intimately acquainted with Trevor's ass.

After setting his phone aside, he pulled up the web site to have a look. When he saw the front page, his mouth dropped open. "Holy shit," he muttered. "Not good."

Ever listen to those modern wannabe rock anthems they put out in churches these days? Well, there's a new kid on the block, and it's getting all sorts of airplay on the local Jesus station. It's a little ditty called "You Draw Me In." I had to look this one up—they have it on their web site now, so you can listen to a preview of it. Anyway, it's full of this really fantastic homoeroticism. Remember the song from about fifteen years ago about getting on your knees? This takes it to the literal next step. I mean, I've never in my life heard such a worshipful song about one dude blowing another. The best part? All these sheeple singing along with it probably have no effing clue what they're really swallowing.

He scrolled down, hoping it would get better, but it didn't. The post went on for about another five hundred words, detailing what Kurt thought inspired the song. He did mention being unsure if it was a reflection of "the songwriter"—who he never named—and his personal life, implying Trevor might have been caught up in Christian pop culture's failure to recognize double entendre. Kurt's intent was clear, though. His rage was directed at the practice of some churches to marginalize gay members while men soaked themselves in erotic lyrics about the Son of God. It bothered Andre too, but he thought Kurt's post was in poor taste, especially since Kurt claimed to be straight.

Andre's stomach clenched, his whole body rigid in his chair. He sat back, exhaling slowly and rubbing his head. His heart thudded heavily, and his hands shook. There was no way he would be able to concentrate on work. He couldn't even pass the account back to Julian without explaining why. His only option to make sure Julian didn't ever catch wind of this development was to keep working on the web site and hope the post didn't get past Kurt's limited following. He prayed most of Kurt's followers weren't the sort of people who would listen to worship music. A post like this one wasn't new for Kurt, and there was a chance it would only be shared by a handful of people who specifically hated contemporary praise songs. Taking consolation, Andre steeled himself and focused on the web site's graphics, doing his best to put what he'd just read out of his mind.

It took less than two days for Julian to discover the blog post. Andre knew he had because Julian was waiting for him when he arrived at work, arms crossed and foot tapping impatiently. His expression said it all.

"Why the absolute fuck didn't you tell me?" he demanded.

Andre sighed. "I was hoping to keep it quiet."

"Yeah, I got that. For what reason?"

Anger surged through Andre. "It wasn't interfering with my job, and I didn't want you to cancel the account just because this tool made fun of my—" He stopped, heart pounding. He hadn't told Julian everything.

The frustrated expression slid from Julian's face, and his eyes popped. "You've been seeing him." He pursed his lips and frowned. "It wasn't just sex?"

"Yes to the first, no to the second. Right on both counts." Andre brushed past Julian and sank into a chair. "I didn't want you to tell me it was a conflict of interest. Kurt's a jackass, and I doubt anyone from Harvest Church reads what he puts out there. I didn't want you to lose a big account for my sake."

Julian's features relaxed. "You still should have said something." He closed his eyes and pinched the bridge of his nose. "I get how hard it's been for you, but have we lost so much that you couldn't talk to me about your guy?"

Andre slouched in his chair and refused to meet Julian's gaze. "I don't know. You've been on me about Trevor since I met him." He finally looked up, and it only took a moment for him to know what he said next could strengthen or sever their fragile bond. "I don't know how to talk to you anymore. Not since Dahlia."

Julian crossed the room and crouched next to Andre. "I've been here," he said. "I've been waiting all this time. Talk to me now."

"It's like he woke me up or something," Andre said. "I told him about Dahlia, and he let me talk. And then we made love. Not just sex, Julian. There's a time and a place for something casual, and you know I've got nothing against any of us giving or getting what we need. This was different."

"Different how?" Julian's brow furrowed.

"It didn't end with one night, and now I'm falling in love with him." Andre's jaw tightened, and he looked down at Julian, daring him to challenge Andre's words. "No, not falling. I'm already there—I love him. I never thought I'd say those words again."

"I believe you." Julian stood up. "It probably is a conflict of interest, but it's one blog post. If you can keep working on Kurt's web site without it affecting you, then go ahead. The minute you can't, you had better tell me, or so help me I will fire your ass."

Andre smiled. "You keep threatening that. I don't think you really would."

Julian's shoulders sagged, and he laughed weakly. "Nah, you're right. But you'd better do a good job. If it becomes a problem, tell me right away, and I'll take the account. Clear?"

"Yes, sir." Andre saluted him and was relieved when Julian rolled his eyes and laughed.

After Julian had gone back into his office, Andre prepared everything for his day and set to work. His stomach roiled when he saw how many likes, shares, and reblogs Kurt's post had, but it mainly seemed to be individuals rather than anything more widespread. He prayed fervently the appeal would die out by the end of the week and Kurt would fade back into the relative obscurity of any other non-celebrity.

He was sorely disappointed. Over the course of the week, the popularity of the one single blog post rose from being seen by the few thousand people who actively cared what Kurt thought to being plastered all over social media. At that point, there was virtually no chance Trevor hadn't seen it, but he remained silent other than a few texts. He'd mentioned it was going to be a busy week, though, so it was possible he'd gotten caught up in things at work. Out of courtesy, Andre didn't mention his work on the blog; if Trevor hadn't seen it, there was no sense in upsetting him during a busy season.

On Friday morning, Andre's phone buzzed with a text. His heart nearly stopped when he saw it was from Trevor, and he wondered if someone at the church had finally made him aware of Kurt's post. All Trevor's text said was, *Guess what?*

Andre sent back, *What?*

It's a surprise. Turn on KXN at 3 during Homeward Bound.

Okay.

Homeward Bound was the Friday afternoon show. They had the latest songs interspersed with games, giveaways, and live interviews. Andre wondered what Trevor was up to, but he didn't ask. Instead, he distracted himself all day with work. At five minutes to three, he turned on the radio and listened to the pre-show ads. Julian briefly stuck his head out to see what Andre was doing, but Andre shrugged at him. Julian closed his door.

The announcer came on. "Have we got some fun for you folks today! Our contest winners will receive a prize package including tickets to the King's Creation Christian music festival in Amherst, Harvest Church's popular CD, and a meet-and-greet with the band. In the meantime, we've got Trevor Davidson and Tom Seltz here with us today to talk about all things music. Give us a call with your questions. Okay, let's kick off the hour with a listen to 'You Draw Me In.'"

The music started, and Andre let it fade into the background. He grinned and typed a text to Trevor: *Congratulations! I'm ready to listen to your sexy voice.* He hesitated for a moment, wondering if it was too forward, then sent it anyway.

A moment later, he had a winking face on his screen. Chuckling softly, he put the phone down and went back to work, listening to the end of the song. When it was through, the announcer came back on.

"Time to take a few calls. Here's one from Brandy, right in Braintree. Hey, Brandy, how're you doing?"

There were more calls, mostly to chat about the songs, when they were going to do a tour, and one about where Trevor got his ideas. Trevor didn't miss a beat, smoothly explaining his deep faith and the way he wanted his songs to have a sensory feel to them. Andre snorted, but he was glad Trevor had prepared an answer—he must have gotten that question a lot. Another set of songs played, they had a game, and then they took another call.

Andre almost choked when the caller said, "This is Kurt in Back Bay."

The announcer said, "Hey, Kurt. What's your question for Trevor or Tom?"

"It's not so much of a question, really," Kurt replied. "More of a response to Trevor's last answer about where he gets his inspiration."

"Okay." The announcer sounded puzzled. "Go ahead."

"Well, you know, I wrote a little something the other day about worship music. You may have read it. I got an interesting comment on my blog this morning, and I thought I'd share it and see what Trevor says." He cleared his throat. "'You're a lot closer than you think when you say worship songs sound intimate. I wish people knew what they were singing about. I doubt Trevor Davidson would keep his job if everyone knew he really was singing about putting his mouth on another man. He likes to go both ways, or so I hear, though I gather this is what destroyed his future marriage.' So, how much of it is true? Is Trevor secretly *gay*?"

"Oh, God!" Trevor's voice was slightly muffled, but Andre heard him in the background.

"Whoa," the announcer said. "I think we should take a break for a minute. Hang in there while I put in some music."

A recent song by a popular artist came on, and Andre sat staring at his computer screen. It took less than another minute for him to completely break, putting his head in his hands and nearly hyperventilating. He gripped his head. It didn't matter whether the comment was from someone who had seen them or someone who had merely guessed accurately at the truth. Trevor would believe Andre was responsible for the comment or at least for spreading it around, given his association with Kurt through the web site.

He eyed his phone, willing a call or text to come through, but it was silent. When he couldn't manage any longer, Andre picked it up and sent a message himself. *You okay?*

It was a full five minutes before he got one back. *Why didn't you tell me?*

Tell you what? Andre responded.

About the post. You knew. You were working on his blog.

I didn't want to bother you with it. When there was only silence in response, Andre tried again. *We'll get through this. Call me, please.*

Trevor's next words tore into Andre. *Leave me alone.*

Andre shoved his chair back and stalked to Julian's office. He wasn't going to let Kurt make a mess of the best thing to happen to him since Dahlia died. He slammed open Julian's office door.

"You can have Kurt's account, or you can tell the motherfucker to go to hell. I don't care what you do, but I'm not going to work on it anymore."

Julian's mouth dropped open. When he recovered, he said, "What the hell?"

Andre tried to get his breathing under control. "He just fucking outed Trevor—incorrectly, I might add—to anyone who happened to be listening to the radio this afternoon."

"Christ on a cracker. What?"

"Do you have any idea how bad—"

Julian cut him off. "Yes, I get it. Trevor's not in immediate danger, is he?"

"I doubt it. He's at the radio station."

"That's not what I mean," Julian said, his voice low. "I've spent enough time around your family to know the drill."

Andre leaned against the doorframe, shaking. He closed his eyes. "I don't know. He's probably all right for now." He lifted his head and opened his eyes. "He's freaking out. No one knew about us except you. I don't even know if he told his roommates. Right now, he's pissed at me for not telling him about the blog post. Maybe he even thinks it's my fault, that I could have stopped it somehow."

"He can't really believe that, can he?" Julian asked, standing up.

"He told me to leave him alone." Andre shook his head. "Maybe he's right. I was working on the web site—I should have done something."

Julian wrapped Andre in a tight hold, letting Andre tense and shudder in his arms. "This is not your fault. You need to find him."

Andre shoved a little until Julian let go, leaving just his hand on Andre's neck. "He won't talk to me, and I don't know how long he'll be at the station. I have to give him time."

Withdrawing his hand, Julian said, "Don't sit on this too long."

"I won't," Andre promised, even though he wasn't sure he could keep his vow.

"Go home," Julian ordered. "You're a mess, and you're no good to me here. If you're up for it later, I'll send you some files to work on remotely. I'll deal with the shithead. I don't want his money if he's in the habit of pulling stunts like this."

"He could ruin your business if you do anything stupid."

Julian glowered. "I'd like to see him try. Son of a goddamn bitch." He smacked the side of his fist against the wall.

"Yeah, okay." Andre's feet didn't want to move, so he remained standing in Julian's office.

"Go home," Julian repeated. "Do you need me to go with you?"

"No. I can manage by myself."

"Good."

Julian gave him a small shove, and Andre used the momentum to return to his desk. He gathered everything together and threw it in his bag, not caring if it all ended up in a crumpled lump at the bottom. He picked up his tablet and almost flew out of the office. He didn't know yet what he was going to do, but he prayed that one way or another, Trevor would come around and they could get through it together.

Chapter Seventeen

Trevor spent the rest of the day and all of the following weekend avoiding Andre's texts and calls. Deep inside, he knew it wasn't logical to think Andre had anything to do with Kurt the Jerk's blog post or his calling the show and making a mess. He certainly hadn't left the comment heard 'round Boston, and chances were good he hadn't even read it. Besides, he'd promised he wouldn't press Trevor to be out yet. Still, no one outside of Andre, Trevor's roommates, and Marlie had any idea what had happened, and Trevor knew Andre had direct connections to Kurt through work. For all he knew, Kurt had dug around in Andre's life, discovered their relationship, and found someone willing to confirm his suspicions. Trying to piece things together made Trevor's head ache.

It was one thing to talk to the people closest to him and another thing entirely for his church and all the adoring fans to know. A public outing was the sort of tabloid fodder the church preferred to kill as quickly as possible, so naturally, the entire congregation likely knew by the end of the weekend. Trevor didn't attend church, appointing Tom to take his place. Tom was kind enough not to say anything, but Trevor heard the curiosity in his voice over whether there was any truth to what Kurt had said.

Pastor Bret suggested he take a brief leave of absence while the church cleaned up the mess. He assured Trevor that one comment on one blog didn't need to mean anything and it was no more than someone spreading rumors. There were two problems with his theory, as far as Trevor was concerned. The first was the damage had been done, and regardless of who it was, it had to have been someone who knew. The second was that it was true. For those reasons, he couldn't face Andre; any chance of being seen together could be taken as confirmation, and without knowing who was responsible, Trevor didn't know who to trust.

Trevor didn't share his insight with Pastor Bret. He simply accepted his two weeks' paid leave and said nothing. The church could easily have asked him to do it without pay or by docking his vacation, but they didn't, and he was grateful. They also didn't immediately fire him, but he supposed they thought it was nothing more than some hateful person spouting off. Not that it mattered to the rest of the population, unfortunately, but the cleanup method was a matter for the damage control team. They would contain the mess before it spread.

That was easier said than done. By the next week, it was all over Christian radio despite Harvest's best efforts. One speculation followed after another—what happened, what kind of person Trevor was, who he had been with. They were analyzing his music, looking for clues to some mystery lover to confirm or deny the anonymous comment on Kurt Vinton's blog. Not only did Trevor refuse Andre's attempts to reach him, he stopped answering his phone altogether unless it was one of his roommates or someone from the church. He had no desire to even talk to family members who had heard the show and wanted to know what the hell was going on.

Out of a desire to punish himself, Trevor listened to Christian news radio. The smooth voice of the noontime newscaster came over the air. "And in other news, Trevor Davidson, the voice of popular praise anthem 'You Draw Me In,' has apparently come out as gay. On Friday afternoon, during WKXN's drive home show, popular satirist Kurt Vinton read a comment from his blog in which it appears Trevor was discovered having an affair with another man during his engagement, which has now been called off. This could shock the entire Christian world. We haven't yet talked to Trevor himself, but a spokesperson for Harvest Christian Community was available."

A new voice came on. "We'd like to clear up any speculation as exactly that. This is all rumor and innuendo. Whoever wrote the comment cannot possibly be informed of all the facts. Until Trevor himself makes a statement, we have nothing further to say on the matter."

"There you have it, folks. They won't confirm or deny the rumors. At this time, people are picking apart Trevor's song lyrics in an attempt to answer the questions raised by this most recent development in the rise of Harvest's band."

Conservatives might not have been kind to other out contemporary music stars, but at least they understood them. They could easily pigeonhole them into a category: nobly remaining celibate, aggressively pursuing a "sinful lifestyle," or playing for their team again after much prayer. Absolutely no one knew what to do with Trevor. He did have some support from a few gay Christian outlets, but he was surprised to find even they mostly wanted him to be another Gay Christian Icon and were thoroughly uninterested in the truth.

There was a small faction of fervent prayer warriors who were determined to uplift him to the Lord that he might not have to struggle with temptation. They seemed convinced he was still a Nice Christian Boy, perhaps acting out some terrible crime committed against his person as a child. Pastor Bret left a message for him that his well-wishers were leaving cards and letters for him at the church and they would hold onto everything for him until his return. Trevor wanted to burn them, but as he didn't have adequate means, he settled for telling Pastor Bret to shred them, a request which was denied.

A second, larger group was equally unhelpful. These were the ones who took up Trevor's cause as some personal mission to point out the oppressive nature of some branches of Christianity. They'd determined that he—and his church—were throwbacks and an anomaly in Boston culture. The only thing that came from their efforts was that Trevor's situation was now news outside of limited Christian circles. He suspected most of the population of the Greater Boston area had no interest in the personal life of a church employee, but that didn't stop any of them from using social media to spread the word. Local stations devoted precious air minutes to speculating about his future in Christian pop music—even the stations playing classic rock.

The blow-up was big enough to land a brief mention on WBZ in between the previous day's Sox score and a report of a traffic jam at Thwaites Place. On another station, a popular non-religious gay talk show host stirred the pot by reminding listeners that bi was just a stop on the Gay Train and Trevor would be announcing his full and active membership sooner or later. After that show, during which at least a dozen men called to say either they'd be happy to mentor him or that he'd better never come near them with his tainted man-parts, Trevor hid in his room under the blankets for the rest of the day. He stopped listening to anything other than NPR, which was about the only radio station uninterested in him, and gave up checking his social media accounts after fifteen friend requests from men he didn't know. Emails through the church site went the same way, especially after being asked by a woman whose mother attended his church if she could be part of his "gay sandwich."

After deleting the message, Trevor brought his lunch into his cave and managed to get crumbs all over the sheets. He snagged a book from the shelf, but he read the same paragraph three times without understanding it. Eventually, he drifted off into a troubled sleep. That was where Nate, Jamie, and Mack found him when they returned to the apartment for dinner.

Nate sat down directly on top of him, waking him and drawing out a pained, "Oof!"

"Get up," Nate demanded.

Trevor stuck his head out of the blanket. "No way. I'm never emerging from this bed again except to make myself peanut butter and jelly toast and get books from the living room."

Jamie flopped next to him and stuck his tongue out. "You got crumbs all over! Ew." He poked Trevor in the shoulder. "You'll have to get up to pee, too."

"Fine. I'll get up to pee. But that's it! I'm living in here from now on." Trevor tried to turn over again, but Nate was still on top of him.

Mack rolled his eyes. "Give me a break, man. This whole thing will blow over soon." He cringed. "Poor choice of words. Sorry."

Trevor shoved hard on Nate, causing him to tip sideways, then sat up. "That's just it!" he yelled. "It's not going to 'blow over.' This is the kind of thing that ruins people. Look what's happened to other singers. They get stuff written about them, read by thousands of angry ex-fans. Remember Jennifer Knapp? An angry woman sent her entire collection of CDs back to her in protest. And the worst part? I get all the fun of 'where is Trevor sticking his dick today' right along with 'how long is Trevor going to be faithful if he gets married.' It sucks in every direction." He glared at Mack. "Pun fucking intended."

"Then think about it this way," Nate said. "At least everyone found out at once. No need to make the announcement one at a time."

"Oh, my God!" Trevor gaped at Nate. "Are you serious? This is not better!"

"They're going to forget about it in five minutes when the next big crisis happens. There's always some public figure being an ass somewhere." Nate shrugged.

"It's not that simple," Trevor insisted. "I'm like their special pet project. Half of them want to hang me, and the other half want to bang me. I can't win. They're not going to let this go."

Mack covered his mouth, and a half-exasperated, half-amused chortle escaped around his fingers. Nate and Jamie both wrapped their arms around him, though Jamie made a face when some stray crumbs flung into the air. Trevor leaned into Nate, too frustrated to say anything else. Nate rubbed his back in slow circles. Mack lowered his hand and leaned against the wall, his legs crossed at the ankles.

"All right, fine," he said. "So people don't forget about it. So what? You still have your job, right? Obviously no one there cares what drama the Penis Police dredge up this week."

Nate and Jamie looked at each other over Trevor's head and mouthed, *Penis Police?* Jamie snickered; Nate coughed.

Mack scrunched his nose at them. "You know exactly what I mean. The super-conservatives and their special brand of whoever they hate this week are forever talking about dicks and where they go. You've heard it. They don't phrase it like that, but it's what it amounts to. Everyone else will forget this happened. They'll try to keep the flames of righteous indignation going for a while, and I guess your church might have to endure some of those traveling bigots with signs protesting shit, but then you'll be free to make whatever the hell kind of songs you want."

"But now everyone is going to question what the songs are about!" Trevor argued. "They've already been informed about the one, and they're starting to pick apart the others—even the ones I didn't write."

Mack let loose a loud guffaw. "Right. Because no other praise songs in the history of the world have ever sounded erotic."

"How would you even know?" Trevor shot back.

Mack uncrossed his legs and strode farther into the room. He grabbed Nate's desk chair and hauled it out, plopping himself on it backward. "Grew up in church," he said. "Surprised?"

"Well, yeah," Trevor admitted. "You always seem kind of confused about my religion."

"More like confused about why you're still in it. My folks' church wasn't like yours at all, but I'm familiar with the music." He lifted one shoulder casually. "Even old hymns sometimes sound dirty, or you can make them sound that way. My cousins and I used to add 'in bed' to all the titles."

Trevor laughed feebly in spite of himself. "You really think this is going to just go away?" he asked.

"No," Mack said. "It'll become less interesting after a while. It's how this shit rolls, Trev. Happens in every industry."

"Besides," Nate said, "think of it this way. Whatever happens next can't be worse than what you've been through. It can only get better, right?"

Trevor scowled at him. "So far, I haven't seen any evidence of anything improving."

"So, it's not even a little bit of a relief not to hide who you are anymore?"

"I don't know. Maybe, but this isn't how I'd have chosen to do things. It should have been up to me how and when to talk about it. I feel...violated, like someone was poking into my personal life." He didn't add how he was sure it was someone he knew. That would have sparked more speculation, and he didn't need his roommates joining the fun.

Jamie rested his cheek on Trevor's shoulder. "I promise, it will get better." There was a heaviness to Jamie's words, and Trevor wondered how much he'd endured in his own coming out.

"Okay," Trevor said. Nate and Jamie let go of him, but he stayed where he was, all three sets of eyes on him.

"So, you'll come out of there?" Nate asked.

Pouting a little, Trevor said, "Yeah, all right."

"Good," Mack said, brushing crumbs off his pants. "But you're cleaning up this mess."

CHAPTER EIGHTEEN

It felt good to be out of his cave, even though he'd only spent one day in there and even though he still had to deal with the small matter of who had caused all the trouble in the first place. He had yet to return any of Andre's messages. In one of his texts, he'd said Julian had threatened to dump Kurt Vinton as a client. Trevor read it as confirmation Andre had nothing to do with it, but he still wasn't ready to pick back up where they'd left off. First he had to hear what his church had to say before he decided if it was worth filling them in on the truth. Then he had to solve the mystery of who had both the balls and the motive to destroy him. Keeping his distance from Andre wasn't going to make his problems go away, though, and Andre wouldn't wait for him forever. Trevor stood to lose one of the best things to happen to him in a long time, which meant he needed to get himself together.

Trevor set to work picking up his personal space. Before he had a chance to take care of the mess in the bedroom, Bret called. Trevor contemplated ignoring it, but in the interest of salvaging what was left of his job, he answered. "Hello?"

"Trevor, hey." Bret sounded weary. "We—that is, the other senior staff and I—think it would be a good idea to meet. Are you free this afternoon?"

Trevor ground his teeth. Bret knew very well Trevor was free; he was the one who had given him a leave of absence. "Yes. What time?"

"Whenever you can make it here. The rest of the staff is still in the office, so the sooner the better."

"Fine. Give me time to get ready." Trevor hung up, his stomach rolling with a combination of anxiety and frustration.

A shower and shave did nothing to relax Trevor. He spent a tense train ride going over what he might say or do to improve his situation, but nothing came to mind. When he arrived at the church, Bret met him and ushered him into a conference room where the other pastors, the senior staff, and the board of elders were seated around the table. Out of the dozen people in the room, only three were women. One was the Director of Youth and Family Ministry, a woman who, like Trevor, had more job title than actual responsibilities. Another was her second in command, the superintendent of Sunday school, who happened to be both Bret's wife and one of the elders. The third was Marlie.

Trevor frowned in confusion, and Marlie shrank back in her chair. She looked down at her hands, folded on the table in front of her, and wouldn't meet Trevor's eyes. Bret cleared his throat, and the entire assembly looked up.

"Well," he said, "let's get this moving, shall we?"

Lew Alden, the senior pastor, addressed Trevor. "Regardless of what else is going on, we're reluctant to let go of you on staff. You've been a valuable part of our team. However, this is a serious concern, and it must be addressed."

Ava Carmichael, Bret's wife, spoke up. "We've been discussing this since the radio broadcast, but until this morning, we hadn't arrived at a decision. Marlie here called us earlier, and we think we now have a viable solution." She exchanged a glance with Bret, her expression troubled.

"The way we see it, you have two choices," Lew said. "You can do what that dreadful radio host suggested and be full-on homosexual from here on out. You would definitely win the Gays for Jesus crowd with that, but you would either have to be single for the foreseeable future or you'd have to find a new job. I can't say for sure whether this church is ready for the kind of publicity you'd earn us outside of Boston if you were to be in a relationship. It might kill your career, or it might not. It's hard to say, since this isn't the usual way people go about announcing their lifestyle."

Trevor gritted his teeth. "Lifestyle. Right. And what's my other choice?"

He smiled, and there was something condescending about it. "You prove you're straight as an arrow."

He sighed. "So how, exactly, do you propose I demonstrate that?"

"I believe Marlie can supply a way." Lew's eyes darkened. "This isn't necessarily ideal for you or for us, but the public is fairly forgiving these days. We're no longer living in the time when every little *bump*"—he emphasized the word in a way that made Trevor's skin crawl—"in the road causes the world to stop spinning."

"I have no idea what you're talking about," Trevor said, glancing at Marlie.

She looked up at him. "I'm pregnant," she blurted.

"What?" Trevor felt as though all the air had been sucked out of him. His head spun. He stared at her, willing her to spontaneously come up with a good reason why she hadn't called him first.

Lew smiled, but there was no warmth in it. "This is how you prove you're as straight as they come. You own your 'mistake' and get married—we can do targeted damage control on that later. For now, it's enough to make a public statement. You get up in front of the congregation, apologize for your behavior, and admit the rest of it was misunderstandings on the part of the Internet. Let people speculate on it being a deranged fan or what have you. Are you willing to take this on to protect your reputation and that of your church?"

"Oh, God." Trevor put his elbows on his knees and buried his face in his hands. "This is not happening."

"Trust me, it very much is," Lew said. "Now, stop stalling and make a decision."

Trevor sat back and stared at his hands while he contemplated. Whether it had happened the way he'd planned or not, he was going to be a father. No matter how awful the choice in front of him, a tiny spark lit inside his chest. It was everything he'd wanted before, to get married to Marlie so they could have kids and live in a cute little cape-style house while he wrote songs and she tended the sick and injured at the hospital. When he looked at her, their eyes met, and he remembered every joy and every heartache they'd shared over a lifetime of friendship and love. An unexpected wave of longing hit him, and he wished he could whisk her away from the prying eyes and meddling souls in the room.

Then he remembered being with Andre, talking and dancing and making love, and the spark died. Marlie could never accept him for who he was. Like all the others, she wanted the illusion—the perfect man who penned pretty but empty lyrics, untouched by his emotion and waiting to be infused by a congregation's collective feelings. No matter how much he'd thought she loved him, it had always had conditions. After the joy of falling for Andre, loving and being loved in return without hiding part of himself, marrying her to appease the church sounded like the worst idea possible. He'd had a taste—even if it hadn't gone anywhere far—of what it could be like to be with someone who wasn't afraid or ashamed of him. Was it so much to ask to have that all the time? Even for the sake of his career, and possibly the tiny life growing inside Marlie, he couldn't do what they were expecting.

After a long moment, he closed his eyes briefly and nodded. Looking directly at Lew, he said, "How can you even ask me this?"

"Ask you what?" He blinked.

"How can you sit there and tell me everything is going to be just fine if I agree to a list of terms and conditions instead of finding a way to move forward? I don't know if I can do what you're demanding from me." Trevor pursed his lips and looked down at his hands, which were clasped on the table in front of him. He was quiet for a long time before he looked up at Lew. "I need time to absorb this. Please give me a while."

Lew's brows drew together. "You have less than a month until you're supposed to be performing at King's Creation. You have to make a decision before then or you won't be going."

"I'll have an answer for you before then."

He stood up and glanced around the table then gave an apologetic look to Marlie before walking out of the conference room. He heard her call his name, but he couldn't answer her. On his way back to the train station, his thoughts drifted to Andre, and he paused to collect himself. Eventually, he would have to answer him, but for now, all he cared about was returning to his cocoon for a while before his roommates came home. He could figure out the rest later, including how he was going to tell Lew he would never be able to go through with their plan, not even to save his job.

Trevor was in no mood to have a conversation with anyone. Instead, he immersed himself in housework, starting with cleaning up the crumbs from the bedroom floor, moving on to picking up his roommate's piles, and finishing with clearing the table after dinner. The whole time, he ran the afternoon's scenario over and over in his mind, working himself into a lather over what he was going to do about even one part of it.

Trevor's phone rang while he was elbow deep washing the dishes. He hollered, "Nate? Can you see who it is?"

"Yeah!" Nate's voice drifted in from the back room. A moment later, Trevor heard him say, "Hello?" There was a pause. "No, he's not available to talk to you, now or ever."

Trevor glanced into the other room to see Nate holding the phone away from his ear. A long string of unintelligible shouting emanated from the phone. Trevor pulled his hands out of the dish water and dried them.

"Never mind. I'll take it. Who's calling?"

"It's Marlie," Nate stage-whispered.

Trevor sighed. He'd known this was coming. "I can't avoid her forever." He grabbed the phone from Nate. "What do you want, Marlie?"

The angry shouting stopped, and there was a long pause. Eventually she said, "I wanted to see how you were doing."

A strained laugh welled out of Trevor's throat. "How am I doing? You tell me how you think I'm doing. Someone pretty much ruined my life and my future career, and then today you had the nerve to show up and drop a bomb on me. So I guess maybe that answers your question. And for the record, I have a few questions myself, starting with whether or not this is actually my baby. We haven't been together in nearly five months."

She sighed heavily. "That's why I called. Yes, of course it's yours."

"We were careful. We always used condoms." He glared, even though he knew she couldn't see him.

"Yeah, and maybe we weren't careful enough the one time. Maybe we didn't use it correctly then or it tore and we didn't notice. It happens, and it really doesn't matter. Everything's out in the open now."

"Right, everything is now a matter of public opinion, you mean." Trevor gritted his teeth, and something occurred to him. "Wait. Was this whole thing your idea? You thought maybe by going to the media you'd get something out of me? You contacted Kurt Vinton as payback!"

"No, of course not! I wouldn't do that to you. You dropped things on me kind of suddenly yourself, but I would never try to get revenge this way." She huffed. "We do need to talk, you know. We have to work this out."

Trevor ignored her last plea. "Well, someone posted that comment on Kurt Vinton's blog, and it seemed like it was on purpose. There are only four people besides the two of us who know the whole story, and none of the others have much to gain from forcing me out. The church is convinced someone's spreading lies about me—or at least, that's what they'd like to think—and you heard their grand plan for how to resolve it. Was that your idea too?"

Marlie was quiet again. "They're not lies if they're true."

"I know, but no one else does, and no one really cares anyway. They're only interested in the gossip."

"Your song, Trevor. You wrote a whole song about someone you were in love with." She paused. "I met him, you know."

"I remember," Trevor said. "On Valentine's Day."

"No," she replied. "I went to the clinic near where I work because no one there knows me. I—" she paused. "I went to get tested because of what you said."

"God, Marlie. Thanks for assuming I wouldn't make sure I kept both of us safe. I made sure I got tested too."

"Well, I didn't know!" she snapped. "Anyway, that's when I found out about the baby. On my way out, I ran into him. I have no idea what he was doing there, but I figured out he's the one you wrote the song for. Do you think he could have gone public?"

"No," he told her. "I wondered at first, but I'm sure he wouldn't have. If you hadn't said it wasn't you, I'd be more inclined to think it was you as some weird kind of revenge. You couldn't even be bothered to tell me right away you were pregnant. You've got to be halfway along!"

"I promise, I didn't do it. And I'm sorry for not telling you, but it's not like I'm the only one who kept secrets."

"Are you serious?" Trevor snapped. "This isn't the same thing at all."

"Your pastor approached me," she said. "He wanted to know if I was aware of anything and if it's why we broke up. I told him about the baby because I wanted to protect you. No one told me they were going to turn it into a way to make you prove anything until right before the meeting."

Trevor dialed it back a notch. "You still should have called me sooner."

"I said I'm sorry." Her voice was small. "It hurt, hearing about you bluntly on the radio. Like it or not, your secret upset other people. I wouldn't have put either of us through it, no matter how angry I was about the reason you wrote the song."

"For your information, I used that as a metaphor—much like how the church took it. It wasn't about what we did or didn't do together. I was more a mess than in love at the time. It was about the feelings I had back then, not that it matters anymore." Trevor closed his eyes and tried not to think about Andre, but it was useless. He missed him, and the awkward, angry conversation with Marlie wasn't helping.

"If it doesn't matter, then why shouldn't we do what we always planned? I can give you what you told me you wanted."

"Because," Trevor said. He swallowed. "I'm in love with him now. We can't make a marriage work based on nothing more than a shared child, but I don't know what else we can do."

Marlie's voice was quiet when she said, "I don't know what to do either. I—" She paused for a long time. "My parents aren't happy."

"And you think us getting married is going to solve all your problems? Why the ever-living hell would you go along with this awful idea?"

He could hear her sniffling. "I don't want to!" The sniffling turned into outright crying. "I don't even want to have this baby!"

"What?"

Trevor waited while Marlie collected herself. Finally she said, "You're right—I don't want to marry you just for a baby. I loved you once upon a time, when we were kids and it was easy, but...I was just doing what I thought I was supposed to do. " She sighed heavily. "I thought we were finally getting to know each other as grown-ups, and then you proposed to me. Some part of me still loves you, but I don't know how to make any of this work without us hurting each other again."

"Oh," was all Trevor could say. "Oh." A hollow ache began in the center of his chest. He'd already admitted back at the church some part of him still loved her, too, for both the girl she had been and the woman she'd become, but he couldn't reconcile it with his growing love for Andre or his anger at her for hiding the truth from him. His eyes stung, and he rubbed them with the pads of his fingers.

"Yeah. And now—I'm talking to you because I still don't know what to do. I didn't feel right about having an abortion, so I didn't. I'm not really—well, if my parents knew I'd even thought about it, they'd have been angry, but I don't think it's a sin or anything. In the end, I couldn't, so I chose not to choose. This is the consequence. Nothing feels like the right decision."

Trevor took a deep breath. "Well, I don't know either." He shook his head to clear it. The truth was, he did know. He knew that despite everything, being a father had always been in his future. It was going to take time to process the situation and come up with a plan, though. "I need to think about this," he said.

"I realize that. Can I—can I call you sometime?"

"Yeah. I mean, we eventually need to do something." He paused. "I do still care about you, but I wish you'd told me privately."

"I know. Me too." Her voice trembled. "Good night, Trev."

He ended the call and blew out the air in his lungs. Nate came up behind him and wrapped his arms around Trevor, burying his face against Trevor's shoulder. Trevor closed his eyes and leaned into it a little, putting his hand on Nate's arm. After a moment, he spun around.

"I'm sorry for everything," he said. "You've been great the last couple weeks, even though I've done so much shit. I shouldn't have used that song. My life is so messed up."

Nate shook his head. "If not that one, then some other song. This would've happened no matter when you told Marlie the truth. If whoever you're with can't handle who you are, they're not worth it, in my opinion."

"Then maybe I'm not worth it," Trevor said. "Right now, I'm not sure I can handle who I am either."

Drawing back, Nate put his hands on Trevor's arms. "What do you mean?"

"The church called me in for a meeting. I don't know how much you caught from that conversation, but they sprang it on me Marlie's pregnant, and she says it's definitely my baby. Their solution to all my problems was for me to make a public apology to the congregation and marry her to solidify my heterosexual validity."

Nate dropped his hands. "You're going to do it."

"I don't know!" Trevor yelled, throwing his hands up. "Neither she nor I want to under these circumstances, but we have to figure this out, and I'm in danger of losing my job if it can't be resolved. Andre said his company might drop Vinton's account because of what happened, and I have no idea what that will do to his career either. I can't let any of them suffer because of me." Trevor inhaled deeply. "I can't marry Marlie because I'm in love with Andre."

Nate sucked in his breath and stepped back as though Trevor

had slapped him. "Y-you are?"

"Yes." It felt powerful to say it out loud. Trevor pounded his fist into his hand. "I wish I knew who the hell had the nerve to make my life public. Marlie says it wasn't her, which makes sense because of the baby. I don't know who else could have—" He stopped and stared at Nate. "Oh, no. No, no, no. You?"

Nate shook his head then nodded, his shoulders slumping. "It wasn't supposed to go so far," he insisted.

"Why?" Trevor demanded. "Why would you do that?"

"I didn't know he was going to read it on the radio! I was angry, okay? You—" He closed his eyes and pressed his lips together. When he looked back at Trevor, there was deep hurt in his eyes. "I loved you, and I waited for you to wake up and figure out you didn't want Marlie. You two were always breaking up, and every time you did, you came right back to me. No matter how many times you said it didn't count, you always did it anyway. All I wanted was for you to stop denying it was only because you weren't getting it anywhere else. When you broke up with her for good, I thought—I thought you might change your mind about us. I offered, but you said you were done with messing around."

"I'd just broken up with my fiancée! Of course I didn't want to jump into anything. You never even gave me time." Trevor backed away, hands held out.

"That's a lie. I saw you," Nate accused.

"Saw me when?"

Nate shuddered. "When he kissed you, out in front of the building, up against his car. Everything I wanted was in that one kiss, and it made me so angry, knowing you'd given it to someone else. New Year's Eve wasn't just about getting off—you'd met someone you wanted more than me."

"So you spread gossip about us?"

"It was an anonymous comment on a blog, venting my frustration. It shouldn't have been a big deal. There was no reason to think it would go anywhere but his audience. I swear, I didn't mean for any of this to happen." Nate reached for Trevor, but Trevor jerked away.

"Well, it did, and you were responsible. I can't do this." Trevor shoved past Nate and began throwing things into a bag. "I'm going to my parents' house for the rest of my leave. You'd better hope I come back, or Mack and Jamie are going to make you room with The Boyfriend."

He turned his back on Nate and ignored him until he heard the door click shut. Only then did he allow himself to fall apart.

CHAPTER NINETEEN

Andre tossed and turned in his bed. He couldn't get the situation out of his mind. He'd tried to talk to Trevor, but all he received in return was silence. Trevor wasn't returning his calls or texts, and Andre was sure Trevor blamed him for the whole thing blowing up because he hadn't warned him. Like a moth to the flame, Andre was drawn to checking and rechecking Kurt's blog, which now had thousands of comments.

In a rare fit of caring about someone else, Kurt had written a follow-up apologizing. He'd called Julian, who had told him he was no longer interested in developing Kurt's professional website without a formal statement. Julian had given Kurt an earful about his lack of ethics in outing someone else publicly. As Andre had done many times in their twenty-year friendship, he thanked God for having his chosen brother be someone who had not only his back but his partner's.

The thought made Andre's throat tighten. He wasn't sure what he and Trevor were to each other anymore. Were they still in any kind of relationship, or had it ended without so much as a conversation? The previous weeks spent slowly getting to know each other had sealed for Andre how far he'd fallen for Trevor and how much he would do to earn his trust back. If that meant leaving him alone until Trevor was ready to talk to him, then so be it. He would wait until Trevor called him. It occurred to him Trevor might never make the next move, but he forced the idea back down because it was far too painful—and too likely—for Andre to deal with.

Andre sighed and got out of bed, dragged on some sweats, and padded out to the living room. He flipped on the television, looking for mindless entertainment. In moments like this he most missed having someone else around the house. He pulled off his glasses and set them on the coffee table then pressed his fingers against his eyes. Andre leaned back against the couch cushions, barely registering what was happening on the television show.

For the first time in months, his mind drifted to Dahlia, who in stressful times would join him, leaning against him and reading a book while he ran his fingers over her smooth skin. He shut his eyes to wall off the lingering grief. He hated when his imagination took him there, fantasizing about having his little girls asleep upstairs and maybe even another one after them. Maybe he and Dahlia would've been talking about adding to their ever-growing family. He'd always wanted to adopt, too; maybe it would've been their next step. The fantasy faded into one of himself with Trevor, their own children surrounding him.

He popped the bubble. Not only was Trevor not speaking to him, it was far too soon to be thinking about building a life together. A tiny voice in the back of Andre's mind suggested that wasn't strictly true, knowing how Trevor felt about having a family. If only Kurt hadn't created this mess, they might be happily shifting toward having exactly the life they both wanted. Anger surging through him, he put on his glasses and got up to clean the house even though it was reasonably tidy—anything to relieve the tension.

He eventually returned to bed and lay staring at the ceiling for a long time. His phone startled him, and he sat up, blinking and rubbing his eyes. The clock on his nightstand read eight in the morning. He hadn't even been aware he'd fallen asleep the night before. The phone stopped ringing. He picked it up, intending to see if the person had left a message, when it started again. It was Julian.

"Hello?" Andre answered.

"Hey," Julian said. "Just checking to see how you're doing."

"Fine, I guess," Andre said. "Tired, but okay. I hope Trevor's all right."

"You hope?" Julian asked. "I thought maybe he'd be there."

"I haven't seen him in almost two weeks. He won't return my calls."

"Aw, shit, man. I'm sorry."

"It's..." Andre sighed and ran a hand over his face. He'd been about to say *okay*, but he changed his mind. "I hate not knowing what he's thinking, and I hate not knowing who left that comment on Kurt's blog."

There was a long silence then Julian said, "So you never got through to him?"

"No."

"He's eventually going to find out who it was, right? I mean, whoever did it—aside from that asshat Kurt—is gonna get caught. You said yourself only a few people knew about the two of you."

Andre swung his feet over the side of the bed. "Could've been his ex. He said at the time she reacted badly. Something's going on with her. I saw her at the clinic when I was there a few months ago helping Grams. Haven't seen her since, but there aren't too many reasons a middle-class white woman would be visiting Grams, unless she's looking for a volunteer position. She said she had some decisions to make."

"And you think one of them was finding a way to publicly humiliate her ex?" Julian sounded incredulous.

"No, not really, but she might have been avoiding her own issues by hurting him. If Trevor would talk to me, I could find out."

"So call him again."

"No." Andre shook his head, even though he knew Julian couldn't see him. "I'm not going to stalk him. He'll call when he's ready." *If he's ever ready*, Andre added silently.

"It's your life." There was a shrug in his voice. "Changing the subject, can you come in a bit early tomorrow? I wanted to run something past you about the business."

"Sure thing," Andre replied. Julian's request piqued his interest and removed his head from the swirling thoughts about Trevor. "Is everything all right?"

"Of course it is. I know you were worried Vinton might pull something to drive away business, but it's been the opposite. An associate was looking to refer me to another client and asked if I was available for the work. I explained why I all of a sudden had some free time, and he was impressed by the stand I took. It led to more business than you and I can handle, so we need a strategy."

"What did you have in mind?" Andre asked.

"I think we need to talk details about where this is going. We'll discuss it in the morning."

The smile in Julian's voice made Andre proud of his friend's hard work. "I'll be there," he assured him.

"Fantastic! I'll see you then." Julian ended the call.

Andre tossed the phone onto the bed next to him. He stretched and rose from the bed. As he laid out his clothes, he did everything he could to clear his mind. A hot shower, a cup of coffee, and a morning at church sounded like just the thing to keep his thoughts away from Trevor.

Andre showered and dressed quickly, putting on a suit and tie. It was too hot for the jacket, but the church would be cool and he was expected to wear it. The little building was about a thirty minute drive from home, and he liked going there. It was the same one he'd grown up attending, and outside of those who had passed away and those who'd had babies, the congregation had remained mostly unchanged. There was a familiar comfort in being among family.

He drove in silence to the church. He'd never liked to listen to the radio on Sunday mornings, wanting to save all his spiritual energy for worship. It might have had something to do with how his mother to that day still put on the early Sunday sermon on television, followed by at least an hour of Gospel Radio Live on one of the local stations. In the occasional fit of homesickness while he lived on the cape, Andre had sometimes flipped the car stereo on to see if he could get something similar out there. Feeling nostalgic, he reached for the stereo, but then he remembered what had been on the air non-stop for almost two weeks. He thought better of it and left the radio alone.

As usual, the service was sparsely populated, but Andre's mother and grandmother waved him over. He took his place between them, noting the absence of the rest of the family. His father was suffering through a summer cold, so he'd remained in bed. Trinity and Krista were home with their new baby, and Phyllice was away for a summer conference. Andre settled in to have his soul filled up. Here at this church, it was all about being set free rather than an emphasis on the wretchedness of souls; he liked it.

The pastor was a tall, wiry Jamaican man with an almost angelic preaching voice. He punctuated his points with low and high sing-song notes, driving home such important concepts as God's love for all creation and the liberation of the saints. At the end of the sermon, the choir, led by an elderly white man with a beard down to his belly and more energy than a toddler on a sugar rush, sang an old hymn with a soaring melody that had all the hat-clad women dabbing their eyes. Andre wasn't sure whether it was the song itself or the impossibly high notes the sopranos hit.

After being manhandled by several motherly women who fussed over Andre on a weekly basis, he made to slip out of the church. As he reached the doors, his mother put a gentle hand on his arm.

"Baby, whatever it is, we're here." She wrapped her arms around him.

Andre melted into her touch for a moment. His mother would never push, but she had a knack for knowing when something wasn't right in his world. His grandmother, too, affirmed her support with a nod and a palm on his shoulder. She wasn't an affectionate woman, but Andre knew she would fight to the death anyone who hurt one of her babies—including the kids at the shelter. He acknowledged her as he pulled out of his mother's embrace.

"I'm all right," he assured them.

"Are you coming for dinner?" his mother asked.

"Not today. I—" He couldn't lie to her. "I'm not up for it, Mom."

"I understand." She kissed his cheek then gave him a sly look. "You could always bring that boy with you again, you know."

"Mom!" Guilt stole over him, both for the secret he'd kept about Trevor and the reason. It still felt like betrayal in some ways, bringing someone else home to his family.

His mother's expression changed. "That's it, isn't it?" She smoothed the front of his jacket. "I don't know what's going on, but whatever it is, you'll figure it out."

"Yeah."

Both women bid him goodbye and bustled out of the church in a cloud of other mothers and grandmothers. Andre stood there for another few minutes before taking off for his empty house.

As he slowed down to turn into the driveway, he frowned. His house wasn't as empty as he'd expected—someone was sitting on his front stoop. His heart jumped, and his stomach lurched, happy and anxious all at once. He parked and got out as quickly as he could manage while trying to keep his cool.

"Trevor?" Andre asked.

"Hey."

"What are you doing here?"

Trevor looked up, and Andre noted the dark circles under his eyes. "I left," he said.

"Left...where?"

"The apartment. I've been staying with my parents for the weekend. I should go back, but I can't." He put his head in his hands.

Andre sat down on the stoop next to him. "What happened?"

Turning his head to face Andre, Trevor said, "I'm sorry I didn't return your calls. I'm sorry I got so upset with you over Kurt Vinton's blog. I'm sorry I said to leave me alone." He choked. "I—"

"Let's get you inside." Andre stood up and offered a hand.

Trevor looked at it a moment before he accepted it and clambered to his feet. Andre unlocked the door and let them inside. He'd barely closed the door when Trevor turned to him, anguish etched on his face.

"It was Nate," he said. "He—" Trevor drew in a gasping breath, trying to get a hold of himself. "He saw us the night you drove me home from the T station, when you kissed me like you meant it."

"Oh, Lord," Andre said. "This was to get back at you?"

Trevor shook his head. "I don't know. He told me he'd been angry, but it wasn't supposed to go that far. What did he think was going to happen if he put something on a blog read by thousands of people? I don't know what to believe." He reached out for Andre. "All I know is how sorry I am for letting my problems come between us."

Andre slid his arms around Trevor. "I understand, and I forgive you."

Trevor exhaled with a soft cry, leaning into Andre and holding on as though he thought Andre might vanish if he didn't. They stayed that way long enough for Andre to hear Trevor's efforts to slow his breathing and bring himself under control. When he had, he withdrew, and a quiet chuckle escaped, relief evident in the sound.

"Sorry," Trevor said.

Andre snorted, but he smiled. "Guess you're speaking to me again, then."

"I am," Trevor agreed.

Andre licked his lips. "Then it's all right if I do this."

He leaned in and waited, and at Trevor's tiny nod he closed the rest of the gap. Their lips brushed long enough for them both to feel the intensity, and then they were swept up in it—tasting, teasing, biting. Already the silent promise he'd made to Trevor to have each other again echoed back to him. A sharp spike of desire lanced his belly, descending in a rush to his groin. He groaned, and that only served to make Trevor gasp and drag him closer.

Like they had twice before, they drifted until they were against the wall, pressing and releasing as they pursued friction. Trevor's hand slid inside Andre's suit jacket, running over the fabric of Andre's dress shirt and making the smooth material glide against his skin. Andre reached down to grasp Trevor's hips, keeping them joined together so they could feel their mutual need as it built. He almost didn't care that he was making a mess of his Sunday best until it became clear they weren't going to slow down. He hauled himself out of the kiss.

"Bedroom?" he asked, needing three breaths to get the whole word out.

"Hell, yes," Trevor said. The words came out as a whine.

Letting up on each other was enough for the circuits in Andre's head to rewire. He considered their previous encounters. They'd taken their time, pleasing each other in turn, but Andre wanted more connection. He wanted to lock their bodies together and feel each other skin-to-skin everywhere until they were both lost. He wanted other things, too, like to have his tongue or fingers inside Trevor and to feel Trevor's hot mouth on his balls, but he craved the whole-body closeness first. He held back a groan.

He was out of time to think about it because they'd reached the bedroom. He shoved the door open with his foot and pulled Trevor inside. Trevor didn't even pause before he was dragging Andre's suit coat off and fumbling with his tie and buttons. Andre tugged Trevor's t-shirt loose from his jeans and attacked the belt buckle. In record time, everything was in a heap on the floor, and Andre didn't even stop to pick up his suit so it wouldn't wrinkle.

They were pushing and pulling toward the bed, toppling down and rutting senselessly against each other. If Andre wanted anything else, he would have to stop them before they were both over the edge too soon. He flipped them so he was on top, grinding down against Trevor. When Trevor arched his back and opened his eyes to look up at him, Andre remained still, gazing back.

"Is this enough?" he asked. "I know you said you prefer blow jobs, but I want you like this so bad I almost can't hold it."

"Oh, God!" Trevor's hand drifted to grip himself. "Shit. Please don't stop. This is fine."

Andre ditched his glasses on the nightstand and pulled open the drawer to extract the lube. He'd bought condoms too, but their prior conversations had led Andre to conclude neither of them was much interested in anything requiring them yet. Trevor's hands shook as he accepted the viscous liquid Andre squeezed onto it. He rubbed his fingers then reached down between them to make them both slick. For a moment, Trevor lay with his hand still, breathing hard.

"Just—just a minute," he said. "God. I feel like I'm going to come if I move at all."

Andre wanted to say something, to acknowledge and agree, but he couldn't. He was so full of the sensation of Trevor below and around him that all he could do was groan and drag him into a kiss, bucking his hips to indicate Trevor had better start doing something.

Trevor let go to wrap his arms around Andre's back. They clung to each other, rocking and thrusting, Andre's lips on Trevor's throat and Trevor's thighs gripping Andre's as they ground together. Trevor moaned quietly, and Andre breathed in the scent of his skin, sending a shiver of desire all the way from the top of his head to his toes.

It barely lasted. Everything tightened just as Trevor yelled and thrust upward, his head tipped back and his face twisted with pleasure as he shot between them. The heat and desperation overtook Andre and he let go, gritting his teeth and burying his face in Trevor's shoulder as he continued grinding against Trevor's dick. Wet heat spread over their bellies, and he sucked in his breath as he slowed his motion.

Andre rolled off, and Trevor curled against his side. He ran his hands down Andre's chest until he reached their combined fluid. His hand stilled for a moment, hovering, and then he trailed his finger through it. He shivered and inhaled sharply before continuing to explore, rubbing and dragging it across Andre's skin and then his own. Neither of them spoke, allowing time to absorb their thoughts. After a while, Trevor broke the silence. He pressed his nose into the juncture of Andre's neck and shoulder, inhaling deeply before speaking.

"I'm sorry."

"Hey," Andre said, lifting one hand to brush Trevor's sweaty locks off his cheek. "You're here now. It's okay."

Trevor shook his head. "It's not. Not just how I acted, the whole thing." He rolled onto his back and stared up at the ceiling.

"There's more."

Andre rolled onto his side and draped his arm over Trevor. "Talk to me."

"My life is shit," he said. "I got pulled into a meeting to clean up the mess Nate made, which in fairness, I contributed to. The pastoral staff blindsided me—they brought in Marlie." He closed his eyes. "She's pregnant."

Andre pulled away from Trevor and sat up. "What?"

"Marlie's pregnant," Trevor repeated.

"I heard you," Andre said. "I just wanted to know if you were serious. Man, you have a bad habit of telling people shit right after you have sex. Are you really that big of a dick?" He rose from the bed and ducked into the bathroom to grab a couple of towels. He tossed one at Trevor, not feeling sorry when it hit him in the face.

Trevor growled and sat up as well then began cleaning up. "When else would you have preferred I tell you?"

"I don't know. Maybe when you showed up on my doorstep all sad eyes and full of how wronged you are?" Andre plucked his rumpled suit coat out of the pile of clothes and clucked, tugging at in in futile hope of restoring its wrinkle-free state.

"You were a little busy mashing your face against mine! I came here to talk to you about all this. I found out about the baby at the damn meeting they hauled me in for. The senior pastor is using it as leverage." Trevor's voice hitched, and Andre turned away so Trevor wouldn't see him roll his eyes. "They want me to marry her and tell everyone the whole gay scandal was just rumors."

Andre turned back around slowly, his heart thumping. He was afraid Trevor would take the opportunity to go right back to pretending, and Andre had no desire to fit himself into a lifestyle of helping anyone hide. He should have known better than to get involved yet again with someone who wasn't open.

"You're going to do it," he said, unable to keep the sound of his breaking heart from tainting his words.

Trevor stood up. "No."

They faced each other, the heap of shirts and pants between them. Andre licked his lips, in fear of breaking the silence and finding out Trevor didn't mean it. While he tried to get his brain into gear, Trevor came closer and put his hands on Andre's arms.

"I talked to Marlie, and neither of us wants to get married solely because of the baby." He sat back down on the edge of the bed and put his head in his hands. "We wouldn't be ready even if things were different." He fell silent except for long, shaky breaths.

Without a doubt, Andre knew what was in Trevor's head. "You still love her."

When Trevor raised his head, his eyes were red-rimmed and wet. "Yes."

A shiver ran through Andre. "And what about us?"

"I'm in love with you, too." A choked sob rose from deep in his chest.

Andre sat down next to Trevor, but he didn't touch him. "I think you're finally being honest with yourself," he said.

Trevor turned his head to the side, and their eyes met. "Is it possible to love two people?" he asked. His voice was small, almost child-like.

Now Andre did reach out to him, drawing Trevor close so his head was on Andre's chest. "Yes." As much as he wanted to explain to Trevor all the reasons he knew it to be true, now wasn't the moment. There would be time enough later.

"I'm scared." Trevor's shoulders shook. "I never wanted to hurt anyone, and now I've done exactly that—to everyone in my life."

Andre sighed. "I would be lying if I said I weren't angry, and I'm jealous, too. But I don't know who I'm jealous of—her because you still love her, or you because you can still have her."

Trevor wiped his eyes. "I'm sorry. I understand if you don't want me like this," Trevor said, dropping his hands. "But I know what I want. I want to be a dad, and I know I can do it." His face showed his determination. "I've made up my mind. I'm going to talk to Marlie about how we can raise our child. I want you to be part of my life, too, even if I have no idea how we'll make it work. If my church doesn't want me as I am, then I'll get a job at freaking Market Basket if I have to. Anything to be the parent I'm supposed to be." He cleared his throat. "And if you don't want me as I am, say the word and I will leave."

The last wall crashed down. All the weeks Andre had spent discovering who Trevor was—the musician, the devoted friend, the devout believer—had pulled him deeper into love with the man sitting there, baring his heart. Andre wanted it all, including a selfish second chance to have a baby in his arms. He couldn't stop the runaway train of his thoughts, carrying him to visions of the two of them together, with Marlie as part of their lives as well. Other people made complicated relationships work; maybe they could too. He drew in a deep breath and forced those thoughts out. They weren't what Trevor needed to hear.

"I want you exactly as you are," he said.

Trevor closed the gap, and they fell against each other, holding on. When they let go, Andre moved back on the bed and lay down. He looked up at Trevor, who waited a heartbeat then stretched out next to him.

"I'm going to quit," Trevor said. "I decided."

"You're—but—your job," Andre said. "What about—"

"I still don't know how I'm going to manage everything," he said. "We were supposed to play a big music festival Labor Day weekend, and now this is hanging over my head. I can go down to the church tomorrow and make my resignation official, but I'm at a loss for the rest."

After he finished talking, Andre remained silent, his mind whirling. Several thoughts occurred to him at once, and grasped Trevor's hand.

"Do you trust me?" Andre asked.

"Do I—yes, of course," Trevor said. His cheeks turned red. "I think the last hour should have sealed that for you."

"I meant, do you trust me to make some phone calls and do a few things? I have an idea, but I need some time to make it happen."

A faint frown crossed Trevor's face. "Can you tell me?"

"Not yet." He leaned in to kiss Trevor lightly. "Please. Give me a week, okay? I'll get to work tomorrow. Don't resign yet."

"All right." Trevor relaxed his shoulders, but his expression remained troubled.

Rather than getting up, Andre tugged until Trevor turned over. Andre folded his arms around Trevor. "Don't worry for now. I've got you covered." He nuzzled Trevor's neck with his nose, inhaling deeply and appreciating Trevor's crisp scent mingled with the lingering aroma of their lovemaking. "Stay here with me," he said.

"Tonight, you mean?" Trevor shifted enough to slide his arms under Andre's and around his waist.

"Tonight, tomorrow—however long you need until you feel like you can go back to your apartment." He trailed his lips across Trevor's jaw until he reached his mouth, placing a reassuring kiss there.

"Yes," Trevor answered, and he pulled Andre closer.

Chapter Twenty

Andre whistled while he rearranged things on his desk and waited for Julian to arrive. An hour earlier, Andre had gone in to sort through financial records and make sure his plan made sense before presenting it to Julian. He'd already sent one email, and he prayed Julian was more in the mood to forgive him than berate him for failing to get permission first. Julian stood to benefit as well; it was only a matter of convincing him.

By the time Julian showed up, Andre had shifted the contents of his workstation no fewer than four times. He almost leaped up when the door opened. Julian's expression ran through a range from still-waking-up to surprised to wary when he saw Andre.

"All right, fill me in," he said. "I know I asked you to come in early, but this borders on ridiculous. You didn't just happen to come to work at such an ungodly hour because you missed it so much over the weekend."

"I have a proposition for you," Andre said.

"Can it wait until I have coffee?" Julian scowled. "You at least did that, right?"

"Yeah, yeah." Andre waved his hand at the coffee pot.

Once Julian had a steaming mug in his hand, he pulled up a chair and settled himself into it with a contented sigh. Andre restrained himself from chuckling. Julian had never been a morning person, but having an almost six-month-old wasn't a whole lot better than having a newborn—especially with a three-year-old in the mix. Julian yawned and scrubbed his face.

"I'm ready any time for your brilliance," he said, gesturing at Andre, palm up.

"All right. So, remember that talk we had about needing to hire more staff?"

"What talk?" Julian asked. "I don't recall that particular discussion."

"The one we should have had after the baby," Andre said pointedly.

"Oh, that one." Julian yawned again. "Yeah, well. We were doing pretty well just the two of us."

"Whatever, Mister Barely Awake. You said yourself we have more than we can manage. It's time we revisit the idea, and I know just the person to hire. Say the word, and she's on her way." Andre sat back and folded his arms, letting it sink in.

The gears clunked. "This isn't a coincidence, is it?"

Andre drew in a deep breath and let it out slowly. "No. Trevor's in some deep shit, and this will help all of us. You get someone to do your promotions and manage our accounts, Trevor gets to 'borrow' her as his publicist, and we all leave happy. I already emailed her about the situation, and she's glad to step in as soon as we need her."

Julian raised his eyebrows. "As soon as we need her, huh? She doesn't have to give notice?"

Grinning, Andre said, "She already did. She was planning to move back to Boston and help out her parents for a while until she found a new job. Turns out they want her expertise for their bookstore. Looks like that's where we come in—we get them as new clients out of the deal."

Julian stretched and stood up. "Call her," he said. "Oh, wait. You already did."

Andre shook his head. "Nah. I emailed. But I'm all over it."

The minute Julian had retreated into his office, Andre pumped his fist. He picked up his phone and placed the call.

"Hello?" a musical voice answered.

"Jagathi? It's all good. You're set to start whenever you're ready."

After lunch, while Andre was going through the files for Jagathi's parents, his phone rang. "Hello?"

"You need to get over to the Lighthouse," Phyllice informed

him.

"What's going on?" Andre's heart rate increased. "Is Grams okay?"

"I don't know." Phyllice's tone went from businesslike to panicked.

"Damn it. I'm on my way." He ended the call. "Julian!" he hollered.

Julian stuck his head out of the office, and his eyes popped when he saw Andre flinging things into his bag. "What's going on?"

"It's Grams. Something's wrong. Do you want to come, or do you need to stay here?" Andre zipped the bag.

"Let me call Elisa's parents so they know I'll be late, and then I'll lock up here. Do I have a few minutes?"

"Yeah, but hurry." Andre shook with tension.

In less than fifteen minutes, they were on their way to the train station. The whole ride, Andre stood. If he could have paced in the narrow car he would have, but he was getting strange looks from other passengers, and people were avoiding him. Julian eventually got up to stand next to him, leaving a hand on his shoulder. Andre managed to calm down enough to make it to their stop without anyone hassling them.

From there, they dashed to the Lighthouse and into the half that served as the clinic. There were two EMS workers there, a tall, lean, muscular man with a neatly trimmed beard and a dark-skinned woman who looked like she was almost half his size. The woman was talking to Joyce, and it sounded as though she was trying to convince Joyce to go to the hospital. Joyce was batting at her with an oxygen mask. Andre stepped over to them, leaving Julian in the doorway.

"Grams?"

Joyce looked up. "I'm fine," she snapped. "I am not having a heart attack, whatever *she* says." Joyce tilted her head at the EMT.

"All right," Andre replied. "Then what's going on?"

The bearded EMT stepped in. "She was complaining of chest pain and shortness of breath." He crossed his arms. "She may be having a panic attack, but she should get herself checked out regardless."

"No," Joyce snapped. "I'm a doctor. I think I know the difference."

"Ma'am, your staff called us because they were worried," the woman said.

Joyce waved the mask again. "I am fine." She drew herself up straighter as though to prove it. "I promise to have someone look at me later."

The EMTs exchanged a glance. The bearded EMT said, "We can't legally force you. Are you refusing medical care?"

"Yes!" Joyce all but roared at them, then sat back in her chair as though it had drained all her energy to yell at him.

After Joyce had signed what looked like reams of paperwork related to her refusal, the EMTs picked up the equipment they'd used and retreated from the office, leaving behind only the disposable supplies. Andre sat down in the chair opposite Joyce's desk, and Julian finally entered. He stood by the wall, arms and ankles crossed.

"Grams, what happened?" Andre demanded. "And why didn't you go with them?"

She slumped back in her swivel chair. "Because I already told them I'm fine."

"Phyllice called me. Please tell me what's going on," Andre begged.

"It's stress, that's all. There's nothing else the matter with me. It doesn't concern you." She turned her steely eyes on him and peered at Andre over the top of her glasses.

"The hell it doesn't," Andre said, glaring right back at her.

Joyce didn't even scold him for his language. She backed off and said, "It was a bad day. A pipe sprang a leak in the staff bathroom, we're out of some of the supplies we need, and three kids under fifteen showed up at the shelter looking like they'd all been in battle. I have no money to buy what we need right now, and I have no idea how we're going to make it to the end of the year. It's only August." She huffed and looked away. "There. Are you happy now?"

"Of course not!" Andre shot back. He knew he was on thin ice, talking back to her, but he thought he might get a pass for being worried about her. He breathed deeply before continuing, "Why didn't you tell any of us?"

Joyce sagged, and for the first time, Andre realized how old she was. "What could you have done? Paid for it all? That's no way to live for any of us." Her hand shook when she rubbed her forehead with her fingers. "I'm failing, baby," she said, waving her hand toward the world at large. "It was good for years, but unless God Almighty sends us a miracle, I'm going to have to close our doors."

Andre sat back, his mouth falling open. He'd known in the

spring they were over budget, but there must have been much more Joyce had hidden from him. He stared at her. At last he closed both his mouth and his eyes, silently praying for whatever miracle his Grams needed. He pulled himself together and opened his eyes then took her hand between his.

"I promise you, we will find that miracle," he said. "I swear it."

"Oh, baby." Joyce reached up and cupped his chin. "I don't think there's anything you can do."

"There has to be a way," Andre insisted. "Let me figure it out." He kissed her cheek. "You've worked too hard to keep all of us safe. Now it's our turn to take care of you."

By that point, Julian had moved farther into the room. He crossed to Joyce and knelt down beside her. "Ms. Bridges, we'll do everything we can."

She smiled and put a hand on Julian's head. "I know you will. Don't be too sorry when it doesn't work out."

"None of that," Julian said. He straightened up. "How is she getting home?"

"I'll call Trin," Andre said. "She'll come get her."

"Do not talk about me like I'm dead," Joyce snapped. "There is work to do here. I don't need to be taken home to lie on a couch somewhere."

"And someone else can do the work for once," Andre told her firmly. He took out his phone. "I'll stay here. Besides, even you can't resist spending the rest of your afternoon with Trinity and the baby."

A faint smile played on her lips, and Andre knew he had her. He made the call then phoned Trevor to tell him he'd be late. As he settled in to wait, he thought it over, but nothing came to mind right away. Anything with the Lighthouse would have to wait until the situation with Trevor was resolved. He rubbed his temples, and when he looked over, Julian wore a slight frown. Andre shook his head. One step at a time, he reminded himself. At least Trevor would be waiting for him at home when he finally made it there.

While Andre was at work, Trevor called the church and told Bret he was still going over the conditions and was taking a sick day. Then he sat by his phone, waiting to hear from someone—anyone—about what they were going to do. Andre didn't fill him in other than to confirm he had talked to someone who could help them, and whatever had happened, it would work out well for his business, too.

He knew he needed to return to the apartment. Jamie had left no fewer than ten messages for him, and even Mack had called. Nate hadn't so much as sent a text, but Trevor hadn't expected anything else. Trevor stalled, hoping to wait until Nate had left for work to stop in. While he hid out in Andre's house, he played the piano, pouring out some of his frustration in song. He didn't trust himself to write anything new, lest he craft another not-quite-for-Jesus ballad. In fact, Trevor avoided anything that could be interpreted as having sexual or romantic undertones.

When he thought sufficient time had lapsed for a safe trip to the apartment, he called for a cab. He could have walked, but it would have been long and hot. They arrived, and Trevor paid the driver but he didn't get out right away, taking a few minutes to gather his strength. Eventually, the driver huffed, and Trevor exited the vehicle. He walked slowly toward the building.

Mack was outside, having a smoke. Nate and Jamie had formed a united front that Mack was not ever to smoke indoors. Jamie hated the smell, but Nate said he couldn't risk the second-hand exposure. He wanted his vocal cords to remain protected, since he needed them fully operational to perform as an opera singer. Trevor hadn't bothered to point out how they all needed theirs intact; that likely wouldn't have made Mack want to quit any more than showing him high school health class brochures on the dangers of smoking.

Mack leaned against the building, blowing smoke into the air and humming softly to himself. Trevor wondered if he was writing a new song, as it was an unfamiliar tune—if it could be called that. Approaching the wall, Trevor cleared his throat, and Mack looked up.

"Hey," he said.

Trevor leaned against the wall next to him. "Hey."

"Are you back?" Mack asked, glancing over at him.

"Not exactly. I came to get some stuff."

Mack snorted and took another drag on his cigarette. "You could at least tell us where you're going to be."

Trevor swallowed. "I'm staying with my boyfriend for now."

With a jerk, Mack turned his head. "Boyfriend?"

"Partner, lover...whatever you want to call it. Yes." Trevor drew himself up, challenging Mack to make a comment about it.

He didn't disappoint. "Didn't know you were seeing anyone. Guess you've gotten over your issues with sucking dick, then?"

"Since when have you cared?" Trevor shot back.

"Jesus. I was just asking," Mack snapped. "I thought you were committed to the straight and narrow. Is that what's going on with you and Nate? He's pissed you're getting it from someone else?"

"It's complicated."

Mack scoffed. "I could write a whole album about your drama."

"Fine," Trevor said. "Go ahead. I'll bet Nate didn't bother to fill you in on all the other shit that went down. Selfish asshole."

"What the hell?" Mack said, dropping his cigarette butt into the receptacle by the door and angling toward Trevor.

Trevor closed his eyes. "Nate made some bad decisions about how to handle things between us, for example outing me on a public blog because he apparently thought I should have picked him. Marlie—my ex—is pregnant. Before you ask, yes, it's mine. I'm on the verge of either quitting or being fired, whichever happens first, because they want me to prove I'm not gay by marrying her. I can't do it to appease—I don't know. The church staff? The congregation? Maybe the entire city of Boston."

Mack muffled a laugh, but it was too much. He uncovered his mouth and let go, putting a hand on Trevor's shoulder. "Oh, man. No. I think Boston would be fine with you as you are."

Trevor smiled in spite of himself. "Probably. But my church won't be, so that's it." He cleared his throat. "Nate's not okay with me, either."

Turning serious again, Mack said, "You were close. Maybe he didn't want to lose you." He lit another cigarette.

"It's not that." Trevor fidgeted. "He wanted more from me than I could give."

"You don't have to justify anything to me. I honestly don't care," Mack replied. "The thing is, though, did you consider whether you were jerking him around?"

"He should have said something! It's not like we were ever a couple. I thought we were both clear about what it meant."

Mack shook his head. "If you're the type of guy who says you only want to be with one person, but you're willing to string along not one but *two* people? I'm not sure I'd have reacted any differently."

"I have no idea what you're talking about."

"You said you and Nate were hooking up between partners," Mack replied. "You and Marlie were constantly breaking up and getting back together, but you never bothered to tell her about Nate in all those years. It's not hard to see how you tried to hold onto both of them while exploring other options, especially now that you're with someone new."

"Oh, but if you and Amelia want to keep up whatever it is you do, that's fine, right? None of that for the rest of us, though." Trevor scowled at him.

"Different situation, bro. First of all, she and I both have other partners at the same time, and we're open about it with each other and anyone else we choose to bring along. Second, I'm not making promises to her I can't keep. She knows my history already, and I'm not holding her off while I wait for better offers. Not only that, she doesn't live with us, so I don't bring any of our shit home. Jamie keeps The Boyfriend out of it for the same reason." Mack paused. "Well, that and he knows The Boyfriend is an asshole."

"Does he?" Trevor asked.

Mack frowned, but it morphed into sadness. He said quietly, "He does and he doesn't."

"So you're not really going to move The Boyfriend in?" Trevor asked, hoping to ease the tension.

"Hell, no." He put out his tongue, revealing his silver stud. "If nothing else, I can't listen to him and Jamie going at it—whether they're fighting or fucking." He dropped the second cigarette into the receptacle. "Work things out with Nate, okay? It'll be better for all of us."

"All right," Trevor said, resigning himself to whatever uncomfortable conversation he needed to have with Nate. "We'll take care of it."

"Good." Mack went back inside, leaving Trevor standing there alone.

After a while, Trevor pushed off the wall and went inside. To his relief, Nate wasn't there. Whatever they needed to say to each other would have to wait. Trevor went through his room, packing clothes and other items into a suitcase. A soft knock on the door startled him, and he looked up to see both Mack and Jamie.

"Look, I'm not going to leave you hanging, you know," Trevor told them. "I'll make sure my part of the rent is covered until I decide what to do. Right now, I can't share a room with Nate, and I doubt he feels any different."

"I know," Jamie said. "That's not why we're here."

"We know it's been bad," Mack added. "I might think you've screwed up as much as he has, but we've got your back. Whatever you need, we're here for both you and Nate."

Trevor could only nod. He stood awkwardly in the middle of the room with his suitcase in hand until Mack and Jamie moved aside for him to exit. On his way past, Mack grasped his shoulder and squeezed. Jamie shrugged and drew Trevor into a one-armed hug.

"Take care of yourself," he said.

"I will."

With that, Trevor walked out of the apartment.

Upon returning to Andre's townhouse, Trevor spent the rest of the day browsing Andre's bookshelves, looking for something to distract himself. By far the best find was a book about bisexual men. Amazed such a thing existed, Trevor sat down to read, and by the time Andre arrived home, he'd finished it. The text was a lot to take in, but Trevor saw himself reflected in a few of the stories. When he finally put the book down, he was both exhilarated and terrified.

Andre was quiet, which Trevor chalked up to whatever he was concocting as a resolution for Trevor's highly publicized woes. Trevor didn't press him on it, instead setting the table and putting out the food he'd cooked. He wasn't much of a chef, but he knew his way around enough to make something edible. They sat down, and Andre's silence continued into their meal.

While he wasn't expecting an analysis of his use of oregano or the elegant presentation of the iceberg lettuce salad, Trevor was puzzled when Andre said nothing at all. He seemed distracted and tense, and Trevor sensed something had happened at work or with his family. Setting his fork aside, Trevor reached out for him.

"Whatever it is, you can talk to me," he said.

Andre sighed and pinched the bridge of his nose under his glasses. He looked utterly exhausted. "It's nothing you can do anything about."

Trevor frowned and withdrew his hand. "You can't know that. It's not like I told you about Marlie and the church expecting you to fix it, and you know there's only so much you can do anyway. Just tell me."

"It's my Grams," Andre said. "She's under a lot of stress, and she thinks she's going to have to close her clinic. Maybe the shelter, too."

"What?" Trevor exclaimed. "Why?"

"Money." Andre shrugged. "Isn't that what it always is? The building needs repairs, and she needs supplies."

"Couldn't they do a fundraiser?" Trevor asked.

Andre's laugh held no humor. "You don't think she's tried? Part of the problem is not having someone on staff to run those events and create publicity. She's relied on the long-standing success of her programs, but everything is bad in this economy. There's not as much support as there should be." He propped his cheek on his fist. "Grams is getting too old for this, but there's no one she can turn it over to. I know she always hoped one of us—my parents or my sisters and me—would take it on, but we all chose different paths. She didn't have a contingency plan."

There had to be something. In the same way Trevor had trusted Andre to help him, he craved the same trust in return. "Let me help you," he begged.

"What can you do?" Andre asked.

"I don't know," Trevor admitted. "But you didn't know what to do either when I came to you. I'll think of something, okay? I know people. Let me get through this crap with my church, and then I'll work on it. Trust me?"

After a pause, Andre said, "All right." He reached out to Trevor. "Don't feel bad when it doesn't turn out like you hoped."

"I promise, that won't happen." Trevor carefully didn't specify which he was committing to. He turned Andre's hand over and linked their fingers, running his thumb over Andre's knuckles.

Andre let go and stood up to walk around the table. He stopped beside Trevor and leaned down to kiss him, placing his palms against Trevor's cheeks. Trevor broke away long enough to rise to his feet then resumed their exploration. Gradually, they picked up steam, their embrace growing needy. This time it was Andre who cut them off.

His voice breathy, he said, "Can we get the dishes later?"

Trevor half-sighed, half-chuckled. "Definitely."

He tugged Andre toward the bedroom and closed the door on the rest of the world.

CHAPTER TWENTY-ONE

The day Trevor called to warn Bret he would be resigning at the next meeting, Bret dropped the bomb before he had a chance.

"Regardless of what you choose, you're not going to King's Creation," he said without waiting for Trevor to speak first.

"Yeah, about that...wait. I'm not fired?" Trevor frowned.

Bret sighed loudly into the phone. "Not yet. Your song has been pulled, and the band will go without you. Any formal decisions can wait until afterward. You are officially suspended through Labor Day. We're postponing a full staff meeting until the festival is over, at which point we'll meet again with the mediator from the district."

"Are you withholding my salary?" Trevor asked, temporarily ignoring the comment about the mediator. "I need to know. I have rent."

"What do you think?" Bret snapped. There was a tense silence. "Yes. It's marked as unpaid vacation time. I'm sorry. I wish you'd come to talk to me before this whole mess. I could have done more to help you."

"Like what?" Trevor's anger flared. "Make me confess all my sins so you could lay hands on me and put me on some kind of monitoring system? Send me somewhere to pray away the gay?"

"No." Bret sounded tired. "This isn't the time to talk about it. We'll discuss everything when we meet in a few weeks. You are allowed to bring in any representation you feel would assist you."

You bet your ass I will, Trevor thought. "Fine," he said. "I'm holding you to that."

When they hung up, Trevor called Andre right away. "Please tell me you have some good news. Otherwise, I'm going to make a blanket fort in your bed, and I'm not coming out until this whole thing is over."

"What?" Andre's laughter rang in Trevor's ear. "A blanket fort? Maybe I should call Phyllice and have her bring the kids."

"Never mind." Trevor huffed. "All I meant is I'll need to hide unless you can find a way for me to get out of this."

"Hell, no. You are not going into hiding. I'm working on it, but I need some time." Andre paused. "Did something else happen?"

"Sort of," Trevor muttered. "I'm on leave until after the music festival, which I won't be attending. Then they're going to drag me in for another meeting, after which I'm sure I'll be fired because there is no possible way I'm going to get up in front of the whole church, apologize for living, and marry Marlie just to get back in everyone's good graces. Of course, they're not paying me for my time off, so I might as well start looking for another job now."

"Don't do anything yet," Andre advised. "We just hired someone I think can help you. Sit tight, and apply for jobs if and when it comes to that. Okay? I promise, I've got you on this."

"Okay, okay," Trevor grouched. "Maybe I'll make that blanket fort after all."

Andre chuckled. "You do that."

Trevor ended the call and slumped down on Andre's couch. He didn't have the energy to move. There was no good reason why the church was drawing everything out, unless they were planning something more than letting him go. He reasoned they might be, considering they not only had to fire him but clean up the image problem he'd created. As much as people loved to watch the train wreck of a good scandal, plenty of those same people would be all too happy to find some fault in how the church addressed it. They could lose members if they didn't tread carefully. It was no wonder they needed him to stay invisible for the next couple of weeks.

While he turned everything over in his mind, his phone rang. Trevor gritted his teeth and debated whether or not to answer. He wasn't in the mood to talk to anyone about anything. During his internal debate, the phone stopped. After a short wait, it vibrated with a message. Trevor's resistance held for another forty-five seconds before he picked up the phone to see who had called.

When he saw who it was, he hurried to call back without listening to the message.

Marlie answered on the third ring. "Hey, Trev."

"What's going on?" he asked. "Your message made it sound important."

She sounded tired when she said, "Are you busy?"

Trevor almost snorted. If only she knew. "Not really." He sighed; he might as well tell her. "I'm on leave, and I only found out a little while ago. Why?"

There was a hesitation. "Can—can you come somewhere with me?"

"Depends. When and how far away?"

"Um, the hospital physicians' office building."

Trevor ran a hand through his hair. "Okay. It'll take a while, though. When do I need to be there, and where am I meeting you?"

"Can you be there in about an hour and a half? It's in radiology. I'll text you the exact address."

Frowning, he said, "Why are you having x-rays? They can't do that when you're pregnant, can they?"

Marlie's nervous, breathy laughter sounded. "No, silly. It's for an ultrasound." She cleared her throat. "So we can see our baby."

Trevor's heart thumped so loudly he wondered if Marlie could hear it on her end of the phone. His stomach flipped, but it wasn't the unpleasant stress cramps he'd had while talking to Bret. Instead, it was a rolling, fluttering sensation which traveled all the way up his sternum and brought a smile to his lips. This might have been the first good thing he'd heard all day.

"I'll be there, sweetheart," he said. "I promise."

"Okay, *dear*," Marlie replied, and her giggle made Trevor flush with happy warmth.

They ended the call, and Trevor shook as he slid his phone into his pocket. He grabbed his keys with his trembling hands, unable to keep the flock of birds from building a nest in his stomach or the ridiculous grin off his face as he shut the door behind him.

Trevor texted Andre from the train. *Something came up. I might be home a bit late.* He slid down in his seat to shove his phone back in his pocket. He glanced up right into the face of another passenger across from him. Like Marlie, she too was pregnant, her belly round and full under her stretched pink t-shirt. Her long, dark, hair lay flat against her back, pulled away from her face with a clip. Conscious now of how much space he was taking up, Trevor straightened his back and drew his legs together. He bounced his knee, and his hands twitched idly as he willed the train to go faster.

They reached his stop, and Trevor flew out of the car. He didn't need to run; there was plenty of time to make it to the outpatient ultrasound clinic. Once he was out on the street, however, he couldn't help it. He dashed up the sidewalk, darting around people. It was a good distance to the physicians' office building, but he knew several reliable shortcuts. By the time he reached it, he was a little winded despite having slowed down halfway there.

It was hot, and he was sure his face was beet red. Sweat trickled down to his collar. He wiped his nose on his bare forearm. For a few minutes, he stood to the side of the main entrance, catching his breath and watching the people entering. He wondered if Marlie was inside already or if she hadn't shown up yet. A glance at his phone reassured him he'd made it there fifteen minutes early. He decided he might as well go inside where it was cooler and he could sit down.

The building smelled like remodeling and fresh paint, and all sounds were muffled by the carpet and the thick walls. People made their way in different directions, but all voices were subdued. Trevor didn't need the directory to locate the clinic—he followed another couple to the correct office. Marlie was seated in one of the chairs. She glanced up when the other couple and Trevor trooped in.

He crossed the room and sat down next to her. "Hey."

"Hi." She smiled then winced as she shifted in her seat. "Ugh."

"You okay?" He wanted to take her hand, but he held back.

"Just have to pee." She stuck out the tip of her tongue. "This is not remotely fun."

"I'm sorry." Trevor wasn't sure what else to say.

Marlie sighed. "It'll be over soon. Meanwhile, I have a question."

"Okay, shoot." Trevor leaned back in his seat.

"Do you want to find out the sex of the baby?" she asked.

Trevor tilted his head. "I guess I hadn't thought about it," he admitted.

"I have, and I don't want to know," she said.

"Okay." Trevor was surprised. Marlie was practical, a planner. "Why not?"

Instead of answering directly, she said, "I've learned a lot in the last few months. Did you know I've been volunteering at the clinic where I got tested?"

"I didn't. Andre's grandmother runs it, but he never said."

Marlie nodded. "I haven't seen him in months. Maybe our schedules don't line up. Anyway, you know what they do, right?"

"Sure," Trevor replied. "She works a lot with homeless kids."

"Homeless LGBT kids, you mean," Marlie corrected him.

"Yeah, I know."

She grimaced as she turned toward him and pressed a hand to her stomach. "There's a trans girl who works there. She's young—sixteen or seventeen, I think. She stayed at the shelter for a while, and now she's in transitional housing. Anyway, I learned some things from her."

"Like what?" Trevor's curiosity was piqued.

"For starters, we can't know whether our baby is a girl or a boy or...well, there are other genders, too." When Trevor opened his mouth, she put up a hand. "I'm not going to do anything like try to have a completely gender-neutral environment. But I don't think we need to start our baby's life with a house full of blue or pink crap because other people have decided it's what we need. I know we could always not tell anyone else, but I'd rather not know either."

Trevor did reach out this time, and he took her hand. "I'm okay with whatever you want. It doesn't make any difference at all to me."

Marlie smiled, and the fluttery feeling was back, zinging from his gut all the way to his scalp. He squeezed her fingers, letting go when a tech came out and called her name. When she stood up, groaning softly, Trevor saw the perfect, round swell of her belly. She rested her palm on it, and warmth pulsed in his chest at the sight. He, too, climbed to his feet.

Marlie took his hand again. "I can't wait to get this done so I can pee."

The whole thing was over almost before Trevor blinked. He tried to keep up and follow what the technician was saying, but the baby mostly looked like a grainy blob to him. He could more or less make out some features, and he saw other things when the tech pointed them out. However, he decided he would have to take the tech's word for it on everything else. Even so, his heart wouldn't stop thudding against his ribcage as he gazed on his tiny peanut for the first time and listened to the whooshing inside Marlie's body, picking out the rapid, soft heartbeat of his child among the other sounds.

"Wow," was all he managed.

They assured the tech they did not want to know the baby's sex, and after a few more minutes, the tech told Marlie she could pee. Trevor nearly laughed at how fast she was off the table and in the adjacent bathroom. He hoped there was no reason he would ever have to endure any kind of medical testing on a full bladder.

When Marlie emerged, she dressed and they walked out together. Once they were in the sunshine, she clasped his hand and swung their arms between them. Trevor stopped several yards from the building and turned to face her. She looked up at him, her blonde hair framing her heart-shaped face. She was smiling, but it faded when he didn't return it. He had loved being with her for the afternoon, but they couldn't pretend, and they couldn't pick things up where they'd left off. They needed something new. Trevor thought about Andre, and he knew what he had to do. It was a huge risk, and he might lose everyone in the process, but he had to try.

"Come home with me," he said. "We need to talk."

Andre had spent the afternoon cleaning out a new space for Jagathi to use. He laughed at once again becoming a cubicle denizen, since there was only one office with a door and it belonged to Julian. If he had to share space, though, Jagathi was one person he could live with. If nothing else, she could regale him with her new adventures in dating. She had the worst luck possible. Her email accepting the position with Julian had contained a long rant about her mother's interference now that she'd moved back to Boston. Jagathi's mother had always been accepting of, if a bit confused by, her daughter's bisexuality. Her lack of awareness had apparently not stopped her from trying to choose potential spouses, however—it had only expanded the territory.

In the middle of preparations, Andre had received Trevor's text. Amusement over Jagathi's predicament faded into worry for Trevor and whatever was going on. Andre tried to put it out of his mind, but his concentration bottomed out. Several attempts to call Trevor yielded nothing, and he didn't return any of Andre's texts.

By the time Andre said goodbye to Julian and headed home, he was a mess. Anything could have happened since his earlier phone call. The tone of the text was indiscernible. It was a relief to finally pull into his driveway. Andre parked and rushed up the steps to the front door.

He heard voices inside, followed by laughter. Trevor's tenor carried into the hallway, and the answering voice was definitely feminine. Andre raised his eyebrows, wondering who Trevor had brought home. He kicked off his shoes, loosened his tie, and set down his bag before chasing the conversation into the kitchen. In the doorway, he stopped short, his mouth falling open.

Marlie had a pepper on the counter in front of her and a knife in her hand. She chopped a piece off and held it out to Trevor, who paused his own cutting long enough to let her pop it into his mouth. She laughed and then made a startled *oh!*, placing a hand on her gently rounded abdomen. Grabbing the knife out of Trevor's grip, she set it down and placed his palm against her. She moved it around until he, too, gasped. He leaned in and kissed her cheek.

A storm of anger, confusion, and jealousy overtook Andre. Once again, he wasn't clear on who the feelings were aimed at—Marlie for the way she held Trevor's attention or Trevor for experiencing something Andre had wanted for so long. He breathed slowly and deliberately in an effort to regain his lost sense of control. They owed him an explanation for why they were in *his* house, in *his* kitchen, but he wasn't sure he wanted to hear it.

"Trevor? What's going on?" he asked, trying to keep his tone civil.

Trevor and Marlie stopped what they were doing and turned away from the counter. Behind them, Andre saw the piles of vegetables and various other ingredients for whatever they were about to cook. More likely what Marlie was going to cook—Trevor was handy with boiling water but not much else.

"Hi," Marlie said, her smile too bright. "We were making dinner."

"I can see that," Andre said. He didn't return her smile. "Why?"

Trevor rubbed his cheek. "It's my fault," he said. "I told her we needed to talk." He closed his eyes and pinched his lips together. After a moment, he looked back at Andre. "Just talk, Andre. Nothing else."

"Maybe I should leave you to it then," Andre snapped. He would have liked to say he didn't know what was wrong with him, but it would have been a lie. The low buzz of fear he'd controlled since Trevor told him about the baby heated deep in his belly, ready to boil over.

"No." The word was clear and firm on Trevor's lips. "This concerns you both." He turned to Marlie, whose eyebrows rose. "I'm sorry I didn't warn you about telling Andre over dinner, but I thought you might refuse to stay."

"If we're going to talk, let's do it," Andre said. He wanted to get it over with, especially the part where his heart ended up torn and bleeding.

Trevor put all concerns to rest in the time it took for him to walk across the room, put his hand on the back of Andre's neck, and lean in for a kiss. When he pulled back, Andre took note of Marlie, her hand hiding a tiny smile. Andre's shoulders sagged, and Trevor slid his hand down to grip his arm.

"While we eat," he said.

Marlie and Trevor finished the preparations while Andre escaped to the bedroom to change out of his work clothes. His hands shook as he undid the buttons on his shirt, and he could hardly slide them through the holes. Half-undressed, he sat down on the bed. Until the knock on the door startled him, he was unaware of the passing of time, too busy trying to keep his mind blank and his emotions in check.

When he didn't answer, the door opened slowly, and Trevor slipped inside. He shut the door behind him and came to sit on the bed next to Andre. Putting his arms around Andre, Trevor drew him in. Andre tried to relax into his touch. Trevor put his hand on Andre's chin and tilted it so he had access to Andre's lips. The kiss was shallow but sensual, as though Trevor were hiding a message in it. Over the next few delicious minutes, Trevor took it from sweet to searing, hungrily exploring as much of Andre's mouth as he could.

At last Trevor pulled away. "I wanted to get as much of that as possible before dinner," he said.

In spite of the tension, Andre laughed. "With Marlie sitting out there waiting?"

"Last I saw, she was pouring us drinks." When Andre opened his mouth to protest, Trevor said, "Just water. I want us all sober for this conversation."

"That sounds bad." Andre wasn't in the mood to mince words.

Trevor didn't disagree. "It might be."

Andre tilted his head. "What's gotten into you today?"

"I went with Marlie for her ultrasound." He put up his hand. "Don't jump to conclusions. I figured some things out, but I guarantee it's not what you think. Marlie and I talked for a long time afterward, and I need you to hear me out. If you want to be rid of me after I'm done, I'll be out of here as soon as we've cleared the dishes."

With a heavy sigh, Andre stood up. "I'm listening."

He threw on a t-shirt and traded his dress trousers for jeans. Trevor led him to the table, and the three of them sat down. For a while, the only conversation was about serving the food. Once their plates were full, Trevor looked between Andre and Marlie. He set down his fork.

"I thought this would be easier over dinner, but I guess not." He looked down at his plate, and all the confidence he'd had moments before seemed to have evaporated.

Andre reached out and took his left hand, and Marlie reached for his right. Trevor twitched and looked up, glancing first at Marlie and then at Andre. He nodded, pressed his fingers against theirs, and let go.

"Talk. We're both here for you," Marlie assured him.

"Okay." Trevor inhaled and let it out slowly, his breath stirring the napkin next to his plate. "I don't know where to begin except to tell you both how sorry I am. When I said we needed to discuss things, I made it all about me and what I want. Instead, I should have started with asking what you want."

Marlie didn't say anything, so Andre said, "I want a home and a family and someone I love to come back to every night."

Nodding, Marlie said, "I used to think I wanted it too. But..." She left it hanging.

"What?" Trevor asked.

"Before all this, I was going to go back to school," she said. "I love being a hospital nurse, but I don't want to stop there." She bit her lip when she looked at Trevor. "I'd already applied and been accepted before you proposed last winter. Now, after working at the clinic, I have a better sense of where I'm headed. I was supposed to start classes at the end of August."

"Why can't you?" Andre asked.

Marlie's hand drifted to her belly. "I have a baby to think about."

"But you also have me," Trevor told her, and Andre's heart squeezed painfully. "Why didn't you tell me?"

She shrugged. "We'd already talked through so many other things. I didn't want to add more to it."

Andre set down his fork. "I wish you would just do it already," he snapped at Trevor.

"Do what?" Trevor turned to face him.

"Break up with me. Go back and play house with Marlie."

Marlie gasped. "Is that what you think this was about?"

"No!" Trevor reached out and gripped Andre's hands. "I want to be the best dad I can be, but I don't want to lose you. You're one of the most wonderful things that's happened to me in the last few months. I love you."

Andre pulled his hands away. "You love her, too. You said it yourself."

Trevor turned his head to look at Marlie. "Yes."

Now was the time for Andre to tell Trevor the rest of the story. A small part of him wished Marlie weren't there to hear it, but he couldn't worry about it now. He rubbed his forehead. "I did that once," he said.

"I don't understand," Trevor answered. "Did what?"

"Tried to hold onto two people. When I was married, I had a man on the side." He held up a finger to silence the others. "I wasn't cheating on Dahlia. She knew. His father was the Bishop—that's like the pastor—at her church, and for obvious reasons, he wasn't out. She started off okay with it, but over time she was less so. Once she was pregnant, she asked me to stop seeing him. She thought it would be bad for our daughters." He closed his eyes. "The last fight we had, I accused her of meaning it would be bad for her if anyone found out. She said maybe Bishop was right and I had the devil in me."

No one moved or spoke until Trevor said quietly, "It was not your fault."

"It might have been."

"No," Trevor said. "You did not drive the car that killed her, and a fight is just a fight. It is not your fault."

Andre didn't argue. "He wanted nothing to do with me after she died because he was afraid everyone would find out about him. I never went back to his church, and I never tried to contact him again. I can't do it. I won't be someone you keep for a little action when it suits you, hiding in that closet you're so fond of while you parade your shiny new wife and baby everywhere. I won't."

"I don't think you understand," Trevor said. "That's not what I'm saying at all."

Marlie cleared her throat. "He means for us to co-parent our child and take our time figuring out the rest. Trevor and I have been friends for twenty-three years, but we're only getting to know each other again as adults. We're not jumping back into a romantic relationship."

Andre saw them exchange a glance, and Trevor gave a brief nod. Marlie relaxed and returned it, her lips curving upward.

"You're okay with that?" Andre wrinkled his brow.

"Very much," Marlie said. "I want more than to be a good pastor's wife, which is exactly what I would end up as if we agree to his church's plan. Not only would all be forgiven, he would be on track to be groomed for higher staff positions. Why do you think he was promoted in the first place? That's not the life either of us wants. I love Trevor, but not in the same way I did as a girl. We work best when we're not trying too hard to be someone else's version of ourselves." Her smile expanded. "I learned a lot from your grandmother, you know. She gave me some good advice—to think about why I was so ready to believe Trevor would get tired of me. It's because *I* was already tired of me, tired of the person I was working to be."

Trevor's eyes were trained on Andre. "It's you I want. Marlie and the baby are part of our family. I'm not expecting you to feel about her the way I do, and I'm not expecting her to love you the way I do. All I want is to build our kind of life, even if it's not conventional." The corner of his mouth lifted. "I'm open to adding to our family any way we choose."

Andre understood what he meant. Trevor wanted their love to be the centerpiece, and he was including permission for Andre to have his needs met as well. Not grudging acceptance the way Dahlia had but instead, the doors flung wide. His head whirled as he tried to make sense of it all. What Trevor and Marlie were holding out to him was a chance for something he wanted but in the most unexpected way. He'd always considered himself open-minded, and he didn't want to be a foolish hypocrite, but a seed of doubt nagged.

"What happens if it all goes wrong?" Andre asked.

Marlie replied, "We figure out something different."

"There's a lot more to it," Andre told her. "We can't go into this unprepared. It doesn't work like that."

Trevor nodded and then snorted a laugh. "We've already been through unplanned sex, an unplanned pregnancy, and an unplanned coming out. I'm fairly sure we can navigate this, too." His half-smile fell. "I've screwed up a lot in the last year, and while I can't undo it all, I also can't expect either of you to fix my mistakes. That's why we're doing this one step at a time. We stay open to possibilities, but we take it all as it comes."

Andre folded his hands in his lap and looked down at them, considering how he wanted to phrase his next question. He decided to be direct. Turning his attention to Trevor, he said, "Is sex part of the deal?"

Trevor's mouth twitched, and a wicked gleam appeared in his eye that almost made Andre chuckle despite the situation. "You and me? Always, as long as you'll have me." He turned serious and glanced at Marlie. "I suspect you mean whether she and I want to have sex. We would like it to be an option, but not until we have some help sorting through things. Most people know they want multiple partners going in, but you're the only experienced one here. We've done everything ass-backwards, and I want us to feel more secure before adding new layers."

"I agree." Marlie smiled. "Andre, your grandmother explained a lot of it to me already. She really knows her stuff. She suggested we find someone to guide us through it, and she recommended a friend of hers who specializes in counseling non-traditional relationships and families." She paused. "This is all new for me—if anyone had asked me even a few months ago if I was okay entering into an agreement with my ex and his boyfriend, I'd have said no. Today, seeing our baby on the screen gave me a new perspective. If I'm strong enough to be Baby Bean's mom, and I'm strong enough to work for my goals, then I'm strong enough to take this on, too." Her face broke out in a delighted grin. "And Baby Bean gets a mommy *and* two daddies. How many kids can say that?"

Trevor laughed, and something in it was so light and free Andre couldn't help the rush of love swelling in him. His Grams had, in her own way, managed to give all of them the foundation they needed to plan their future. Thinking of her reminded him he had yet to come up with a way to honor the work she'd done for so many years. Andre took a deep breath and pushed those thoughts aside to focus on Trevor and Marlie.

"All right," he said. "Let's figure out how this is going to look for us."

Chapter Twenty-Two

Trevor woke up alone in bed. He'd overslept and missed Andre departing for work. The memory of how they'd spent their night after Marlie left rose to the forefront, and Trevor grinned. She'd gone home, and the first words out of his mouth had been to ask if he could show Andre how loved he was. The sex had been a little rougher than Trevor had anticipated; they'd both been too eager to reconnect for it to be slow. As Trevor stirred, he winced. It was definitely his ass, not his neck, that was sore this time, even though it had only been Andre's fingers. He was glad he wasn't at the apartment fielding Jamie's nosy questions.

The ache wasn't unpleasant, though, and Trevor enjoyed lingering over the details while he dragged out bringing himself off. Afterward, he let his mind wander to other matters. He'd settled things with Marlie and Andre, and while they still had a long way to go, having all of them on the same page felt good. Only his job and his strained relationship with Nate were left. Trevor snorted then stretched and rose from the bed. Somehow, navigating his newly blended family seemed far easier than either of the other things.

He still had no idea what Andre was planning on the publicity front. The anticipation nearly destroyed him, but all Andre would say was, "You'll see." Trevor couldn't discern any good reason for keeping him in the dark, but he went along with Andre's plan for the sake of showing his trust.

The good news was Trevor had been able to start answering his phone again. As Mack predicted, the initial media furor had died out. With Kurt's apology, removal of the original post, and agreement not to fan the flames, it was no longer a fascinating topic to anyone outside Christian circles. Inside was another matter, but at least the messages propositioning him had stopped.

After a shower, he sat on his bed in his underwear, contemplating his options. Of his two remaining troubles, Nate was the more easily addressed. He couldn't do anything about his job until the staff meeting. If Trevor recalled correctly and the schedule hadn't changed, it was Nate's day off. Mind made up, Trevor sorted through the dresser drawer Andre had cleared for him, searching for something to wear.

Just as he was zipping his shorts, his phone rang. When he saw who it was, he hurried to answer. "Hello?"

"Trevor?" a mellow woman's voice replied.

"Irina?" Trevor said. His heart beat faster, and his palms were clammy. He hadn't spoken to her since his leave started, and he wondered what the band had said about his absence from their rehearsals. He was sure she'd heard all the rumors, but her reaction was an unknown quantity. He tried to make his voice smooth as he asked, "What's up?"

"You tell me," she said. "I just got off the phone with my business manager because your publicist called her."

"My what?" Trevor frowned. "I don't have a publicist."

"Apparently you do, unless a complete stranger called my manager. She had some interesting news." Irina's voice was dry.

"And what would that be?" As far as Trevor was aware, there hadn't been any new developments in his situation. What happened to him shouldn't have affected her.

"We were both supposed to open on the first day of the festival, but she informed me you won't be there."

Trevor cleared his throat. "No, I won't, but the band will be."

"Because of what happened?" she asked.

"Of course. They see me as a liability now." He swallowed around a lump.

She took on a brusque tone. "That's ridiculous. If they don't want you, then they surely don't want me."

"I—what?" Trevor frowned. "Of course they want you! You're already becoming a sensation. Everyone wants to see you!"

"Well," she said, "that's only because there's a lot about me the public doesn't know. Listen, if they've banned you, I'm not going either. I won't let them decide who is worthy of singing about Jesus."

"You can't do that!" Trevor almost shouted into the phone. "It's too short notice. The festival is next weekend! That would be career suicide."

"It might be," she agreed. "However, it's about time I took a stand. They would manage if I got sick and went to the hospital, so they can deal with my absence for a different reason. I'm going to make a few phone calls. I'd like to do something, and it might help both of us. Are you game?"

Intrigued, Trevor asked, "What did you have in mind?"

"Uh-uh. Phone calls first, then I'll tell you." There was a teasing tone in her voice. "You'd better call your publicist, though."

"I already told you I don't have one." He huffed.

"Must be someone the church hired, then. Are you with me or not?"

Trevor closed his eyes. What did he have to lose? "All right," he said. "Say the word, and I'll do whatever you need me to."

"Good. Later, sweetie. Oh, and Trevor? Don't let this get you down. You're not alone. I'll talk to you later." She ended the call.

For several minutes, Trevor stood there with the phone in his hand, irritated to now have two people keeping him in the dark about what they had planned for his career—or lack thereof, if his gut feeling was right. He stuffed his phone into his pocket and threw on a t-shirt. There was no point in sitting around waiting for Andre or Irina to provide him with details. He was down to one problem he could resolve alone.

Trevor snagged Andre's keys on his way to the door. His stomach growled, and he glared down at it as he remembered skipping breakfast. He didn't think he would be able to eat much anyway, so he ignored it and headed to the apartment.

He let himself in, making as little sound as possible. As he tiptoed across the living room, he tripped on something and banged his shin on the coffee table. He clapped a hand over his mouth to muffle his grunt of pain. Looking down, he noted the mess on the floor and rolled his eyes. Without him, the other three were hopeless about housework. Disappointment wrapped around him at how the previous few weeks had gone. He missed the other guys.

As he reached the hallway, both doors opened, and three heads poked out. Trevor bit the inside of his cheek to keep from laughing.

Jamie's face lit up when he saw Trevor, and he popped out to pull Trevor into a tight hug.

"You're back!" he said. "We've missed you."

Trevor looked back at the mess in the living room. "I can see that," he replied, and Jamie shoved his shoulder.

Mack emerged next. He was less warm, but he reached out to grip Trevor's arm. "It's good to see you."

Nodding, Trevor said, "You too."

At last Nate came out of the other room. His eyes met Trevor's, but he looked away. "Hi," he told the floor.

Trevor sighed. He'd known it would be awkward, but Nate wouldn't look back up. Trevor squeezed Jamie's arm and brushed past between him and Mack. He stood right in front of Nate. Behind him, he heard Mack and Jamie disperse and begin rattling around in the kitchen.

"Can we talk?" Trevor asked, keeping his voice low.

"Yeah." The word came out on a sigh, and Trevor couldn't tell whether it held relief or resignation.

They entered the room they'd once shared, and Trevor sat down on his bed. His half of the room looked as though it hadn't been touched since he'd gathered his things and left for Andre's house. Nate's bed was rumpled, but he'd managed to contain most of his belongings. He perched on the edge of his own bed.

"I wasn't sure you'd ever want to talk to me again," he said.

"I wasn't sure either."

Nate nodded. "I promise, I wasn't trying to destroy you."

"I believe you," Trevor answered him. "What you did was still wrong. Even though you didn't use your name, you still made a public statement about me." When Nate opened his mouth, Trevor put up a hand to stop him. "I'm not even all that pissed about ruining my career. I could have fixed it if I'd really wanted to. I'm angry that you took the choice away from me."

"I'm sorry." Somehow, Nate managed to shrink himself, no easy feat for someone his height.

Trevor ran his hand through his hair. "Andre's grandmother runs a clinic and shelter. Maybe it wasn't all that big a deal for me to have you tell everyone—I'm safe, for the most part. Not everyone is. If I'd been one of those kids, what you did could have killed me."

"I know." Nate put his head in his hands.

After a pause, Trevor stood and went to Nate's bed. He sank down next to him and put his arms around Nate. Leaning into him,

Nate pressed his cheek against Trevor's shoulder.

"I was wrong too," Trevor said.

Nate shifted away. "How?"

"Mack reminded me I was stringing you along. He said I always treated you like I was waiting for a better offer." Trevor cleared his throat. "Maybe I was."

A frown darkened Nate's face. "I don't understand."

"You and Andre aren't the only guys I've been with. Other than Andre, it wasn't any more than with you, but I should have been honest." Trevor moved so he leaned against the wall, and Nate mimicked him.

"Why didn't you ever say anything?" he asked.

"I was too afraid of the consequences to let myself fall in love with another man," Trevor told him. Before Nate could answer, he continued, "It wasn't your fault. I care about you, and you've been my closest friend, but I didn't feel about you the way I did with Marlie. I had myself convinced that's all it should be with any other guy, a physical thing I had to get out of my system before settling down to my real life with her. Instead of telling you the truth, I let you think I kept coming back to you because I was in denial about us. The truth is I knew deep down I had the capacity to love anyone, regardless. I used you to hide what I was scared of admitting to myself. What I should have done was tell you no in the first place and not let it go on for so long."

Nate was quiet for a long time. "And now?" he finally asked.

Trevor had known this was coming. "And now I'm with Andre. I fell in love for real." He swallowed around a lump that had begun to form in his throat. "I'm with Marlie, too, in a way."

Nate stared at him, eyes wide and lips parted. "What?"

"It's complicated."

"I can see that," Nate muttered. "What I don't get is how Marlie's okay with it. She barely tolerated Jamie and me."

Trevor let out a nervous chuckle. "I'm not exactly sure how she came around either. She's been volunteering at the Lighthouse, so she's seeing things differently than before. We talked last night, she and Andre and I, and we're still figuring it all out. He and I are in a relationship, and maybe we'll eventually get married. I don't know—I'm not ready yet. She's going to be part of our lives too." He coughed. "In a lot of ways, but mostly because we all have to figure out how to co-parent."

"If it's a problem, why involve Andre at all? It's not his kid."

Nate wrinkled his nose.

"Because he's with me. It's like any other relationship involving stepparents," Trevor told him. "Marlie will be around as well, which is why we're being open."

Nate frowned. "So…like, you're with both of them?"

Trevor shook his head. "Not exactly. You don't jump into a relationship with two people because of a baby any more than you'd jump into one with a single person. We need time to figure everything out between us. But I love both of them, even if I'm not sure where we're all headed together."

"Is Andre into her too?" Nate asked.

"That's a pretty personal question, but I'm gonna let it go because it's you and I feel like I owe you. No, Andre has no interest in her outside of friendship, and even that's touchy right now. He's managing the whole situation pretty well, but it's rough for him. He has a lot of feelings about Marlie and the baby—he lost his wife while she was pregnant, and he's still dealing. It's going to take a while for all of us to adjust."

"I seriously can't imagine sharing myself or my partner. Too much room for jealousy. Can't you just be with him?"

"He has to 'share' me in a sense anyway because I'm not going to abandon Marlie to raise our child alone," Trevor said. "And it's not about making sure no one gets jealous. Jealousy happens, and the only thing we can do is take care and address it when we need to. This is about creating a family, even if it's not like everyone else's. We'll work it out in our own way, and you'll have to trust that it's not your job to watch after us."

Nate whistled. "This is a big change. Speaking of jobs, what about yours?"

"I don't think I'll broadcast to the universe that we're working through what kind of relationships we have, but I'm not hiding it either. The church can fire me, or I can quit. Either way, they're invited to bite me if they don't like it."

"I…wow," Nate said. "Wow." He blinked rapidly a few times. "Since when did you grow a spine?"

Trevor glared at him, but he realized Nate was right and sighed. "I went with Marlie for her ultrasound. I saw our baby." He shook his head, remembering his dazed awe. "I figured if I can't stand up for what I need, how can I stand up for my kid?"

"That does make sense," Nate agreed.

"Yeah. Which is why I'm not pissed at you anymore. You might have picked the last possible way I wanted to do things, but I should have done it myself ages ago." Trevor blew out a breath. "I'd like to come back here for a bit. I'm not quite ready to stay with Andre all the time, at least while we're working things out. Can you live with me for a few more months?"

"Just a few?" Nate asked. There was a definite air of disappointment about him.

"Until our lease is up. If things are going well, I'm moving out then. It'll be enough time to think about starting over with Marlie and Andre and the baby."

Nate nodded. "Of course."

The tension had lessened, but it still hung between them, heavy like the humid August air. Trevor wondered if they would ever regain what they'd lost. *Time*, he thought. *We need time*. As he was about to say something else, his stomach emitted a loud rumble. They both laughed.

"Don't know about you, but I haven't eaten yet," Trevor said. "I'm starving. Let's go see if Mack and Jamie made us a make-up breakfast. I heard them doing something out there."

They rose from the bed, and Nate reached for the door. When he opened it, Mack and Jamie nearly fell on top of him. Trevor was torn between choking back laughter and wanting to smack both of them on the head for eavesdropping. Nate beat him to it. He shoved Mack, who was closer, until he stumbled backward into the wall. Jamie ducked out of reach, but Trevor caught him around the middle and held on.

"Oh, no you don't," he said when Jamie squirmed and squealed in protest. "You stay right here and take the consequences."

"Were you two listening in?" Nate demanded, keeping one hand on Mack's chest to hold him in place.

Mack and Jamie exchanged a glance, and Mack grimaced. Jamie had the good graces to blush. He bit his lip then opened his mouth to speak, and Mack shook his head. Jamie ignored him.

"We were trying to tell if you were going to have an argument or hump like bunnies," he admitted. "It was too quiet, so we came to the door."

"Oh, my God!" Nate exclaimed. "Just because you and The Boyf—"

"How much did you hear?" Trevor asked, cutting Nate off before he put his foot in it.

"Not much. We got here in time to hear you ask Nate if it was okay to come home," Mack said.

Trevor took a deep breath. "Okay. Well, you're eventually going to find out anyway, so I'll fill you in over breakfast." He looked over at Nate. "There's nothing going on between us—no arguing and no sex."

Mack nodded, and Nate removed his hand. Trevor let go of Jamie, and the four of them made their way back to the kitchen. Trevor hung back a bit, watching the others. After they ate it would be three down, the rest of Boston and the Christian music scene to go.

CHAPTER TWENTY-THREE

The other guys still had their day jobs, so for the next couple days Trevor was as alone in the apartment as he'd been at Andre's. He spent the time picking up the rooms, though he left anything alone if he could smell it or it gave him shivers. Fortunately, it only amounted to a handful of laundry items, including a pink satin thong peeking out from behind the television. Trevor had no interest in finding out who it belonged to or what it was doing there.

He texted Andre to meet him at the apartment. Trevor wanted to return the car without the temptation of staying at Andre's another night. It might not have been the bravest way to handle it, but he needed both a little breathing room and time to himself for a few days. With Nate at rehearsal and the others at work until late, he could do whatever he liked to relax. It had been ages since he'd been comfortable with his own company, and it brought a relieved smile to his face to have such confidence.

The phone call Trevor received mid-afternoon almost changed his mind. He peered at the unfamiliar number, his stomach lurching. Hoping it wasn't another random person riding the residuals of his brush with infamy, Trevor answered.

"Hello?"

"May I speak with Trevor Davidson?" The woman on the other end rolled her r's slightly.

"This is Trevor. May I ask who's calling?"

"My name is Jagathi Prashad. I work with Andre Cole, and he asked me to call you," she said.

"Uh...okay." Trevor furrowed his brow. "What's this about?"

"I will be acting as your publicist," she informed him.

The pieces clunked into place. "You've saved me some detective work finding out who you are. Irina Clay-Jones told me you called her manager already."

Jagathi laughed lightly. "I did, and I believe Irina had an idea for you both. When I called again, her manager had all the details. Do you have a moment to discuss it?"

"Sure," Trevor replied.

For the next hour, Jagathi gave Trevor all the information she had. They talked through the strategy for both Irina's plan and the staff meeting, arriving at a conclusion Trevor thought might bring something good out of all the negativity. When they ended the call, he was mentally, if not yet emotionally, prepared.

Andre arrived to pick up his car, and Trevor met him out in the parking lot. His resolve wouldn't hold if he took Andre upstairs. They would end up in bed, and Trevor would be back at Andre's house before he had time to process it. Disappointing as it was for both of them, Nate hadn't been far off the mark with his crack about Trevor developing a backbone. More than ever he needed to remain confident.

"Hey," Andre said, leaning in for an all-too-brief kiss.

"Mm," Trevor said, his reply muffled against Andre's lips. Withdrawing, he said, "Guess who called me?"

"Someone from work?" Andre guessed.

"Nope." He tilted his head. "Jagathi..." He tried to recall the name. "Prashad, I think?"

"Oh!" Andre exclaimed. "Yes, my associate."

"Uh huh. She claimed she was my publicist."

Andre fidgeted. "She sort of is. We hired her for other reasons, but I hoped she might do something for you, too. She has a lot of connections." He cringed. "Are you mad?"

Trevor shook his head. "It was a surprise, but I'm not upset. She had some good ideas." He grinned. "Irina called me this morning with an idea of her own, and it seems to have panned out."

"Oh?" Andre's eyebrows shot up.

"I think I'll keep that part a surprise for now." Trevor laughed at Andre's scowl. "Two can play that game, you know. Jagathi's idea for my job was good as well. She suggested the church would be better off creating some good publicity out of the situation rather than fighting the bad. They want the problem to go away, but she thinks they should embrace it."

"Yeah?" Andre leaned against his car. "What did she want to do?"

"She suggested the church put some effort into building bridges with LGBTQ-plus communities. There are some organizations..." Trevor's voice trailed off as the idea occurred to him.

"What's wrong?" Andre asked, his brows drawing together in concern.

Trevor turned to him and put his hands on Andre's arms. "Not a damn thing," he said. He planted a sloppy kiss on Andre's lips and then one on his cheek. "I'm pretty sure I just figured out how to solve both our problems."

"I—what?" Andre flattened himself against the car, his mouth open and his eyes wide.

"If we get my church on board, we can save my job and your grandmother's clinic in one go," Trevor said. "Leave it to me. I'll talk to Jagathi, and we'll work out how to get what we need." He let out a whoop. "This is perfect!"

Andre's laughter was shaky and not quite as exuberant, but he pulled Trevor in for a tight hug. "I trust you."

"Like I trusted you," Trevor confirmed. "Now, go home, and I'll get to work." He kissed Andre again and sent him off, certain his plan was exactly what they both needed.

Once everything was at least temporarily settled, Andre brought Trevor back to his townhouse. Trevor's meeting at the church was in less than eighteen hours. Rather than sitting at home annoying his roommates with his nervous energy, he spent the night doing the same to Andre. The difference was that Andre didn't mind; he was anxious as well, though he tried to keep it under control for Trevor's sake.

They sat together at the dining room table, having a quiet dinner together. While they ate, Andre asked, "How much are you going to tell them?"

Trevor shrugged. "No more than I have to. I'll need to let them know about you, of course. For now, I can tell everyone Marlie and I will be co-parenting our child. It's the truth, and since we haven't all settled into anything definite yet, there's not much else to tell anyway."

"Sounds about right," Andre agreed.

He was still tense during conversations when Marlie's name came up, but Trevor had found a number of small ways to provide reassurance. Not all of them were physical. Andre was the beneficiary of Trevor's gestures of romance, and he loved every second of it. When he'd been with Dahlia, he'd been the one to shower her with affection and gifts; no one had ever done the same for him. It left him feeling like a boy with a first crush, and he treasured every token of Trevor's love. The previous day's offering had been a splurge purchase of a rainbow-dyed rose which sat in the middle of the dining room table. They were sharing the current day's treat, a cupcake from a specialty bakery around the corner from Trevor's apartment.

When they were through, Trevor stood up and began clearing the table. As soon as the food was away and the dishwasher humming in the background, Trevor pulled Andre into his arms. Andre sighed with contentment. They both needed to relax, and he hoped he knew where this was going.

"Come with me," Trevor murmured against Andre's ear right before he put out his tongue and touched the shell lightly.

Andre shivered but made no protest as they found their way to the bedroom and partially undressed. They lay in bed, stripped down to underwear and t-shirts. Trevor leaned in and kissed Andre lightly, running his hand down Andre's side. Andre sighed; he wanted to do that forever. Trevor's warmth against him was comforting after the long day.

Andre retreated just far enough to speak. "What you're doing is so brave," he said.

Trevor chuckled. "We'll see how brave a move it is after the meeting."

"At least we have a little time together tonight. We don't have to worry about it until morning." Andre kissed him again.

"Mm," Trevor replied.

As they continued to kiss, sucking on each other's lips and tongue, a thrill rose up Andre's spine. No matter how many times they'd done this in the previous few weeks, each time was exciting. Uninvited, thoughts of Marlie drifted to the forefront of his mind, questions about what Trevor had enjoyed with her and whether he wished Andre were more like her when they made love. He forced the stray feelings away and concentrated on the man in his arms.

Trevor clearly sensed his anxiety and withdrew. "Okay?" he asked.

"Yeah," Andre said. "I'm a little distracted."

"I can imagine. Let's take care of that, shall we?"

Andre settled down into the pillows, leaving his hand on Trevor's hip. He applied gentle pressure, squeezing and releasing. Trevor relaxed into the touch, closing his eyes. Andre slipped his hand farther back to cup Trevor's ass. His fingers slid over the cotton-covered mounds then traced the crease. Trevor inhaled deeply and mimicked the motion. The sensual touch brought Andre out of his swirling thoughts and into the moment as arousal bloomed. He leaned in and took possession of Trevor's mouth with his own. Bringing his arm up, Trevor draped it over Andre's waist and rested his hand on Andre's lower back.

They moved closer together, their kisses heating up and their legs twining together. Andre grasped Trevor's ass more firmly and dragged him so they were pressed together. Both of them groaned at the contact and the frustration of too much clothing. Trevor pulled at the confining material of Andre's underwear, catching his thumb in it in his haste. Andre laughed breathlessly and adjusted so he could take his own off. When Trevor sat up to pull his t-shirt over his head, Andre took the opportunity to do the same. As soon as they were fully naked, they lay back down and resumed their kissing.

Trevor's hand wandered down between them, and he took them both in his hand, bringing them together to full arousal. He pushed Andre onto his back and began a slow rhythm with his hips, rolling them against Andre's until they were both breathing hard and arching into each other.

Andre pulled his lips away from Trevor's. "Turn...around," he said between gasps.

"What?"

"Just—just do it," he panted. "I want you to fuck my mouth while you suck me."

Trevor's intake of breath was sharp. "Oh. Oh, yeah." The words came out as a whine, and the need underneath them had Andre bucking up against Trevor.

"Please," he begged.

Slowly, Trevor extracted himself from Andre's legs and turned so he straddled Andre's head. He bent forward and gave an experimental lick, causing Andre to inhale audibly. Dizzy with want, Andre needed a moment to regain control. The mere thought of having each other like this was almost enough to push him over the edge; it had been far too long since he'd done this with anyone.

"God," Trevor said. "Touch me."

Andre brought his hands up and ran them over Trevor's thighs. Trevor was a natural blond, and the hair on his legs was light and sparse; the coarse swatch between them was a pale brown. Andre's fingers wandered there, fondling the curls and then extending to encircle his shaft. Trevor moaned, and his legs trembled.

Andre angled his head and touched his tongue to Trevor's hole. With a shout, Trevor bucked backward, and Andre jabbed more firmly. He licked and probed, drawing a string of profanity from Trevor's otherwise unoccupied mouth. Andre buried his tongue inside Trevor and used his hand to apply just the right amount of pressure to his balls. When Trevor was reduced to incoherent moaning and writhing, Andre withdrew, needing something to satisfy his own aching need.

"Suck me," he demanded, keeping his hands on Trevor's ass and squeezing.

Trevor obliged, first mouthing around Andre's sac and then trailing his lips and tongue upward until he reached the tip of Andre's erection. He took only the head in at first, teasing the slit and making Andre squirm. Andre pushed a little until they both lay on their sides so they had a better angle. They both needed the connection, joining their bodies and feeling as much skin-to-skin as possible. Andre took Trevor's dick in his mouth and began a slow rhythm. Trevor paused his own actions briefly then swallowed Andre down and matched the pace.

The room filled with the soft slurping and the occasional throaty moan as they worked each other. Andre used his hands to touch Trevor's legs and backside, tenderly stroking his soft skin. As Trevor closed in on his climax, he held onto Andre's hip, kneading and keeping him close. He shifted to grab Andre's waist.

Pulling off, he paused long enough to say, "Gonna come".

Andre sucked harder, and Trevor tightened his hold as he returned his mouth to its task. His fingers and toes flexed, and his groan of pleasure was muffled by Andre's dick. The vibrations were enough to send Andre spiraling into orgasm just as Trevor released down his throat. Andre's back arched, and the flash of tingling heat starting in his groin spread outward, dragging out the pleasure of his release.

Andre rolled all the way onto his back, and Trevor rested his head on Andre's thigh. They rubbed each other's bellies and chests as they descended from the ceiling. Andre didn't want to let go, but Trevor withdrew so he could turn around again. He draped his arm across Andre, and Andre joined their hands. Neither of them moved or spoke, lying with their fingers entwined and their legs pressed against each other. They slid into a contented sleep, all worries lost in the exchange of love and pleasure.

CHAPTER TWENTY-FOUR

When Trevor and Andre showed up for the meeting at the church, all of the people from the previous meeting were already there, as well as Marlie and three people Trevor didn't know. One was a pretty, plump Indian woman, dressed for business with her hair pulled into a smooth bun at the nape of her neck. A second looked to be teenager of around sixteen or so. The third was a white-haired man in a suit and tie. Before Trevor and Andre entered the conference room, the woman and the girl stepped out, closing the door behind them. Andre gave both of them quick hugs. Trevor was surprised; he hadn't realized Andre knew the girl.

"This is Jagathi Prashad, my associate," Andre said, indicating the woman to his right. "And this is Lina, who works at my grandmother's shelter." He frowned. "Come to think of it, what are you doing here?" he asked her.

She smiled. "Jagathi asked me to be here. She said she has something for me to do."

Trevor grinned. "It has to do with that thing I said was a surprise," he told Andre.

As they stepped into the room, Andre caught his eye and gave a reassuring nod. Trevor's heart thudded, and it was all he could do to keep still. He took a seat beside Marlie, who offered a tentative smile. The others took seats around the table, and Trevor was comforted by the presence of Andre on his left and Marlie on his right. She reached out under the table and squeezed his hand, and he returned her smile.

Introductions were made all around. The white-haired man turned out to be Marcus Annable, the mediator from the denominational conference. He was only there to listen, not to make any decisions. Since nothing Trevor had done was explicitly prohibited in the conference by-laws, his church was responsible for disciplinary action. Jagathi indicated she was Trevor's representative, which raised a few eyebrows, but no one made any objections.

"I think we're all clear on why we're here," Lew began, looking around the table. He turned to Trevor. "I suppose you've had time to consider your options."

"I have." Trevor swallowed. "I'm not going to take your offer."

Bret's eyebrows shot up, and Lew frowned. "Can you explain why?"

Trevor stole a glance at Andre, who nodded. On his other side, Marlie touched his elbow. For a moment, Trevor closed his eyes, gathering strength. He thought about the baby growing inside Marlie, and his resolve returned. Opening his eyes, he took a deep breath and let it out slowly.

"I can't marry Marlie under these conditions. It's not fair to her, to me, or to our child. I'm already in a relationship with Andre." He put a hand on Andre's arm. "I refuse to stand up in front of everyone and fake the shame I don't feel over creating a family in a way a few people disapprove of."

"I see." Lew's frown remained firmly in place.

"I don't think you do," Trevor said. "I'm not sure you ever will."

Bret sighed. "This doesn't leave us with many options."

"Right," Lew agreed. "We were clear on what it would take for you to stay."

Trevor met his angry gaze. "Before I say anything else, I need to know a few things. Is the problem that I'm in love with another man and that I won't marry the woman carrying my child? Or is the negative publicity the issue?"

Lew's eyebrows rose. "A combination of all of the above. I think we might have been able to work around your...differences if they hadn't been so public."

At his words, Trevor balled his hand into a fist and bit back a growl. Beside him, Andre put a comforting hand on his knee. Marcus made a few notes on the page in front of him and looked up at Lew. He cleared his throat.

"May I?" he asked. When Lew motioned to go ahead, he continued, "Is there any other option for reinstating Trevor? While it's up to you how to proceed, I would be interested in what alternatives have been proposed."

Trevor relaxed and looked over at Jagathi. "I believe Jagathi has an idea," he said. "She is currently representing my interests as a public figure."

Jagathi handed a stack of papers around the table. "I understand you would like to mitigate the effects of the negative attention your church has received," she said. "Your method of handling it is counterproductive and won't do more than appease your congregation, if that. It might even fail there, if enough people are uncomfortable with church staff stepping into private relationship matters."

Lew pursed his lips, but he accepted the paper and skimmed it. "Perhaps you could explain in more detail."

"Of course," Jagathi agreed. "You might be able to satisfy a few church members with a brief Sunday morning announcement and a forced apology—which, in my opinion, is entirely unnecessary. You are also unlikely to stop the rumors and speculation outside your church, and there are many who will not believe your official statement. Instead, you might try embracing the subject. Turn the situation into a way to do some good in the community."

"We're listening," Bret said, folding his hands on top of the table.

"Trevor is not the only member of your church hiding his identity. Your church has no explicit policy on gay, lesbian, bisexual and transgender members. Your denomination allows for welcoming environments but takes the position it's up to individual congregations whether they choose to do so. This is a good time to become fully affirming, as other churches have done. As part of your stride forward, I propose a partnership with one of the local homeless youth shelters. That's where this young woman comes in." She turned to Lina and put a hand on her arm.

Lina fidgeted for a moment then looked up with confidence. "I'm Lina Hawling. I came here because my parents said if I didn't stop 'pretending' to be a girl, I could leave and find somewhere else to live. Andre and his sisters brought me to the Lighthouse, where they took good care of me and helped me get on my feet. I work there now, and I'm saving money to go to school."

Jagathi nodded. "The shelter could use a long-term partner in order to stay afloat. Doing this now, you'll be out in front. You will send a message that you not only embrace Trevor but you are willing to do as your Bible says and love your neighbors. Instead of a small ripple from a single apology, you will create a big ripple of positive press." She glanced at Trevor. "Either way, we have in place a way to spread the word."

The room fell silent. The other staff members looked around at each other, none of them meeting Trevor's or Jagathi's eyes. At last Lew spoke.

"We need a few minutes to discuss your proposal," he said. "Give us half an hour, and we'll have you back in."

Trevor's knees shook as he stood up. He nodded to the others, and Andre and the women followed him out into the hallway. He led them to the break room, where they sat down at one of the round tables.

"And now we wait," he said.

Exactly twenty-eight minutes later, Bret stuck his head in the break room. "You can come back now."

His expression was neutral, but Trevor had a bad feeling about it. He nodded and stood up, followed by the others. They all trooped back into the conference room. They had barely shut the door and reclaimed their seats when Lew cleared his throat.

"We've made a decision," he said. "I'm sorry, Trevor."

Trevor blew out the breath he hadn't realized he was holding. Slowly, as though waking from a dream, understanding dawned. "You never had any other course of action planned."

For a moment, Lew looked like he might protest, but then he nodded. "If you had really wanted to do as we asked, you would have said something sooner. It's been several weeks. Your lack of discipline and obedience toward authority is as much a problem as anything else you've done."

"Obedience to authority?" Trevor repeated. "We're not talking about my work ethic or how I've treated members here or whether I was difficult about making changes to church policy. This is my life we're talking about! You'd like to dictate to me—and maybe other members—who we have relationships with and under what circumstances. No, thank you." He sat back in his chair.

Lew leaned forward. "This is about the kind of image we have when someone walks through our doors. You're not someone only attending weekly services or even someone with membership rights and responsibilities. How will it look to people if we aren't making an effort to show our staff in solid, stable family structures based on standard biblical principles?"

"It will show them anyone is welcome," Trevor answered. "Pretty much like Jesus, actually. And what about the other stuff? I can accept being let go—I was anticipating it. What about the shelter?"

"I'm sorry," Lew said, holding out his hands palm-up in a helpless gesture. "If you aren't here, we see no reason to deeply invest in a new project. We have several ministries to help the community already."

"You mean several ways in which you try to draw people in before you help them," Trevor snapped. "I've sat on this long enough, dealing with your methods of outreach, to know exactly what you mean. It's not about caring for people. It's about growing in size so you can post this week's notches in your 'saved' belt."

Lew rose to his feet and pressed his hands on the table. "We do care," he said, his eyes flashing. "We care about people's souls as much as their physical needs."

"If you really cared," Trevor said, glaring around the table, "you'd all be jumping at the chance to help the shelter. People like Lina and Marlie and me will always exist, and as long as we exist, there will be people who would rather we didn't—or at least wish they could shove us into a corner and pretend we're not there."

"That isn't what we're doing," Lew said. "We can accept people like you, but we also need to consider people who believe what you're doing isn't right or moral."

"Exactly." Trevor stood up, his back straight. "You don't want me gone because some jerk with a keyboard saw fit to publicly out me. You want me gone because I'm a bisexual man fathering a child with a woman I'm not married to, and I'm not apologizing for any of it. Instead of letting me deal with my own shit"—there was a collective wince at his swear—"you tried to cover the whole thing up with fancy words and forced promises. I'm not going to lie anymore for the sake of your image." He drew in a deep breath and let it out slowly. "I had hoped when I went public with my story I would have good news and your blessing, but I'm not surprised to find the opposite."

Trevor turned around and stormed out, slamming the door to the conference room behind him. It made a satisfying bang, and he imagined all fifteen people inside the room jumping at the noise. The thought drew a humorless smile to his lips, and he strode toward the front foyer. Before he made it to the double doors, he heard the rush of feet behind him.

"Trevor! Wait!"

The tapping quickened, and before he knew it, there was a hand on his arm. He turned around to look straight into Marlie's steady brown eyes. Trevor sighed in regret; he hadn't waited for the others after his angry speech. Marlie clasped his hand, and Andre came up beside him to wrap an arm around his shoulders. Jagathi and Lina stood in front of him.

"It's okay," Marlie said. "We'll get through this."

Trevor shook his head. He turned to Andre. "I am so, so sorry. I thought I could fix everything for both of us, if only they would listen. I should have known they wouldn't." He dropped his head to Andre's shoulder.

"Sh," Andre murmured. "It's all good. I understand."

"We'll find a way," Jagathi promised. "We'll save the shelter, one way or another."

Andre let go of Trevor. "I don't know," he said. "There probably isn't much anyone can do."

"Don't say that!" Lina exclaimed. "We just need some hope."

"And a miracle," Andre muttered.

The door to the conference room opened again, and Bret stepped out. He motioned to Trevor. "Can I speak to you a moment?"

Trevor glanced at the others then nodded. He followed Bret around the corner to the staff offices. Bret shoved some things off a chair and closed the door.

"I'm sorry," Trevor blurted out the minute they had privacy. He sank into a chair and covered his face with his hands.

"Trevor," Pastor Bret said gently. "Look at me."

Slowly, Trevor uncovered his eyes and raised them to meet Pastor Bret's. He lowered his shaking hands to his knees, which he gripped tightly while he waited for Bret to lay into him. The flogging never arrived.

Instead, Pastor Bret said, "I'm proud of you for what you did."

"Y-you are?" Trevor stammered.

"Absolutely. You have no idea how big a favor you've done me." Bret reached across the desk and clasped his hand.

"I have?"

Letting go of Trevor, Bret sighed. "It was what we needed to start making some changes around here."

Trevor frowned. "Such as?"

Bret pinched the bridge of his nose under his glasses. "First of all, you aren't the only one in this church or even the only one on the worship team. You're simply the first who came forward and refused to apologize for who you are." He sighed. "The real problem is this church. We've long been promoting a 'live and let live' policy on a lot of things, believing that would let us focus on people instead of issues. That's not necessarily a bad thing—a church can't go from zero to sixty when it comes to social change. We can't stay in this place, though. We need to move on."

"What are you saying?" Trevor asked.

"I'm saying you're right." Bret tilted his head. "Do you know much about the history of this church?"

Trevor nodded. "At least, I know about how it started. Basement of another church, right?"

"Yes, among other things. Lew was one of the founding members, and now he's the senior pastor." Bret folded his hands. "When this church opened its doors, it was just before same-sex marriage was legalized here. A faction of people built their ministries on battling the inevitable because they saw our state as having gone too far. Lew and the other original staff wanted to offer a 'neither here nor there' option where we didn't state public support either way." He sighed. "Lew is not native to Boston, and he's from an older time when such things weren't possible. A number of evangelicals were defining themselves in opposition to both Catholicism and left-wing politics." Bret snorted. "Which in Boston can sometimes be the same thing."

Trevor's laugh was shaky. "This church is different from the one I grew up in," he admitted. "No one really talked at all about any of it."

"I don't know why Lew refuses to admit your way is better than his. He's not ready for us to be affirming, but he also knows he can't reverse direction and make an official policy against membership, either. He thinks avoiding a position will let us keep our place in Christian radio outside of Boston while still allowing for what he calls 'differences of opinion.'" Bret paused. "I believe we need to take a stand and do it all at once, like removing a bandage. Sure, we'd lose people, but we have thousands of members. I doubt it would create a dent that wouldn't be filled with people glad to find somewhere welcoming. Myself included."

Trevor's mouth dropped open. When he'd mostly recovered, all he managed was a weak, "What?"

"I'm no different from you. Why do you think I wanted to hire you in the first place? I read you at your interview. You used inclusive language, which almost no one but an insider would have. I wasn't certain, but I perceived you as open-minded at a minimum." Bret's smile was strained and sad. "There are other ways in which I suspect you and I are alike. You didn't come right out and say it, but my guess is your relationship with both Andre and Marlie is complicated."

Briefly, Trevor considered not answering. Realizing he had nothing left to lose, he said, "Yes."

"Right." Bret sighed. "My wife and I have a complicated relationship as well." He coughed. "With another couple."

"Oh," Trevor said, too stunned to formulate more words.

"Not anyone from church. These are people we've known since we were your age. The relationship developed slowly and started as more...play partners, in the beginning. We love them—as though our individual relationships are units joined together. A marriage of marriages, I suppose. Not one person at this church knows, even though I wish we could be honest with everyone."

"Would becoming affirming really change that?" Trevor wondered aloud.

Bret shrugged. "I don't know. What I can tell you is how angry I am Lew convinced the others to fire you so quickly. He doesn't want our level of truth." Bret reached out to Trevor. "Ava and I fought for you as hard as we could, but no one listened."

"I believe you."

With a smile, Bret sat back. "I did know exactly what your song was about, by the way."

"You—you did?" Trevor's face heated.

"Yes. I pushed for you to include it because I loved knowing the secret and having someone else on staff who shared mine, even if you didn't know it." Bret stood up and circled his desk.

Trevor rose to his feet as well, and Bret wrapped his arms around him. For a long moment, Trevor poured his disappointment into their embrace, letting Bret absorb it. Eventually, he pulled away.

"I'll keep in touch," he said.

"Please do," Bret replied. "I want to know how things are going. I'll be here for you, especially if you need someone to talk to about navigating unconventional spaces."

With one last look at Bret, Trevor pulled open the door and stepped out to look for his family.

Chapter Twenty-Five

After the meeting, Andre's efforts to convince Trevor to tell him the big secret he was still keeping were futile. He only got the question out once, and Trevor's answer was, "You'll see," spoken with a grin. From that point, Trevor seemed to have a sixth sense for when Andre was about to broach the subject because he found new and creative ways to stop him before the question left his lips. Of course, Andre was benefiting from the arrangement, and if he pretended to ask a time or two in order to reap the rewards, what Trevor didn't know wouldn't hurt him.

After a week of this, Trevor popped into the office unexpectedly one afternoon. He had Irina with him, and Andre lost his words when he saw her standing *right there*. Jagathi, on the other hand, rose from her desk and greeted Irina warmly.

"It's nice to finally meet you in person," she said, extending her hand.

"Likewise," Irina responded, a smile gracing her lovely face as she accepted the handshake.

Andre thought they held on a bit too long, and he cleared his throat. He raised his eyebrows at Trevor, indicating he'd like an explanation for their appearance during work hours. Before Trevor could say anything, Julian stuck his head out of his office.

"What's all the—oh!" He stepped out. For a moment, he looked to be as speechless as Andre had been. He pulled himself together.

"Irina Clay-Jones. To what do we owe the pleasure?"

Andre rolled his eyes behind her back; Julian was laying it on thick. Trevor spotted Andre's facial expression and suppressed a laugh. He winked and reached out to brush his fingers against the back of Andre's hand.

Stepping forward, Trevor handed Julian a magazine. "There's a Boston-based magazine for Christian performers—*Stage Lights*. This is the LGBT-plus off-shoot, *Lights/Out*." He chuckled. "I didn't even know there was such a thing. Here's the print edition, and the web version was up this morning. There's a pre-recorded interview that should be airing on WKXN in"—he looked at the clock on the wall—"about fifteen minutes, if you want to hear it."

Jagathi and Andre peered over Julian's shoulders to read it. When Andre saw the responses to the interviewer's questions, his jaw dropped. He looked up at Trevor, whose face broke out in a wide smile. He stepped closer and drew Andre away from the others.

"I love you," he said. "I don't care about saying it in front of thousands of people, and I don't care that your entire office staff—all three of you—are hearing me say it now." He rested a hand on the back of Andre's neck. "I love you," he said more quietly.

Instead of kissing him, Andre drew Trevor in to hold him tightly. "You are absolutely the best thing that's happened to me since moving back here," he murmured in Trevor's ear. "I love you too."

They broke apart and turned around to find three sets of eyes fixed on them and three amused grins. Andre ducked his head, but he smiled, and beside him Trevor shook with silent laughter. When everyone had calmed down, Andre addressed them.

"Well? What are we waiting for? I want to hear that interview."

They flipped on the radio, enduring a few unfamiliar songs before the announcer came on. "In news sure to rock the contemporary Christian music scene, established gospel artist Irina Clay-Jones and emerging contemporary worship songwriter Trevor Davidson have both made bold announcements. In a pre-recorded interview with Cherrie Barlow, they answer questions about what it means for the future of their music. Here's the interview in its entirety."

After a brief bit of introductory music, a woman's voice came on. "This is Cherrie Barlow of WKXN, your home for the best in Christian contemporary music. Today, I'm sitting down with Irina

Clay-Jones and Trevor Davidson to talk about some of the recent things happening with both of them."

They chatted for a few minutes about general music-related topics, and Andre tapped his foot, anxious for the important part of the interview to arrive. It didn't take long for Cherrie to bring it up.

"Trevor, you've been surrounded lately with some controversy, correct? Why don't you tell us a little about that."

"About six weeks ago, Kurt Vinton—who has since apologized, so please no trolling his blog over this—published a post saying I'd written a song about..." He cleared his throat. "Sorry. About an intimate act. It set a whole chain of events in motion."

Andre looked at Trevor, whose face had gone beet-red. Trevor cringed visibly, and he said, "I seriously hate listening to myself talk."

The others shushed him, and he fell silent.

On the radio, Cherrie continued, "I take it there's more to this story."

Trevor's nervous laughter followed. "Sure, of course there is. In case there was any question at all, I'm bisexual. Not gay, not straight. Not half-and-half. Not hiding or pretending or confused or whatever other words you want to use for it. I know who I am, and I'm ready to be myself. I'm in a relationship at this time. I don't mind talking about it, but for their sake, I'm not going to get into specifics."

"That's fair," Cherrie said. "Now, Irina, the result of this was your refusal to play the King's Creation music festival in Amherst. How did that come about?"

"As I said to Trevor at the time, if they didn't want him, they didn't want me. I don't talk a lot about my private life, but to show my solidarity with Trevor, I'm using this as my public coming out. I'm a gay woman, and I'm proud of who I am as much as I'm proud of my music. I'm honored to be able to sit here with Trevor, speaking our truth together."

The interview continued, both Trevor and Irina discussing other aspects of their music and their careers. As the interview was about to conclude, Trevor asked Cherrie if he could say one more thing. Curious, Andre stole a glance at Trevor, but his face was neutral and his eyes were fixed on a point on the wall.

"I may not know what's in store for my own future, but I'm not the only one in need. Because of my situation, I've become familiar with a wonderful organization in Quincy. The Lighthouse is a shelter for homeless LGBT-plus youth, and there is an attached clinic providing free and sliding-scale health services to underserved populations. Right now, they're struggling. Not only do they need your prayers, they need your help to continue caring for people who need them. Please consider contributing financially." He gave the Lighthouse's physical and web addresses.

The interview ended, and Andre turned to Trevor. "Oh, my love," he said.

"I don't know if it will do any good," Trevor said. "But I couldn't sit here and do nothing when I had a willing audience. You're not upset?"

"No," Andre assured him, leaning in to kiss Trevor's cheek. "Not even a little."

"I think this deserves a celebration," Julian declared. "My house, Friday night. Trevor, feel free to invite your friends. That is, if they can deal with a preschooler and a baby."

Andre laughed. "Maybe we should have it at my place. That way, you can get a babysitter and have a real night out."

"Fair point," Julian agreed.

"We'll be there," Trevor said. "Irina, what about you? Want to join us?"

She looked over at Jagathi. "Will you be there?" she asked.

Jagathi's eyes popped. "I—that is—am I invited?"

Julian gave an exasperated sigh. "Of course you are."

"Then yes, I'll be there." She smiled.

"I'm in," Irina said, and her eyes never left Jagathi's.

"Friday night it is," Andre said. "Now, shoo. We have work to do."

After work, Andre stopped by the clinic. They'd closed for the day, but a few of the volunteers were still there shutting the building down. On his way in, Andre almost ran into a slim, athletic woman with her black hair pulled smoothly back from her face.

"Sorry!" she exclaimed. "Andre, right?"

If Andre could have blushed, he would have. His neck began to sweat. "Nia. Hey," he replied. He had never called her after their one date, and guilt tugged at his gut.

She smiled. "How are you?"

"Good," he managed to say. He cleared his throat. "And you?" He mentally smacked himself for his lack of conversational skill.

Nia didn't seem to notice. "Not bad. What are you doing here?

They're closing up."

"My grandmother runs the place," he said. "What about you?"

"Trinity said they could use a physical therapist, so I'm putting in some hours here," she replied.

"That's great." There was an awkward pause then Andre said, "I'm really sorry I never called you."

To his surprise, Nia laughed. She took his arm and led him to the chairs in the waiting room. "I wasn't upset. Trinity convinced me to give it a try, but I wasn't interested in more than a fun night out so I wouldn't spend Valentine's Day moping over the loser whose ass I'd dumped." She laughed again.

Relieved, Andre relaxed into the chair and chuckled. "I'm sorry about the loser," he told her.

"Nah. He really was no good. You gave me a fun time, and I got to see a band I like."

Andre coughed. "Glad you enjoyed it." Changing the subject, he said, "So you'll be spending some time here, then?"

"Yes. I was listening to the radio, and I heard this place was in trouble. I'll do what I can to help." She smiled and reached out to squeeze Andre's hand. "Guess that means we'll see each other around."

He wanted to tell her he was in a relationship, but he was afraid he'd misread her meaning. In the interest of not saying something embarrassing, he replied, "I guess it does."

They stood up, and Andre said goodbye to Nia before turning down the short hallway to the offices. He poked his head into Joyce's and waited for her to hang up the phone before stepping in and greeting her with a kiss.

"Hey, Grams."

She smiled up at him. "I've been fielding calls all day," she said. "Seems we've had some unexpected donations, and several people have volunteered to do repairs for us at cost or for free." The smile faded. "It's wonderful, but it's only a stop-gap. I might not have to close at the end of this year, but at best we have one more." She sighed.

"We're still working on it," Andre said. "Please don't give up hope."

"Oh, baby," she said, reaching out and patting his cheek. "I'm not worried. The year will give me a chance to figure out how to shut down without destroying my finances. It's a gift you've given me." She winked. "You and that young man of yours."

Andre ducked his head at the mention of Trevor. He looked up at Joyce. "You can't close," he told her. "There are too many kids who need this place."

Joyce took off her glasses and set them on her desk. She leaned back with her eyes closed, her hands folded on her stomach. When she opened her eyes again, her gaze was fierce. "I am an old woman, Andre. I can't do this forever, and there's no one to take my place. I have wonderful volunteers, but none of them want to take over full-time. We have a board, but they're all people with other jobs too. I already told you it would take a miracle to keep this going."

"I know." Andre's shoulders slumped.

"Enough of that," Joyce said, putting her glasses back on and becoming business-like. "We have work to do."

Andre threw himself into it, but his disappointment remained at the back of his mind. One way or another, he would find a way to make sure his grandmother's legacy didn't end with her.

There were enough people in Andre's small townhouse to spill over onto the back deck. Somehow, he'd managed to convince Phyllice and Trinity to come with their partners but without their children. All three of Trevor's roommates had joined them as well, along with various people's significant others. One of Trevor's roommates—Jamie, Andre thought—had brought a man who looked familiar.

"Who's the guy over there?" he asked Trevor.

"Oh, he's The Boyfriend." Trevor shrugged.

"Yeah, I sensed that. Does he have a name? Also, I think I've seen him somewhere."

"We don't use his name." There was something dark in Trevor's response. "He probably looks familiar because he was there when I proposed to Marlie last winter."

"I see."

Andre followed their interactions. The Boyfriend constantly had his hands all over Jamie and didn't seem to want to let him out of his sight. It was unsettling for a reason Andre couldn't pinpoint. It might have been the way Jamie didn't look like he was into it. Andre filed it away in the back of his mind and wandered into the kitchen to see what was going on out there.

Trinity cornered him. "Hey, baby brother," she said. "You've been busy lately."

"Mm-hm," he acknowledged. This was going somewhere; he

would have to wait until she got around to it.

Sure enough, she smacked him on the arm. "You didn't tell me Irina plays for my team!"

Andre let loose a loud guffaw. "Is that all?" he asked.

"I may have to buy all her music from now on," Trinity declared.

"And Krista will be all right with that?"

Trinity snorted just as Krista walked up and put her arms around her. "She's not the jealous type."

The words hit Andre funny, but he managed a tight smile and a shake of his head. He was distracted when Trevor arrived a moment later, followed by Irina and Jagathi. Trevor grabbed a soda out of the fridge and popped the top, leaning against the counter. Irina had a formal air about her, but she didn't seem uncomfortable. Andre almost choked on suppressed laughter, however, when he saw Trinity's eyes go big and her mouth open and close a few times.

After several attempts, she finally managed to squeak out, "Hi!"

Irina's smile was warm, and humor flickered in her eyes. "Hello yourself." She extended a hand. "Irina."

"I know who you are!" Trinity said then cringed. "I love your music."

"Thank you," Irina replied. "Speaking of..." She turned to Trevor. "I am so sorry about your job."

He shrugged. "It was bound to happen."

"That doesn't make it right." She put her hand on his arm. "I'd like to make you an offer."

Trevor's eyebrows shot up. "Oh?"

"I'm looking for someone who writes songs, plays the piano, and is familiar with jazz and other swing styles. Know anyone who fits the description?" She winked and pressed a business card into his palm.

Grinning, Trevor replied, "I might."

"Good. I need him to get in touch with my people this week to set up a meeting and an audition." She withdrew her hand and headed for the kitchen door. Looking back over her shoulder, she said to Trinity, "Nice to meet you."

Andre thought Trinity might faint. He caught Krista's gaze, and she rolled her eyes. Leaving the two of them alone, Andre threaded his fingers with Trevor's, and they returned to the living room. Marlie was on the couch, talking to Trevor's roommates. Jamie, who was still tangled in The Boyfriend's uncomfortable embrace on the love seat, looked up when Andre sat down to her right. Trevor squeezed himself in the middle between them.

"Trev says it's your grandmother who runs the Lighthouse," Jamie remarked.

"She does." Andre's stomach tightened.

"I know the place," Jamie continued. "Um...from a long time ago. I'm sorry to hear it might close."

"Yeah," Mack put in. He looked up at Trevor. "You should've told us, man." He shoved Trevor's knee. "You know we'd do what we could to help."

"What could you have done? None of us have the kind of money Ms. Bridges needs to run the place." Trevor sighed. "We're still working on it."

Mack snapped his fingers. "I know!"

"What?" Jamie moved away from The Boyfriend's embrace, causing him to huff dramatically. No one paid any attention to him.

"Well," Mack said, "what about a concert? Remember the one we did at the bar? They raised money and supplies for shelters."

"Yeah, but, like, where would we have it?" Jamie and Mack were talking as though they already had the whole thing planned, and Andre chuckled at their enthusiasm.

"Dunno." Mack shrugged. "We'd find a place."

The lightbulb went on. Andre said, "I think...hey, Julian!"

Julian looked over from where he was talking to Elisa and a petite dark-haired woman Andre thought was Mack's friend or girlfriend. He said something to the women and stepped around them to where Andre was sitting.

"What's up?" he asked.

Andre pulled out his phone. "Can you text me Curtis' number? I think I might have a new plan."

"Curtis from the bar?" Julian's brow furrowed in confusion.

"That's the one. You did some work for his man, right? Can't remember his name, but Curtis did all the stuff with the payments and everything."

"Oh, right. Sure, I'll send it to you." Julian pulled up the number. "Done."

Andre grinned when the phone vibrated in his hand. "No guarantees, but it's a start, and maybe it'll buy us time until we can figure something else out."

Trevor raised his eyebrows, and Andre mouthed "tell you later" at him. Conversation moved on, and Andre relaxed, letting it flow around him for a few minutes. He was about to get up and see if anyone needed anything when he heard Marlie exclaim, "Oh!" She giggled.

Turning to her, Trevor put a hand on her belly. A small pang of jealousy settled in Andre's chest. He thought he'd suppressed a sigh, but he must have made some noise because Trevor looked over his shoulder at him.

"Can he?" Trevor asked Marlie.

"Of course," she said.

She reached around Trevor and grasped Andre's hand, drawing it to the round swell. For a minute or two, she moved it around then smiled when they both felt the flutter. He looked into her eyes, and he saw the same pleasure and joy reflected there he'd seen on Trevor's face after the ultrasound. Once again, the thrill transferred to Andre unexpectedly, and his own heart threatened to burst from it. He laughed, and Marlie squeezed his fingers before letting go of his hand. He withdrew from Marlie and sat back, still stunned.

Tears stung his eyes, and he let himself indulge in a moment of thinking about Dahlia. She wouldn't have wanted him to spend the rest of his life grieving for her and their babies, but would she have been okay with how he'd moved on? He hoped she would have and that she'd have been proud of the growing love he already felt for the child he was going to help raise.

Trevor leaned against him and pressed a light kiss to Andre's lips. "Amazing, isn't it?"

Andre knew he didn't just mean the baby. He meant everything they'd been through since January, together and apart. He wiped his eyes and answered, "It sure is."

He slid his arm around Trevor's shoulders and kissed his temple. Whatever the future held, he had no doubt they would get through it together.

ABOUT THE AUTHOR

A. M. Leibowitz is a spouse, parent, feminist, and book-lover falling somewhere on the Geek-Nerd Spectrum. She keeps warm through the long, cold western New York winters by writing romantic plot twists and happy-for-now endings. Her published fiction includes her novels, *Lower Education* and *Passing on Faith*, as well as a number of short works, and her stories have been included in several anthologies. In between noveling and editing, she blogs coffee-fueled, quirky commentary on faith, culture, writing, and her family at amleibowitz.com.